When Apples Fall

Nancy Wilkens

Llumina
Press

ISBN: 978-1-62550-424-1 (PB)

Chapter 1

Some days, I think I'm like the Germans who claimed they knew nothing about the concentration camps when all the while they were cheering the Nazis on at rally after rally.

Other days, I think I was just another victim in a long line of victims.

When night falls, her face appears in the darkness of my room like some hideous, luminescent sea creature. I wake with a shiver when she visits.

Sitting up, I wrap the sheets around my body in an attempt to ward off the chill. She doesn't open her mouth, but I hear her speak. The question she whispers is always the same: "Why didn't you save us?"

When I put my foot down on the floor to go to her, she disappears, and I am left to try and come up with an answer that will free my soul.

Doctor Stone says that if I talk about it, if I get things out into the open, that I might be able to put it all into perspective. I don't know if it will work, but I have to try.

If I write it down as I remember it, maybe I'll be able to figure out where things went wrong. Maybe I'll be able to figure out why the babies died.

This is how it happened.

Chapter 2

Father Regan opened the door, walking straight to Sister Margarita. Bending down, he whispered in her ear.

She jumped up from her seat, a penguin jack-in-the box, but quickly smoothed down her habit and composed herself.

"Continue with your reading, children," she said.

Father shut the door tightly as he ushered her out.

Voices echoed in the hall, followed by a wave of muffled sobs. I focused my eyes on the frosted glass in the door in an attempt to penetrate it. As usual, my super powers failed me in my time of need.

Father Regan returned alone. He went to the front of Sister's desk, leaning his hands behind him for support. Clearing his throat several times first, he made the announcement. "Boys and girls, I have some very sad news to tell you. President Kennedy has been shot." His voice cracked. "I think we should say a silent prayer for the president and his family."

All I could see was Mother's face, sad and angry at the same time.

She'd blame me. She always did.

"Amen."

When I opened my eyes I was startled to see tears rolling down the old priest's face, almost as if he was one of us: real... human... flesh of our flesh. He brushed the tears away with the back of his hand before making the sign of the cross over our heads.

"Bless these innocents, Holy Father. Now, children, I want you to gather your things and go to the cloakroom and put your coats on. We'll be going to the courtyard. Your mothers have been called and will be coming to pick you up."

None of us moved, too shocked by it all.

"Go now, children."

We got up and did as instructed, silent lambs following the good shepherd. He led us down the hall until the slowpoke classes ahead of us stopped moving.

Glancing across the hall, I caught sight of Sister Margarita sitting on the sofa in the faculty lounge. She was fingering the beads on her rosary as she clutched them to her chest. She began to recite the magic words: "Hail Mary, full of Grace. Blessed art thou among women. " She said it with an urgency that frightened me as her nimble fingers worked the beads. After she finished one verse, her needle got stuck at the beginning.

"Hail Mary, Hail Mary, Hail..."

A hand appeared, fumbling on the door frame like Thing from *The Addams Family,* until the door finally closed. Suddenly, the logjam of pupils broke up and we continued down the steps, outside into the bright sunshine of a crisp autumn day.

I watched with envy as my classmates began to be picked up by their mothers. Unlike mine, their mothers did not make a spectacle of themselves or embarrass them on purpose. My fondest daydream was that someone would take mercy on me and enroll me in a mother-daughter exchange program. If only daydreams came true...

Soon there were only three of us left: Tony Carappacio, whose mother didn't speak English; the weird kid nicknamed Bug, who would eat any insect for a nickel; and me, fatso ten-year-old Gerri Moran.

I kept squinting until my eyes were mere slits, straining to see Mother. She was often late, especially when others were waiting for her. Maybe she had forgotten about me. I should be so lucky.

I decided to play the waiting game I had made up long ago to distract myself when Mother was late picking me up.

Turn this way, turn the other way, she'll be there.

No.

Hop on one foot, hop on the other, she'll appear.

No.

I had gotten up to round four when her tiny frame, oversized sunglasses, and black-and-white polka dot kerchief appeared at the edge of the yard.

Everyone get ready to curtsy; Queen Lizzie has arrived.

She gave me a royal wave. I returned the gesture with pretend enthusiasm.

Her unbuttoned trench coat flapped as she promenaded down the red carpet toward her loyal subject. As she approached, she held her arms out, and I ran to her as expected. She hugged me with a grip that left me struggling for breath.

"Come on, let's get out of here."

Suddenly, Sister Angela's broad body blocked our path. "How nice of you to join us, Mrs. Moran."

Mother squeezed my hand so hard it made me wince. "Excuse me?"

"I was beginning to think you weren't coming. Tardiness is a sinful habit. It sets a poor example for the young when their elders are constantly late."

Sister Angela looked at me. I lowered my eyes, filled with shame. Mother perched her sunglasses on top of her kerchief, eyeballing her adversary. Putting her hands on her hips, she rocked onto the balls of her feet to make herself as tall as possible. Moving closer to Sister Angela, her eyes directly in line with the nun's habit-shrouded nipples, Mother went on the offensive. "Well, excuse me, but some of us aren't married to Christ. Some of us have husbands made of flesh and blood, real men whose needs have to be met."

She flipped her sunglasses down. "Come, Geraldine, let's go home to our family."

Mother began marching me out of the courtyard. We were half-a-dozen steps on the other side of the chain link fence when Sister Angela called after us. "God Bless you, Elizabeth Moran! I'll say an extra prayer for your soul during Mass."

Mother stopped abruptly and turned on her heels. She ran to the fence, but the object of her venom had disappeared within the walls of her sanctuary.

"Stupid fucking cow," Mother said.

A shiver flew down my spine. She had called Sister Angela the f-word!

She grabbed hold of the fence and shook it with a ferocity that made the birds in the nearby trees scatter. Turning around, she noticed my shocked expression. "What's the matter with you?"

"You can't call a nun that bad word."

Mother ran over to me, took me by the shoulders, and broke into an impish grin. "They're just people, Gerri."

"But you said they're married to Jesus."

She gave me an annoyed pat on the head. "I can say anything I want. You wouldn't be going to that school if I hadn't made a promise to that old woman."

That old woman was my grandmother. If there was one topic Mother could talk about without end it was how everything my grandmother said or did was part of a conspiracy to ruin her life. She wrapped her hands around my throat, shaking me playfully.

"You're a funny kid, Saint Geraldine. Let's go home so you can preach to the choir."

We walked briskly through the neighborhood of rundown buildings owned by absentee landlords. As our tenement came into sight, I spotted Grandma and Aunt Colleen sitting on their lawn chairs, the usual suspects in the usual place.

Mother bent down, kissing Grandma on the cheek as she whispered in her ear.

Grandma was Mother's mother. She lived with Aunt Colleen in the apartment above ours. Her face was wrinkled, but her eyes were still bright. You could never pull a fast one on Grandma. She had you pegged from the moment you were born.

Aunt Colleen was Mother's sister. She had flaming red hair, a face full of freckles, and deep blue eyes. Her laugh had more than a hint of a girlish giggle. At least once a week, Mother would warn me not to believe everything Aunt Colleen told me. She said she was fond of telling tales out of school.

Once when I was playing hide-and-go-seek, I overheard a group of neighbors from the building talking about her. That bony old crone, Gertrude O'Connor, said that she wasn't right in the head and shouldn't be allowed near civilized beings.

Franny Boyle's mother said she should have been put away a long time ago, and wouldn't let her daughter near her.

In spite of the danger, I felt closer to my aunt than anyone else in the world. She was the one person I could share my deepest secrets with. I just knew she would never tell.

Looking back, I suppose it wasn't the secrets I could tell her that worried the grownups. It was the ones that Aunt Colleen could share with me that terrified them to the quick.

Only a few weeks before, with no prompting by me, she took me to her bedroom and taught me the real names of all the naughty body parts. According to her way of thinking, it was completely proper to use the real names. She explained that people were afraid to do so because they were ashamed of their own bodies.

Anyone other than Aunt Colleen would have left it at that; however, it was always that extra step that made her truth dangerous, but extremely exciting to an impressionable young mind.

A moment later, she proceeded to remove her clothes and point out each unmentionable area as casually as you check off items on a grocery list. Worst of all, she made me recite the names back and spell them out as if we were judge and contestant in an obscene spelling bee.

She was my favorite person in the world. Spending time with her was like riding in a bumper car without a seat belt.

On that sad November day, when Mother was so utterly devastated by the news of JFK's assassination, I approached Aunt Colleen and began to stroke her silky shock of bright red hair. Suddenly, she pulled herself into a ramrod straight position. She broke into a mischievous grin as she announced, "My boyfriend is dead."

I looked at Mother and watched her cheeks grow crimson as her hands balled into fists. "You bitch!" she screamed.

My heart began to pound furiously. Having enough sense to know better than to get caught in the middle of their fray, I backed up.

In an amazing leaping motion, Grandma sprang out of her seat, throwing her body in front of Aunt Colleen to shield her from Mother's wrath. Grandma stood her ground as she said in her never-lost brogue, "Now, Lizzie, you know she doesn't know what she's saying. It's not her fault. Don't go making something out of nothing, for Mary's sake."

Mother shook her fist. "It's never her fault, according to you. She knows this isn't something you joke about. This is the president we're talking about. Even Colleen isn't that crazy."

The ever-present knot in my stomach grew harder, a granite nodule. Mother had called Aunt Colleen the one word that she knew would hurt her more than any other: *crazy*. It was the word uttered in hushed tones by outsiders. True or not, family did not use it, an unwritten rule you did not break.

Aunt Colleen began to whimper, the cry of a wounded animal caught in a trap of her own design.

Grandma wrapped her arms around her, wagging her finger at Mother as she said, "For shame, Elizabeth, for shame."

Mother dismissed her with an icy-cold stare. Grabbing my arm, she began to drag me in the direction of the building. Aunt Colleen's cries grew louder and more pitiful as we moved away.

Mother led me upstairs in a rampaging whirl of rapidly winding turns, venting her rage on innocent baby strollers and tricycles, cusswords flying through the hall. Charging into the apartment, she slammed the door behind her, nearly hitting me in the head. She paused for a moment to catch her breath as she unbuttoned her coat and threw it at me. "Hang it up. Then put the kettle on. Oh, and bring the Oreos, too. I'm sure you know where they are."

Orders given, she took off for the living room while I headed to the kitchen.

She was right, of course. I did know where she hid the Oreo cookies, inside the large yellow mixing bowl on the top shelf of the cabinet nearest the refrigerator. The Milky Way bars were behind the gravy boat, Mallomars in her night table, Hershey bars in her sewing box.

If she didn't want me to eat sweets, why did she make them so easy to find? It was a rigged contest from the start. But like a sucker at the carnival, I could not resist the temptation the barker laid before me: *Step right up, little lady, win yourself a box of shame.*

I retrieved the cookies before putting the kettle on. As I arranged them on the tray, I momentarily considered unscrewing the tops and spitting on the cream. The screech of the kettle brought me back to reality. *Better hurry. If you keep Queen Lizzie waiting, it's off with your head.*

In my haste, I forgot to use a potholder and burned myself on the handle. I ran my hand under cold water and the throbbing subsided for a moment. When I withdrew it, the pain returned. But I held in my tears.

Rule one: Never let her see you cry.

If she found out how clumsy I had been it would just be an excuse for her to use it against me.

Chubby girls have chubby fingers that cannot grip.

So I dried my tears and brought the tea in silently, carefully, praying that the creaking floorboards would not betray me with gossip about my failure. I sometimes believed Mother possessed the sorcery skills of a practicing witch. She always seemed to know what I had been doing without asking.

The living room shades were down, curtains drawn. Mother was staring at the television with a glazed-over look when the kind-looking grandpa with the horn-rimmed eyeglasses announced the bad news: "President Kennedy is dead."

Mother pounded her fist on the coffee table as tears streamed down her face. She did not seem to notice me.

"I brought the tea and cookies."

She looked up. "Come sit next to me, Gerri Girl." She pulled me to her lap for just a minute before pushing me onto the lumpy sofa. "Damn it, Gerri, why didn't you remind me how fat you are?"

She went back to staring at the television, hypnotized by the altar. Mother sipped her tea slowly as she listened intently to the news. Every so often she would shake her head, before letting out a deep sigh. When I tried to slip off the couch, she grabbed me by the arm, pulling me back without saying a word. Eventually, she loosened her grip to take another cookie, and I managed to wiggle a couple of inches to the right.

Half an hour later, the apartment door opened, and I listened as a pair of cautious footsteps approached. Billy, the eldest, went to Mother, kneeling before her as if he were going to ask for her hand in marriage. "I'm so sorry, Ma."

She pulled him up to her, brushing a lock of hair from his forehead. "Sit next to me."

He climbed over the coffee table, shoving me to the side as he sank into the timeworn sofa. Mother leaned her head against his shoulder, as if she were his child.

We had just settled in when the door was flung open. Paddy Boy came stomping in, shirttail hanging out, hands behind his back.

"Hi, Ma," he said, presenting her with a pathetic-looking bouquet of violets. Judging by the dirt-encrusted roots dangling from the bottom of the bunch, it was obvious he had pilfered them from someone's garden. "I hope you like them."

Mother took them and inhaled, making a great show of it. "They're beautiful, Patrick. Come sit next to me."

Billy slid over, pushing me into the arm of the sofa. We settled into an uneasy silence, all of us together, yet alone.

I glanced up at the portrait of Kennedy that hung over the television set. Flickers of light cast ghostly shadows across his face. His image above mirrored the one on the television screen below in a macabre display of double exposure. My flesh became goose-pimply.

Afternoon turned to evening. Daddy's heavy footsteps echoed through the hallway as he fought his way past clotheslines and roller skates, spewing his daily confession of rage at life. "Damn lace curtain slobs. Drunken pigs, the lot of them." He headed straight to the refrigerator.

The whoosh of Daddy's first beer of the night was soon followed by one of his classic belches, echoing through the flat like an ocean liner lost in the fog—S.S. Frankie Moran.

As he entered the living room, Mother ran to him with outstretched arms. He wrapped his massive limbs around her diminutive frame, caressing her shoulders with a tenderness that belied his size. Silently, he took her hand and led her to their bedroom, locking the door behind them.

Paddy switched the television off.

"She was watching that," Billy said.

Paddy stuck his tongue out at him.

Billy began to rise, but stopped as we heard Mother begin to cry. It was barely perceptible at first, becoming progressively louder, quieting down for a moment, only to start up again.

I covered my ears, but it did no good. You could never escape from Mother.

Paddy Boy got down on all fours and began to creep along the wall.

Billy gave him a death stare. "Stop playing the fool."

Paddy defiantly wiggled his butt in Billy's direction.

When our wiseass brother arrived at our parent's bedroom, he cupped his hand and put his ear against the door. Suddenly, it opened a crack. Paddy froze.

It shut again and he slithered back to the couch, climbing onto the cushions just as Daddy stepped out of his lair. He stood in the doorway a moment, one hand on his hip, the other on the doorjamb. He did not seem to be focusing on anything in particular. Shutting the door behind him, he lumbered to us.

"I want you kids to be on your best behavior. Your mother's having a rough time of it. We all need to pull together and be strong for her. Do you understand me, team?"

We nodded in unison. *Yes, Coach Moran, we'll win one for "The Gipper." Rah, rah, rah.*

"Good."

Orders given, he went to the kitchen and began to search through the cabinets and refrigerator for the perfect meal.

Skilled chef that Daddy was, he made us hot dogs and beans. I helped him by setting the table. Billy and Paddy washed and dried the dishes, something they had never been asked to do before. It was not men's work.

Rule two: Men did men chores and women did women chores.

Who was I to argue with a system that God must have made? After all, you never saw a picture of the disciples cleaning up the dishes after the Last Supper. We all know which of the two sexes must have been stuck with that chore.

Still, to his credit, Daddy made sure we washed and brushed our teeth. He even made sure we did our homework, something he had never done before and would never do again.

Mother did not come out of her bedroom the rest of the evening. Daddy brought a dinner plate in to her, but she left it outside the door, food untouched.

It took me a long time to get to sleep that night. I kept having a dream where demons whisked Mother to hell for calling Sister Angela that awful name. Even as the devils stuck her with their pitchforks, she called them bad words and told them to go where they already were.

I woke the next morning with a start at the sound of her voice above me. "Gerri."

I opened my eyes to find her black-veiled face hovering over me.

"Wake up, sleepyhead. Put on your black velvet jumper and white blouse. I've already packed a bag. We're going to visit Aunt Peggy."

Less than half an hour later, we got on the elevated line that took us into Manhattan, and we boarded a commuter train headed to the northern village of Ferrytown.

Peggy Donovan was Grandma's sister. She lived in a large Victorian house that would have been described as a fixer-upper, large and showing its age, not unlike Aunt Peggy. Right behind the house was Lake Owl's Head.

When we arrived at Aunt Peggy's, the lumbering ox greeted us at the door as if she had been expecting us. She motioned to the straw mat in the vestibule to remind us to wipe our feet. Clean soles or not, Aunt Peggy always made you wipe your feet.

We followed her into the parlor. It smelled like peppermint and mothballs, sweet yet nauseating. It smelled like Aunt Peggy.

She and Mother sat on the shrink-wrapped sofa. Taking a seat in the oversized wing chair, I tried to make myself small.

"How are you holding up?" Mother asked.

"Oh, as well as can be expected. I'm not one to complain, mind you. But since you asked, my bunions have been aching something awful. Oh, and my stomach is acting up, as usual."

Aunt Peggy glanced at me, prior to continuing in a softer tone of voice. "Oh, and you know my female problems are getting worse."

Mother looked at the television set and back to Aunt Peggy, who, in turn, looked at the TV and back to Mother. A moment later, she broke into an embarrassed smile, the kind of grin Paddy Boy called the "I've just stepped in it look."

"Oh, I'm so sorry, Elizabeth. I should have realized you were talking about Mr. Kennedy. I know what he meant to you... I mean, to all of us. Let me get you and the little one a cup of tea."

Before Mother could answer, Aunt Peggy fluttered off to the kitchen as she tried to shake the crap she had stepped in from her bunions. Mother rolled her eyes, almost sending me into a fit of laughter. I controlled myself by biting my lower lip.

When Aunt Peggy returned with the tea tray, she set it down with a resounding crash and pointed at the television set. Shaking her head, she put her hand on Mother's shoulder. "He was a good man, our Johnny. The world was a better place for having him in it," she said.

Mother lifted her hand to Aunt Peggy. She grasped it and pulled herself down to the sofa. After several awkward attempts, they hugged with a stiffness verging on cardboard. Their artificial display almost made me grateful they'd left me out of their circle of love... almost.

Over the course of the next few days, the television became our altar. The three of us sat watching events unfold as if they were just another one of Grandma's soap operas.

"You're watching history," Mother said.

"Yes, history," Aunt Peggy chimed in.

"It's something you'll always remember," Mother said.

"Yes, always," Aunt Peggy repeated.

"I think I'll name my next child John."

"I think..."

"Yes, it will definitely be John this time."

"Are you... with child?"

"Yes."

Aunt Peggy shook her head.

"Another one, is it? Well, at least you're following the teachings of the church. That's more than can be said for a lot of young ones."

I lowered my head.

Mother pinched my cheeks as she laughed. "Not you, silly. She's talking about the birth control sluts."

"Elizabeth! Little pitchers have big ears."

Mother let out a giggle, but quickly contained it. Replying in her most solemn voice she said, "I'm sorry, Aunt Peggy. Sometimes I think I must have a bit of the devil in me. I pray every night for salvation. Isn't that right, Gerri?"

I nodded.

"Well, try to keep your wicked impulses under control. This is neither the time nor the place." Aunt Peggy got up. "I'm going upstairs to take a nap. Maybe you should, too, my dear. You have to take special care now."

"Maybe in a little while, Aunt Peggy. Pleasant dreams."

When Aunt Peggy was tucked away in her bed, Mother helped herself to a box of the fancy chocolates our aunt kept hidden in the china closet. I watched as she sucked the fillings out, tossing the shells in the wastebasket.

The next day after lunch, Aunt Peggy found the empty box and waved it in front of Mother's face. "What happened to my chocolates?"

At first, Mother turned red. I thought she was going to confess. What else could she do? Instead, she pointed at me. "She did it. I'm always telling you what a little glutton that one is. Now you see it for yourself."

Aunt Peggy looked at me with scorn as she made a clucking noise with her tongue. "Oh, Geraldine, for shame."

I couldn't speak. It was as though my lips were glued together like one of my dolls.

"She can't even defend herself she's so filled with guilt. Gerri, go to your room."

Aunt Peggy shook her head as I walked past with my head hung low. "Oh, Elizabeth, it must be that husband of yours who makes her such a selfish child. I told you no good would come of marrying him. I warned you. An apple doesn't fall far from the tree."

That's when my lips became unglued.

"How dare you talk about my daddy like that? You don't know him. He's good and kind and loves us."

Mother got off the couch, yanked me by the hair, and began to slap me, over and over, until Aunt Peggy intervened. "Lizzie, the baby."

Mother let go of me and I ran upstairs and locked myself in my bedroom until the following morning when she called me for breakfast. She'd be sure to attack me. But I had come up with a plan to follow when I went downstairs. I would strike first.

Aunt Peggy was at the refrigerator, her back to Mother. I went to her, holding my arms out. "I'm sorry I ate your candy, Aunt Peggy."

She gave me a pat on the head at arm's length, the way you might touch a skunk if you were forced to. "I forgive you, angel. But we must not give in to impulses. No good can come of it."

"I understand. I promise to try harder, Aunt Peggy."

"Very well. You can pour my coffee now, child."

I looked at Mother and tried to will her with my brain waves to tell the truth. I could not penetrate her defenses. She just bit into her toast like a lioness devouring a fresh kill. My belief in the possibility of super powers vanished. I balled my hands into fists, but fast relaxed them.

Rule number three: Don't let the predator savor the blood of her victim.

I sat down and ate my cereal, munching, crunching, like a ravenous beast.

"Gerri, slow down and eat like a lady," Mother scolded.

I put my spoon down.

"Yes, Geraldine, good manners indicate proper breeding," Aunt Peggy added.

Breeding? What did she think we were... a pack of dogs?

I nodded before slowly lifting my spoon to resume eating in a way that even Queen Lizzie would approve of. After all, Mother had to be the foremost expert on etiquette. Who else would know the proper curse word to use when addressing a nun?

Chapter 3

As they stood in the doorway the following week saying goodbye, Aunt Peggy and Mother confirmed plans.

"You're coming up for the summer, aren't you, Elizabeth?"

"Of course, Aunt Peggy."

"Good."

"I'll send your love to Frankie and the boys."

"Frankie? Oh, of course. He's not going to spend the whole summer with us, is he, dear?"

"Now, Aunt Peggy, you know very well that he has to work."

You could see the relief in Aunt Peggy's eyes.

"They'll be up for the Fourth of July. That's what we agreed to, isn't it?"

"Yes, of course, dear. I don't object to Frankie or the boys. It's just that, well, they're so messy, aren't they?"

"Well, I do have to agree with you there. But Gerri and I will clean up after them, won't we?"

I nodded, even though we both knew it would be Gerri, not Lizzie, doing any cleaning. Mother's cleaning method consisted of delegation, followed by a swift departure to parts unknown.

Business deal concluded, hugs and kisses negotiated, we began the trek back to the city. I must have dozed off after we changed trains to the elevated line, because the next thing I remember is Mother shaking me by the shoulders to rouse me.

"Come on, Gerri Girl. We're going for a treat."

She took me to the Shamrock Diner. We plopped down in a big, comfortable booth in the back.

The waitress came and handed us grease-stained menus. They matched the smoky curtains and torn seat cushions. I ran down the entree selections with my fingers. It was a list of mostly high-fat and calorie-laden dishes.

I glanced at Mother. She had been monitoring me. Her lips were pursed with censuring disapproval.

"What'll it be, ladies?" the waitress asked.

"I'll have the cheeseburger deluxe platter with a side order of onion rings and a large chocolate shake," Mother said.

"And for you, young lady?"

"A cup of chicken noodle soup and some iced water, please."

"Is that all? A young lady needs to keep up her strength to grow. How about some fried chicken?"

Mother's forehead wrinkled. "How's about you mind your own business? A young lady needs to watch her figure."

The waitress flipped her pad shut.

As she walked away, Mother said in a voice loud enough for everyone in the restaurant to hear, "What can you expect from that type? It's so typically low-class."

The woman stopped for just a moment, but decided to ignore the verbal jab as she went back to her corner.

Mother grinned, joy etched into every facial muscle.

Round one to Killer Moran.

"So, Gerri, did you enjoy the trip?"

"Yes, because it was just us. Billy and Paddy always get to go places."

"Yes, it's good to get away from the men. We can take care of ourselves when we need to. We're not as helpless as your father likes to think we are."

She began flipping the knobs on the mini-jukebox that sat between the ketchup and sugar. She settled on a page, dropped her coins in, and depressed the same set of buttons repeatedly. A big band number began. Mother began tapping on the table with her utensils.

Totally absorbed by the show, I jumped when the waitress laid Mother's shake down with a violent thud. She took a couple of straws from her pocket and tossed them on the table. She put my iced water down, taking a napkin to wipe the condensation dripping down the glass.

The waitress walked away with a jiggling swagger.

Mother frowned. The counterpunch had caught her off guard. She had to recover points from the judges. She threw the straws to the floor, raised the shake to her lips, and took a healthy swallow. A chocolate foam mustache appeared over her upper lip. She looked like a rabid dog, overflowing with sweet chocolate madness. My taste buds ached with envy.

Don't look at her.

Drink your iced water.

Putting the glass to my lips, I maneuvered a cube into my mouth and bit down on it.

"Geraldine, a young lady does not crunch her ice," Mother said.

Another ten minutes passed before the waitress returned with our food. She dropped Mother's plate with a crash of china.

She laid my soup down, putting a napkin and tablespoon to the side. Reaching into her apron pocket, she dropped half a dozen cracker packets to the left of my bowl. "For you, miss."

Mother reached over and scooped them up. She opened her handbag, clicking them tightly shut in their prison cell.

The waitress blinked rapidly several times. "Will there be anything else?" she asked.

"No, you can leave," Mother replied as she waved her away as if shooing a fly.

Triumphant, her combination of punches hitting her adversary squarely on the chin, Mother ripped into her burger. Bloody juices oozed out, dripping from the sides of her mouth. She took her napkin, dabbing daintily at the animal fluids.

The smell of meat permeated my nostrils. Tendrils of aroma clawed their way to the nerve endings of my brain, blinding me with bloodlust. I stirred my soup, and tornadoes of steam rose. Taking an ice cube out of my water, I plopped it into the bowl. It did not do the trick; when I drew in the liquid, it scalded the flesh inside my cheek. But I could not let her see my pain. She would interrogate me: Why couldn't you wait? Why did you have to rush? Why are you such a shameful glutton?

Swallowing my pain, a warm feeling of satisfaction spread down to my gut. I had kept it to myself. She would not hurt me this time.

After we had been eating for five minutes, Mother put her burger down. "I have something to tell you, Gerri." She interlaced her fingers, cupping them under her chin. "Why don't you come over here?" Mother moved over and I slid in. "This is a secret between us girls. I haven't even told your father yet. Give me your hand," she said. She placed it on her tummy, below the waist. "We're going to have a new baby. This is where it will grow."

(Aunt Colleen had made me memorize the word: w-o-m-b-womb. The womb was the room for the baby. "When a man loves a woman, he gives her his seed." Paddy had warned me not to swallow any watermelon seeds or a baby would grow inside of me.)

"Gerri, are you listening?"

I nodded.

"Anyway, since you're getting older, I think you can take on some baby chores. Of course, this means you won't be the baby of the family anymore."

"I'm not a baby now."

"Take it easy, little one. It's just that with your father and brothers, I have my hands full already. So, do you think you'll be ready to help out when the new baby arrives?"

"Yes."

"Do you promise to be my little helper? Do you promise to always be there for me when I need you?"

"I promise."

"And what do we say about promises?"

"A promise is a promise."

She planted a hard kiss on the top of my head. "Oh, look. I didn't finish my shake," she said. She pushed it toward me. "Take it. You deserve it."

I hesitated, afraid it might be one of her tricks.

"It's all right."

I raised the glass and inspected it. She had left a lipstick stain on one side.

"Thank you." Turning it to the unstained side, I poured the remains into my mouth. At first, the chocolate tasted sweet. When it touched the raw wound on the inside of my cheek, however, it stung. Ignoring the pain, I forced myself to finish it.

But I had swallowed the golden elixir too fast and could not stop myself from letting out a Daddy-sized belch, just as the waitress came back. She laughed and said, "I'm so glad you had something besides soup."

Mother scowled, eyes narrowing to slits.

The waitress tore the check from her pad, put it on the table, and walked away, no doubt convinced she had been the winner.

"Tramp," Mother muttered. She took the check and inspected it, almost as if she was hoping to find an error before removing a bill from her wallet. She reached for the ketchup, unscrewed the cap, and dropped globs of sauce strategically across the bill. I could see her eyes light up as she carried out her wicked plan. When she was done, it was clear that no matter how the waitress tried to pick it up, she could not avoid coming into contact with the saucy mess. "Come on, let's go," Mother said.

When we arrived at the entrance, she stopped and turned back to look at our booth. Mother smirked as she watched the waitress wipe the bill off, her eyes twinkling with delight over achieving glorious revenge. "That'll teach her. No one crosses Lizzie Moran and gets away with it." Victorious, the champion had taken the belt again.

On the walk home, a question popped into my head. I tugged on Mother's coat sleeve to get her to stop. "I was just wondering," I began. She waited for me to continue. "Do you think we could get a girl this time?"

"We're hoping for a boy. We're going to name him John."

"Oh."

"But that's a good thing, Gerri Girl. It means we'll always have a special bond. Nothing can ever come between us." She got up and we went home, hand in hand, till death us do part.

Chapter 4

Soon the Christmas season approached. Every year, our school would put on a pageant consisting of both secular and religious performances. No matter how fate had treated you before, if you landed a choice part at Christmas, popularity would follow into the next year. Now, I knew I could never get a major part like Virgin Mary. A role like that would be assigned to a beautiful, thin goddess with a name like Cecilia or Nanette. If I could play an angel, or—dare I dream—the innkeeper's wife, I would be satisfied.

But there would be no heavenly role for me that year, as our class was designated to put on a production of *Frosty the Snowman*, a play that only has two major roles.

Sister Angela lined us up on stage to look us over, peering up at us over the half-glasses perched on the end of her nose.

Bobby White was picked to play the boy who creates Frosty. This came as a surprise to no one. After all, he had the kind of looks that even children knew entitled him to special treatment. The supporting roles were filled one by one, and soon only Johnny Boyle and I were left without parts. Johnny stood there with a cocky grin as he bowed to his friends.

"What are you smiling about?" Sister Angela asked as she climbed onstage and grabbed him by the back of his collar.

"Well, it's obvious I have the part. He's a snowman, not snow woman." She let go of him, went to the lectern to leaf through script pages as though attempting to verify the validity of his assertion.

"Come here, Mr. Boyle."

She rolled up the script, making us think she was going to hand it to him. Instead, she began to hit him on the back of the head with it.

"Hey, what gives?"

When she finally ceased whacking him, Sister pointed to the side of the stage. "You'll pull the curtain open and shut. Pride is one of the deadliest of sins, young man."

Johnny Boyle stomped his foot and made an unsuccessful plea for his case. "But Sister Angela, she's a girl."

"So am I, Johnny Boyle. So am I."

That afternoon I went home by way of the park. When I got to the playground, I saw Aunt Colleen sitting on a bench tossing pieces of bread to a squirrel. I ran over to tell her my good news. The squirrel ran up the nearest tree.

"Now look what you did. You made him leave."

"I have something important to tell you."

"We have to get him back." She placed pieces of bread at the tree roots, making a trail back to the bench.

Scrambling down, the twitchy rodent gobbled up each piece in a greedy frenzy until he got to the last one. Suddenly, Aunt Colleen trapped the creature under a cardboard carton. "Gotcha!" she shouted as she flung her body over the box.

"What're you doing? "

"Mother told me I could have a pet if I could get one on my own and take care of it."

"But, Aunt Colleen, it's a squirrel."

She looked at me as if there were nothing unusual in her choice. "I think I'll name her Princess." The carton began to move, so she sat on it.

I looked at my watch as I backed away. "It's getting late. I have to go home now. You know how Mother gets if I'm late."

"On second thought, I think I'll call her Lizzie. Lizzie the Second."

As I neared the fence, she called after me. "What did you want to tell me?"

For some reason, I just blurted out the first word that popped into my head. "Nuts."

Her forehead furrowed and I realized she thought I meant her.

"I mean the squirrel. You should feed him nuts."

"Well, shit, Gerri, you're a regular Einstein, you are."

I stuck my tongue out at her and walked away, mouthing the word *nuts* over and over to myself as I went. As I approached our apartment building, a snowball slammed into the back of my head. Turning around, I spotted Paddy Boy standing across the street.

"Don't you just love the snow?" He gathered a pile of it from the hood of a car and began to head in my direction.

I ran up the steps to our flat, Paddy at my heels all the way. He tackled me to the kitchen floor and shoved the icy mess down the front of my blouse. Looking up, I saw Mother standing over us. She began to kick him as if he were a football and she were trying to clear the goal post. "Track snow in my house, will you?"

He rolled off of me, shielding himself from punishment with his arms. "Oh, Ma, don't be mad. Gerri has to learn to deal with snow. She's going to be playing a snowman." He knew that would spark her interest, and during that momentary lapse in her desire to kick the smartass out of him, he made a dash back downstairs.

"Is that true, Geraldine?"

"Yes. I'm going to be Frosty in our play."

"Well, isn't that something. They picked *you*?" She eyeballed me for a moment before arriving at her logical conclusion. "Oh, they must have gone by the shape of your body. When is it going to be?" Just then, the phone rang, and she ran off to answer it.

For the next week, I managed to avoid answering her question by making myself as scarce as possible.

Rehearsals, meanwhile, progressed at a steady pace. With each passing day, I grew more confident in my ability to play the jolly, fun-loving creature everyone loved. During dress rehearsal, however, I was standing in the wings when I felt a chill go down my spine. Sweat had been pouring down my back for the past hour. My legs grew wobbly, and it became a struggle to stay upright.

You can't be sick, you have to go on.

That night I got down on my knees to pray for deliverance. "God, if you just let me be Frosty, I promise I won't eat any more candy bars for the rest of the year." Sometimes sacrifices have to be made for the sake of art.

Despite my deal with Our Heavenly Father, I woke to a feeling of nausea the next morning that took even *my* appetite away. I looked at myself in the mirror and decided I would fight it. This was my chance for stardom, and nothing was going to stop me. So I pasted on my bravest face, put one foot after another, determined to meet my adoring fans.

In spite of my efforts, Mother had managed to find out what afternoon the play was going to be performed. Although it would mean missing her soap opera shows, she vowed she would attend. "I wouldn't miss Gerri Girl's performance for anything in the world. She could be another Oliver Hardy," Mother said.

"Don't you mean Laurence Olivier?" Daddy asked.

"Not with her figure."

The day of the show, I tried my best to pretend she wasn't there when I saw her sitting front row center. It was difficult to do, considering she was the only mother there dressed as if she were attending a Broadway opening, complete with feathered hat, white gloves, and pearls. I thought that if I wished hard enough, maybe the magic in my hat would make her invisible. The power of belief in miracles dies hard.

Rubbing my palm on the brim, I closed my eyes and said a silent prayer for deliverance.

Please, God, make her disappear. Please, make her leave.

Opening my eyes, I was disappointed to find it had not worked. So I focused on my lines and attempted to will myself to change from child to snowman, a happy soul without a mother, created out of love and loved by those who created him.

A few minutes later, I made my grand entrance. During my jolly dance, the audience burst into a round of applause. Their reaction caught me off guard. It was a new feeling, and it took me a moment before I was able to let the warmth wash over me. It felt like hot chocolate slathered with whipped cream.

Even my toughest critic's presence couldn't ruin my debut. She could not penetrate the ambrosia of approval, the sweet nectar of unconditional love.

By the end of the play my head was swimming, lights spinning around me. I didn't know if it was the thrill of a winning performance or the effects of the flu. It did not matter. As we took our bows, my heart filled with sheer joy. In that magical moment, I was overcome by a feeling of pure and complete happiness, unlike any emotion I had ever felt before. It was bliss.

Johnny Boyle pulled the curtain shut just as I fainted.

When I came to, Mother was cradling my real head under one arm and my snowman head with the other.

"How are you, Gerri Girl?"

"Was I good? Did they like me?"

"Yes, of course. But don't forget, you were good because you get your artistic talent from me."

I was stunned, nearly falling back to the floor from the shock. She had said I was good!

Slowly, I sat up. As I did, Mother grabbed my cheeks and pinched the flabby flesh. "Of course, you'll have to lose a lot of weight if you want to act. Lard butts never make it to Broadway."

I melted back into my costume as the hurtful words echoed in my head.

Thumpety thump-thump,
thumpety thump-thump
 look at Frosty go.
Look out for Mother,
she'll push and she'll shove you
into the dirty snow.

Chapter 5

Spring burst on us in waves of cool, breezy days interspersed with teasingly warm ones. On one of those lush spring days, Mother took me on our annual pilgrimage to buy our Easter outfits. She picked out a selection of dresses for me to try on, each dowdier than the last. As I modeled for her, she stroked her chin as she passed judgment.

"Your body isn't right for that waistline. That color's too bright for your pasty complexion. That would be better on someone like me. No, no, that won't do. You'll ruin that beautiful design with the way you slouch."

Finally, she found one she said suited me to a tee. It was a charcoal gray suit with a matching jacket. She found a black and white bonnet with a tacky plastic rose stapled to the front. The elastic from the skirt pinched my flesh. I looked at myself in the mirror: *Junior Queen Frump.*

"You look adorable," Mother said.

She had made up her mind. There would be no changing it.

It was on to the ladies' department.

I stood outside the dressing room while she narrowed down her own model-size choices. After twenty minutes, she emerged wearing a beautiful lavender dress with a plunging neckline. A double row of pearly white buttons ran down the front. Her pillbox hat was a slightly darker shade, with a small purple feather on the side.

"What do you think, Gerri? Do I look like a movie star?"

"Audrey Hepburn."

It was true. She knew it, too. Everyone was aware that she never missed an opportunity to have you tell her just how fabulous she looked. It was funny how she never returned the favor. Never.

When we got home that day, Mother made me hang my suit up in my closet. She left her dress up on the coat rack in the hall for her legions of fans to admire. Every day for two weeks, I passed her royal gown and resisted the impulse to grab a pair of scissors and cut it to shreds. What right did she have to look so beautiful when she was so mean? It just wasn't fair.

In spite of how I felt, Easter morning arrived on schedule, on one of those overcast days where the sun plays hide-and-go-seek in the clouds. As I opened my eyes, I spied a hot pink basket on my dresser. I slid on the scatter rug as I ran to read the tag: "Happy Easter. Love, Peter Rabbit."

A stuffed yellow duckling with black bead eyes sat on a nest of green cellophane. His lips were sewn together as if to prevent him from revealing some deep, dark ducky secret. As I stroked the tuft of feathers on top of his head, I decided to name him Mr. Quack. There were two bottles of nail polish labeled "For Young Ladies", one pink, the other clear. I opened the pink bottle and sniffed the contents. The smell made me woozy.

Dumping the rest of the goodies on the bed, I surveyed the loot. Besides the duck and polish, there was a comb, a manicure set, and a lace handkerchief. It took a moment for me to realize something was wrong. I searched again. There had to be more. Where was the chocolate rabbit? There were no marshmallow chicks, not a single jellybean. In fact, there was no candy at all.

A thought hit me in a flash: *Paddy must have stolen my candy!* He was always taking things that weren't his: violet plants, beer, cigars. I went to my brother's room to retrieve my property.

"Paddy, are you awake?" He was lying on his bed, eyes closed. A sudden burst of sunshine hit the mirror, illuminating Paddy's grinning chocolate-smeared face. Guilty!

Digging my hands into his basket, I snatched a chocolate egg. He jumped up and grabbed the basket from me. "Keep your paws off, missy", he said as he gave me a gentle slap on the hand.

"But you took my candy."

"Are you calling me a thief? Gerri, I didn't take anything from you."

"No? Then tell me, where's my candy?"

"Can I help it if our darling mother thinks you shouldn't get any? I'm not the one making you get on the scale every week. Think about it, little sister."

Mother was the culprit. I should have known.

Billy sat up.

"Give her some candy."

"Excuse me?"

"You heard me."

"Oh, all right."

Paddy took a fistful of jellybeans and began to pelt me.

I retreated to my room. As I was dumping the contents of my basket into the trash, Billy appeared in the doorway. He dug into his robe pockets and began to stack jellybeans and malted milk balls, and, yes, marshmallow chicks on my dresser. Finally, he put a golden foil-wrapped rabbit in the center. I sniffed it, and the smell of chocolate intoxicated me with sweet perfume. Billy kissed me on the head and we embraced. As we were pulling apart, Paddy rapped on the open door.

"Oh, isn't that sweet? Billy, you're such a fairy boy."

I was about to take cover, ready for a second jellybean assault, when I saw him reach into his pajama top. Instead, he gave me a wonderful surprise. "Abracadabra," he said. He revealed a fluffy toy lamb, shoving it into my chest as he tousled my hair.

"Oh, thank you, Paddy. It's so pretty." As I kissed him on the cheek, a crimson blush appeared on his face, and he wiped away my "girl germs" with the back of his hand.

"No need to get sloppy. I'm glad to be rid of it. What would a man want with a little girl's toy?"

Billy tapped him on the shoulder. "Come on, tough guy. We have to get ready for church. You know how Mother likes to get there early to show off her clothes."

"Yeah, I know. She'd take Father O'Meara's robes right off his back and put them on if she could get a compliment out of it."

After they left, I went to my closet and took the hideous gray suit out and lay it on the bed. Resigning myself to my fate, I put it on and looked in the mirror, but this time I did not see *Junior Queen Frump.* This time I just saw me, and it was fine.

I retrieved the polish, comb, manicure set, and handkerchief from the trash pail and put them back in the Easter basket. Lifting the green nest, I buried the candies in the bottom to hide them from prying eyes. Raising the chocolate rabbit, I began to unwrap it. The foil made a crinkling sound. I stopped to lock the door. Just as I was about to bite into the left ear, she called, "Gerri, are you up?"

"Yes."

"Well, hurry up. I want to see how you look in your suit."

"Okay."

"Was the Easter Bunny good to you?"

"Yes, thank you."

"Oh." She sounded disappointed.

"Well, snap to it, slowpoke. I just hope you haven't gained more weight since I bought you that suit. I can just imagine what people would say if it split during Easter Mass."

As I listened to her walk away, I raised the rabbit to my mouth and bit the head off. I ground the candy eyes between my teeth and imagined they were Mother's perfect fingers being pulverized by my canines, never able to point her accusing digits at me again.

There goes Peter Cottontail, hopping down the bunny trail.

Hide your candy, Mother's on her way.

Chapter 6

At the end of June, we prepared to spend the summer at Aunt Peggy's house. Mother made sure there were enough clean clothes to get our men through the first month. "After that they can run through the sprinklers in the playground," she said.

They would not want for food. Grandma would cook for them... and cook... and cook. She was fond of saying, "Once famine is in your blood, you never take a meal for granted."

Having done our best to fortify the genuinely weaker sex during our absence, we packed our bags and left them to tough it out.

It was unusually warm for upstate the day we arrived. As I dragged our bags through the open screen door, Mother called, "Aunt Peggy, are you there?"

"I'll be right down," Aunt Peggy replied. She appeared at the top of the stairs. "Come in and wipe your feet." She lumbered downstairs, letting out a sigh every few steps to remind us of her burdens.

Mother grabbed my arms for support as she lowered herself onto the sofa. As her belly grew, she used me more frequently like a dog playing fetch. "Gerri, get me..." Two minutes later, "Go get me..." I grew more fearful with each passing day that she would tie a collar around my neck and start calling me Rover.

When I sat down, my perspiration-soaked clothes stuck to the plastic slipcover as though I were caught in a Venus flytrap. Leaning forward, I tried to free my thighs by shifting, but it did not work. I could only pray that Mother would not poke fun if I had to move, but could not get up, due to my predicament.

"How was the trip?" Aunt Peggy asked.

"Hot," Mother said.

Aunt Peggy clapped her hands together. "Where are my manners? Let me get you and Geraldine some cold lemonade. You must be parched after that long trip." Before we could answer, she waddled off to get the refreshments.

Leaning back, Mother positioned herself to catch the breeze from the ancient iron fan whirring on the floor below the window. She kicked off her Keds as she shut her eyes. Water droplets appeared on her brow, descending slowly like a sled down a baby hill.

Aunt Peggy returned with a tray holding two glasses of lemonade and a couple of sugar cookies.

Mother opened her eyes. "That looks delicious."

We raised our glasses, taking healthy swallows. Our lips puckered simultaneously, and Mother's eyes actually crossed.

"What's wrong?" Aunt Peggy asked.

"It's a little tart," Mother replied.

Aunt Peggy slapped her forehead. "Oh, my word, I must have forgotten to put the sugar in!" She dropped the tray with the cookies on the coffee table and clopped off to the kitchen.

As soon as she cleared the doorway, Mother said, "Cookies, Gerri."

I frantically passed a cookie to Mother, taking another for myself. Biting down hard, I hit into a flavorless pile of bland nothingness. No, it wasn't just flavorless; it was gritty, as though the cookies had been made with sand instead of flour.

Mother reached into her handbag and pulled out a couple of tissues. She spit the cookie mush into hers and then passed me one to do the same. I handed it back to her, along with the remaining cookies. Wadding them up, she buried the evidence deep in the recesses of her purse, where half-rolls of Lifesavers collected lint and stray hairs.

Aunt Peggy reappeared holding the sugar canister the way a priest raises the chalice as he performs the sacred rite of Holy Communion.

"This should do the trick," she said.

She removed the lid, scooping a stingy half-teaspoonful into each of our glasses. Judging by the amount of sweetener the old miser doled out, you'd have sworn she was giving away California gold dust instead of Domino's refined white.

When she lay the canister down on the coffee table, she noticed the cookies were gone. The self-satisfied grin of a successful pastry chef spread across her face.

"Oh, I see you finished the cookies. Let me get you some more."

As soon as she was out of sight, Mother said, "Canister, Gerri."

I passed it to her and she scooped two heaping spoonfuls into our glasses, stirring briskly. Hoisting her glass, she tapped it against mine. "Cheers."

Sweet relief spread through my mouth.

"Now, that's what I call good lemonade," Mother said.

Aunt Peggy returned with a plateful of the lethal cookies. As she settled down in the oversized wing chair that was her throne, she tried to tempt our taste buds, cheerfully saying, "Have some more; I have two dozen left."

Looking into Mother's face, I could see her wheels begin to spin by the darting movement of her eyes.

"Well, Aunt Peggy, I have to be honest with you."

"Yes?"

"I'm feeling a little tired. I think I'd like to take a nap, if you don't mind."

Aunt Peggy leaned forward. "Of course not, dear. I should have realized you'd be tired considering your... condition. Let me take you up to your rooms."

"No, we'll show ourselves up. You've done too much already."

"I won't argue with you. To be honest, I'm feeling a little tuckered out myself. I'm not used to all this company, you know."

Inching herself to the end of the couch, Mother held her arms out for me to help her up. She leaned on me while we walked to the stairs. We had only gone up a few steps when Aunt Peggy called after us. "I'll call you when dinner's ready. I'm making a special meal to celebrate your arrival. It's a secret recipe handed down through the family."

"Thank you, Aunt Peggy. Geraldine and I will be looking forward to it." Mother turned around, holding her stomach in mock agony as she put two fingers in her mouth and pretended to vomit. When she was done with her dramatic moment, she whispered in my ear, "Julia Child she ain't."

Opening the door to my bedroom, the pungent aroma of mothballs burned my nostrils. I dropped down on the bed, pulled the sheet over my head, and closed my eyes, hoping I'd dream of Twinkies and soda pop.

When I woke, the setting sun was a bright red-orange fireball in the sky. I went to the window and pulled the screen up. Golden sparkles shimmered across the surface of Lake Owl's Head like thousands of Christmas tree lights dancing over the water.

I don't know how long I had been standing there, mesmerized by the display, when Mother's voice broke the spell. "Gerri, dinner's ready."

"I'm not hungry."

In a rage, Mother flew through the door and wagged her finger in my face. "If I have to eat it, you have to eat it. You're going to eat it, and you're going to compliment the way it tastes... and you're going to offer to clean up afterward."

"But she's the worst cook ever."

She took my cheeks in her hands, jiggling the flesh.

"God knows you could stand to miss a meal or two, that's for sure. But we do not insult our host. Not when I've worked so hard to get to this point. Not when we're so close..."

She looked into my eyes. "I have a plan."

That came as no surprise. Mother always had a plan. Sometimes I used to think Lucy Ricardo got her harebrained schemes from Mother.

"I'm going to insist that you cook our meals the rest of the summer. Our storyline is that you're going for your cooking merit badge and need all the practice you can get."

Of course, her plans usually involved work for me.

"Oh."

"All right, miss, put on your best face and let's go down together. After all, what do we say about birds of a feather?"

"They flock together."

"Correct."

Crossing my fingers behind my back for luck, I followed Mother down, silently praying that God, in His merciful wisdom, would not let this meal be our Last Supper.

Chapter 7

As I stood at the stove cooking breakfast the next morning, Aunt Peggy and Mother discussed my schedule.

"I think we should have Geraldine help out with some chores," Aunt Peggy said.

"What a marvelous suggestion, Aunt Peggy," Mother replied. She got up and put her arms around me from behind. "She could certainly use the exercise. Isn't that right, Gerri?" Suddenly, she began to poke me in the side repeatedly with her index finger. "Isn't that right, chubby?" She kept jabbing her finger into my flesh, but unlike that masochistic Pillsbury dough boy, I found nothing to giggle about.

"You'd never believe how lazy this one is. "

I could no longer tolerate her taunts and extracted myself from her grasp. Done with her hurtful attack, she sat down, while I concentrated on the frying pan. The food was ready.

"Eggs are done. Let me have your plate, Mother."

Just as I was passing them to her, I lost my grip, and they fell onto her lap.

"Damn it, Gerri! Look at my pants!"

"I'm sorry. It was an accident."

Grabbing a towel, I got down on my knees and began to wipe the gooey mess away.

She ripped the towel from my hands, throwing it to the floor.

"Just leave it and go outside and work in the garden. You can't be trusted near food. You're useless."

As the screen door shut behind me, I knew I had sealed my fate. She'd find a way to get back at me. She always did. Still, that did not stop me from fantasizing about my own plans for revenge.

As I began to pull weeds from the vegetable patch, I imagined I was plucking the hair from Mother's very stylish hairdo. It was delightful. That afternoon, as I peeled the potatoes, I pretended I was shaving Mother's perfectly shaped eyebrows off; as I snapped green beans, I dreamed I was breaking her poking finger in half. My skin tingled with guilty pleasure as I kept daydreaming.

Later that day, my imagination pushed my thoughts in another direction. As I was sweeping the kitchen floor, a vision of Cinderella popped into my head. What if I really was a princess waiting to be rescued from a life of drudgery?

I came to the conclusion that it could not be true. Cinderella was good. I may have been the one left to clean the cinders while the others went to the ball, but the princess in disguise never wishes harm to befall her enemies. Cinderella never thought about torturing her evil relatives. She just waited for the prince to take her away. And Mother had convinced me a handsome prince would never take me away. She had told me many times that Prince Charming did not put the slipper on the chubby stepsister's foot. There would be no happily ever after for me.

Chapter 8

We had been at Aunt Peggy's for a week when she left to attend her annual Hummel collectors' convention. I would be alone with Mother until Daddy and the boys arrived the day before the Fourth of July.

Aunt Peggy, being the model of efficiency that she was, made a chart of chores to keep me busy until she returned. She posted it on the refrigerator door with a magnet shaped like a pickle that read "Heinz 57 Varieties." Mother told her where to put it, saying, "Gerri will never miss it if you put it on the refrigerator door. It's her favorite appliance."

As I was polishing the coffee table the day Aunt Peggy departed, Mother called me to the dining room. "I need you to get that vase down from the top of the china closet."

I climbed on a chair, teetering precariously as I stretched to reach the porcelain.

"Be careful. I don't want anything to happen to it."

Cradling it carefully with both hands, I passed it to Mother.

She turned it over and looked at the bottom. Laying it on the table, she took a notepad from her pocket and wrote something down.

As I stepped down from my perch, I saw that she had a list of household items.

Mother whirled me around by the shoulders. "What are you looking at, nosy?"

I shrugged.

"I'll bet you don't know. Well, let me tell you something. I've worked my whole life to get my hands on this stuff. No one's going to stop me now." She smacked me on the top of the head with the pad. "You promise me you won't tell anyone about my list." She grabbed my arms. "Do you promise?"

"I promise."

"And what do we say about promises?"

"A promise is a promise."

"Good."

She pulled me to her and kneaded my shoulders as though I were Thanksgiving stuffing being prepared for the bird.

"Now, go put on your swimsuit. I think you deserve a little break."

As I headed upstairs, she called after me. "One more thing, Gerri."

"Yes?"

"Try not to spill any more plates of food. Nothing is ever just an accident."

Chapter 9

The next couple of days passed without incident. But on the third day, all hell broke loose.

Mother was asleep, so I thought it would be safe to go for a swim. I heard her call to me as I came in the back door, sopping wet, tracking lakeside mud through the house. "Gerri, get up here!"

My heart pounded when she let out a scream that sounded like the shrill screech of a seagull. Pulling my towel around me, I began to shiver as I crept upstairs, scared to go up, but even more scared not to. As I turned the corner, I caught sight of her reflection in the dresser mirror. She was clutching at the sheets as she writhed in agony. She spotted me, and my stomach began to ache. "Where the hell have you been? Get in here!"

I tried to cover my suit with the towel, but when she saw how I was dressed, her eyes narrowed to slits. "Have you been swimming? Who gave you permission to go swimming?"

I shook my head.

"You just wait until I can get hold of you."

Suddenly, her eyes grew wide, and she erupted into the seagull screech again, followed by a string of cuss words that would make a longshoreman blush.

My eyes were drawn to the sheet, focusing on the sea of red at the far end of the bed.

"It's coming. The baby's coming."

I backed up.

Her eyes rolled back in her head as her face contorted into a twisted mask. Finally, the pain subsided.

"Go get help!"

I froze, unable to move, unable to speak.

"Snap out of it, you useless pig!" Reaching on the nightstand, she grabbed the alarm clock and flung it at me.

I ducked, and it crashed against the wall with a resounding clang-clang-clang, just as the seagull screech returned.

I covered my ears, but I could not drown her out, so I turned and ran away as fast as I could, down the stairs, out the back door to the shore of Lake Owl's Head.

Look straight ahead, don't look back.

Keep going, keep going, run away.

Don't look back or you'll turn into a pillar of salt.

Kicking up pebbles, a hundred of her heads crunched beneath my feet, scattering in all directions like gravel beneath the wheels of a speeding car.

I ran and ran, side burning, fiery flesh punishing me. Wet granules pummeling my cheeks, screeching bird overhead, I ran to the cottage, pounding on the door with the last fibers of my strength. Just before I passed out, I managed to utter one word that came out like a curse to the shadowy figure that opened the door: "Mother."

Chapter 10

The kind man in the cottage was able to revive me to get the story. An ambulance came to take Mother to the hospital, and John was born. The rest of the day is a fuzzy blur in my memory. I do remember that I tried to stay out of the way, making myself as invisible as a chubby girl can.

Aunt Peggy had to cut her convention short to stay with me. She did not keep her displeasure with the situation to herself. As she came to the door, she dropped her bags with a thud. "Bring them upstairs," she said.

As soon as she saw the bloodstained mattress, her eyes landed on me with an accusatory stare. "It's ruined. We'll never get it clean." She shook her head. "If someone had been where she was supposed to be this never would have happened. Who could that someone have been?"

I had no reply as the tears welled up in my eyes. As they began to fall, she had no words of comfort in her cold voice. "Go downstairs and wait for your father. We'll have to put up with his antics as well, I suppose. If he had any sense of responsibility at all, he'd never have left your mother alone with such a selfish child."

I swallowed my tears as rage began to ball up in my gut. As I was about to open my mouth and defend Daddy, she hit me with another pounding blow. "I just hope God will forgive your sins. He doesn't look fondly on little girls who break their word."

How could I answer her? It was true. I hadn't been to confession all summer, and now I'd have to tell the priest about my horrible sins!

"Well? What are you waiting for? Scat."

I ran to the kitchen and pulled out the piece of chocolate cake Mother had been saving behind the grease can in the back. Just as I was about to sink my teeth into it, an automobile horn began to blare.

I ran outside to Daddy's waiting arms.

"There's my favorite girl. How are you, my love?" He planted a raspberry kiss on the top of my head.

"I'm okay. I'm sorry I wasn't a good girl."

"Not a good girl? What are you on about?"

"I wasn't here to help Mother."

He rolled his eyes.

"Nobody can help her. She's what we call a hopeless case."

He took my hands, bending down to eye level with me.

"So, what do you think of my moustache?"

I hadn't noticed he had grown one until he pointed it out. It was barely perceptible.

"Do I look like Clark Gable?" he asked as he tweaked it between his fingers.

"It's nice but..."

"Yes?"

"Mother won't approve."

He grinned like a cat caught in the canary cage. "Hmmm... you might have a point."

It was at that moment that Paddy scrambled out of the car, tossing a paper airplane at my head. "What a knucklehead! Daddy's not afraid of a woman, are you?"

Daddy picked the plane up. "Did I ever tell you how many planes my battleship shot down in the war?"

Billy climbed out of the car. "Half a dozen, right?" he asked.

Daddy tossed the plane to him, and he flew it back to Paddy Boy.

"Too bad the planes were all ours," Paddy taunted.

Daddy turned red, grabbing my brother by the wrist. "Let me show you how they ended up." He picked Paddy up, bear hugging him to his chest as he carried him from the back of the house. "Billy, give me a hand."

Billy joined in, taking the struggling Paddy's legs as they grew closer and closer to their destination. They took their victim to the dock, dangling him over the water. As they prepared to throw him in the lake, he begged for mercy.

"I'm sorry. I didn't mean it. You were a war hero, Daddy."

I thought Daddy was going to let him go, but Paddy could not resist one more barb. "Too bad you're afraid of your itty bitty wife now."

With one swift jerk of his arms, Daddy dropped my smart aleck brother into the drink. "Cool off, little man. I'm bigger than you, I'm stronger than you, and you will never defeat me."

Daddy walked off the dock and took me by the hand, leading me back to the house. As we got to the screen door, he bent down to ask me a question. "What do you really think about my moustache? Does it make me look sharp?" He looked at me like a child looks for approval.

"I don't like it. It tickled when you kissed me."

He smiled. "Come on, let's get rid of it."

He got his shaving kit from his suitcase and we went up to the bathroom.

"Well, I was planning on getting rid of it soon. But if you say I should do it now, I'm going to do it." He collected shaving cream from the can and lathered it over his upper lip. I stood transfixed as he transformed back into the clean-shaven Daddy I knew and loved. He washed the soap off and towel-dried his face before admiring himself in the mirror.

"I have to admit, I am one handsome devil."

He tossed the dirty towel into the hamper like he was playing basketball. "Do me a favor, Gerri."

"Yes?"

"If anyone asks, it was your idea to get rid of the moustache."

"Okay."

He hugged me. "How's about we have a little snack? I'll bet if we look hard enough we'll find something good to eat in the fridge."

"I know what we can have." I split the cake and a tall glass of milk with him while he told me his war stories and I pretended I had not heard them a thousand times before. When Aunt Peggy came into the kitchen, he stood up and bowed.

"Wipe that moustache off in my clean house," she said.

It was a moment before I realized she meant the milk one. He stuck his tongue out at her before rolling it slowly over the creamy rectangle above his upper lip, finishing off with a wipe of the back of his hand.

"Vulgar lace curtain trash," Aunt Peggy muttered as she stomped out of the room.

"Oh, well, she won't be around forever to look down on us," Daddy said.

"I hope not," I replied.

He burst into laughter before pouring two more glasses of milk for us to make matching father-daughter moustaches that we licked off in unison, creating vulgar lace curtain memories.

Chapter 11

"**I**'m afraid to see her," I said.

Paddy put his hand on my shoulder. "You can't keep avoiding her."

"I know."

"The longer you wait, the harder it'll be."

"It's just that..."

He bent down and looked into my eyes.

"She needed me and I ran away. I broke my promise."

He grabbed me by the shoulders, shaking me furiously. "She has no right, do you hear me?"

I began to tremble, frightened by the sudden violence of his reaction.

Paddy composed himself, relaxing his grip. "Sorry. I didn't mean to scare you. I just can't stand it when she treats you like you were some kind of a dog or something." He gave me a playful punch in the arm. "But if you don't stand up to her, you deserve it. Just promise me one thing."

"What?"

"Promise me you'll come to me if you get into trouble."

I nodded.

"No, say it."

"I promise."

"Good. Now, go to bed."

The next afternoon, when Daddy and the boys were swimming, I gathered my courage and knocked on Mother's door.

"Come in."

She was in the rocker giving John his bottle. I lowered my head and went to her, kneeling at her feet. She glanced at me. I focused on the rug.

"Get up, Gerri." She took my hand, placing it on John's cheek. "Isn't it soft?"

It was, and I would have liked it if the little stinker had not smelled of poop.

"Do you want to hold him?"

She got out of the rocker.

"Sit down."

She handed him to me, positioning my hand under his damp melon head. Suddenly, he opened his eyes and grasped my pinky with his fingers, clamping onto me like a leech. I found it scary for someone so small to be so strong. I felt a panic rise up in me and pried his fingers loose, passing him back to a surprised Mother.

She put him down in his crib and went back to the rocker, taking the blanket from the seat before she sat. "Here, Gerri, cover him."

I took the blanket and laid it gently across his tiny frame.

Suddenly, Mother flung a Raggedy Andy doll at my head. I picked the poor victim up and put him in the crib beside John. Mother leaned forward in the rocker, pointing at me. "That's right, don't you forget." She folded her arms across her chest. "You're Mother's Little Helper."

Chapter 12

The following day, Daddy and the boys went back to the city. I was waving goodbye as they drove away, just as Aunt Peggy's friend pulled up in her black Cadillac to drop her off from town. She jumped back a step when Daddy honked the horn as he passed by. Composing herself, she called me over. "Come, Geraldine, fetch the groceries."

I ran to her, and she dumped the bags into my arms. She stuck her head in her friend's car window to say goodbye before the woman drove off, without bothering to acknowledge my presence. Aunt Peggy pointed to the front door for me to follow her.

"I trust Mother is feeling well today."

"Yes, but she says she's tired. John's crying keeps us up half the night."

"Yes, I have noticed he is on the noisy side. But I suppose that's how those creatures are."

"What do you mean, Aunt Peggy?"

"The male of the species are born loud. They don't have the natural refinements we possess. We have to break them until they can behave like civilized beings. I suppose we'll just have to deal with the young one as best we can until it gets trained."

I wondered if she thought Mother had given birth to a puppy, instead of a human being. If I looked in her grocery bags, would I find dog biscuits?

"Come, let's check on Elizabeth. Leave the bags on the kitchen table for now."

I followed her inside. She began to trudge upstairs, stopping every two or three steps to catch her breath. I followed half a dozen steps behind, afraid her massive bulk might come crashing down onto me as she wheezed her way up.

"Elizabeth, I'm home."

"In here."

Following my aunt, we stopped outside the half-open bathroom door.

"Come in."

Aunt Peggy pushed the door open the rest of the way, revealing Mother luxuriating in a tub nearly overflowing with bubble bath foam. Pointing to the toilet, she said, "I'd offer you a seat, but the little prince is on the throne."

Aunt Peggy gasped when she saw John sleeping in his baby carrier on the closed toilet seat lid.

"Good Lord, Elizabeth, is that sanitary?"

Springing to an upright position, Mother splashed tub water on the floor, suds dripping down her chest to reveal her swollen breasts.

Aunt Peggy averted her gaze.

"Don't worry, Aunt Peggy. I won't let John's germs contaminate the john. A few shots of Lysol and you'll never know he's been there."

"Don't be vulgar, dear. Save that type of humor for the other side of the family."

Mother winked. "You're right. I've missed your guidance so much, Aunt Peggy. Let me give you a hug." Mother rose to her feet, exposing the fullness of her womanhood.

"No, no, too much to do. Come see me when you're decent," Aunt Peggy said as she fled down the hall in terror at the thought of Mother's flesh touching her.

As soon as she heard Aunt Peggy's bedroom door shut, Mother put on her robe. "Well, I guess we know how to get rid of her in a hurry."

She picked John up. "Follow me." We went to her bedroom, and she put him in the crib. Fluffing up her pillows first, she climbed into bed.

"Have a seat," she said as she indicated with her hand for me to sit next to her. She opened the box of Whitman chocolates Daddy had bought her and plopped one in her mouth. "You know, Geraldine, I trusted that you'd be there for me, and you let me down. Can I count on you?"

"Yes."

"Can I ever truly count on you again? You made a promise and you broke your word."

"I'm sorry."

"That's not good enough. I want you to swear."

She rifled through the night table, but didn't find what she was looking for. I could see by the way her eyes lit up she had an idea. She placed one of my hands on the chocolate box while she raised the other. "Do you solemnly swear you'll always be Mother's Little Helper?"

"I swear."

She let go of my hand. "Good. You can have one chocolate to seal your oath."

She held the box open while I studied the printed guide on the inside of the lid. When I chose the orange cream-filled one she said, "No, that's my favorite."

As I started to put it back, she snatched it from me and dropped it in the wastebasket, "No, it's contaminated now."

She examined the index.

"Here."

She handed me a maple walnut-flavored candy, clearly the worst tasting one in the box, and held it to my lips. I opened my mouth and accepted the heavenly host, crunching the nutty bits while trying not to make a face.

"Thank you."

Finding no napkin to clean her holy fingertips, she wiped her chocolate-smeared digits on the bottom of my blouse.

"Okay. Now I want you to take John for a walk around the lake. The carriage is by the back door."

I gazed at my sleeping brother and couldn't understand why she would want to disturb him. But duty called, so I picked him up, holding him close.

"Take your time. A couple of turns around the lakeshore should do it. Heaven knows you could use the exercise."

The reason behind her plan to pass my brother off to me became clear when I saw her reach for the remote control to click on her soap opera. As I passed in front of the set, she waved me away, just as the melodic voice from the television speaker said, "As sand in the hourglass, so are the days of our lives."

It became a daily routine for me to take John for afternoon walks around Lake Owl's Head. At first, I was unsure how to tell whether he was crying because he was hungry or needed to be changed, or just because he wanted to say, "Look at me. I am here." But I soon learned to tell the difference.

As our time together grew, I started to make up games. I would shake his rattle behind my back. "What's that?"

He'd turn his head from side to side while I switched hands. I always got a kick out of how excited he seemed when the toy miraculously appeared before his eyes. I was Gerri the Magnificent.

Even changing his diaper became a game. I would hold my nose and say, "Who made this smelly mess? Are you the stinky baby?" John would smile and coo, but never admit his guilt, choosing instead to use his baby charm to seduce me into forgiving him his vile acts.

Still, I don't think I bonded with him until the end of the fourth week, the time when Mother began to become a "slack-a-bed" as Aunt Peggy phrased it. One day she just didn't get up. Then she stayed in bed the next day and the day after that, until she started to resemble one of those zombies that Paddy Boy was always talking about.

Often, she didn't seem to notice when I lay John down in his crib. She just stared blankly at the television set or into space. Aunt Peggy tried to coax her up by saying, "It does no good to give in to slothful tendencies, Elizabeth."

Turning her face to the wall, she would reply, "I'm just too tired to get up today. Maybe tomorrow. I am just too exhausted."

One afternoon when I returned with John, I found she had managed to move his crib into my room. I can't say that I really minded all that much. My baby brother was starting to grow on me. Anything I said or did was okay with him, so long as he got his bottle. There was no judgment, no criticism of how I was doing my job.

The evening when I read him, "The Three Little Pigs," I fell in love with him.

"I'll huff..."

There was a hint of a squeaky voice.

"And I'll puff..."

Again, there was a barely discernable sound.

"And I'll blow the house down."

I heard a full-fledged baby giggle and felt a thrill unlike any I'd experienced before. I pulled him to me and felt his peach-pit heart flutter against my chest. We fell asleep together that night, baby brother and big sister, united as one.

The second week in August, Aunt Peggy and I were eating breakfast when Mother appeared at the table acting as if her previous month-long self-imposed exile had all been a dream.

"I'm ready for breakfast. What have you got good to eat?"

Aunt Peggy sprang from her seat. "Anything you want, Elizabeth. I'm so glad to see you up. We'll start you out with bacon and eggs and toast. Is that all right?"

"That would be great, Aunt Peggy."

As she turned her back to go to the refrigerator, Mother put her index finger in her mouth and did her pantomime-gagging act. I bit down hard on my toast to stop myself from laughing.

Just as we were finishing our meal, John began to cry. I began to get up, but Mother pushed me back down in my chair. "No, Gerri, it's my turn."

I didn't know why, but her sudden decision to look after John made me afraid.

When she was gone, Aunt Peggy said, "Don't forget she's his mother, Geraldine. She was your mother first. She just has to remember how she treated you." Then I knew why I was afraid.

"After you do the dishes, I'll show you my new Hummel figurine. She reminds me of you with her plump figure."

"Thank you, Aunt Peggy. I can hardly wait."

The rest of the morning, Mother stayed upstairs while I did my chores. She didn't come down when Aunt Peggy called her for lunch, so my aunt sent me upstairs with a sandwich for her. I found her in bed watching television.

"I made you a tuna fish on rye with chopped celery, the way you like it."

She said nothing, just pointed to the night table, and I put the tray down.

John was in his crib in my bedroom.

"Come on, baby. Let's go for our walk."

I circled the lake three times before heading back. When I arrived home, Mother was standing on the back porch, arms folded, narrowed eyes pinpointed on me. She flew down the steps.

"Where have you been? What are you doing with my baby?" She snatched John from the carriage, slapped me hard across the face, and ran inside.

I walked up the steps, collapsed on the porch swing, and curled myself into a ball. The rain started just as the tears began to flow down my cheeks. I swallowed them, their bitter salt burning my throat. Finally, when I had no more tears left to shed, I became a hard and thorny cactus.

You can't hurt me. My fingers are chubby, but my skin is tough.

I pulled myself up, wiped my cheeks dry, and went inside to keep my promise. I was Mother's Little Helper. I could not let her down.

Chapter 13

One Saturday morning, Daddy drove up to take us home. We were waiting out front when he pulled up with a squeal of tires, sending gravel scattering in all directions beneath the station wagon wheels. When he got out of the car and stretched, he made his biceps muscles dance. His cap was tilted to one side, toothpick dangling from the corner of his mouth. Daddy took his cap off with a flourish as he bowed.

"Your carriage awaits, my fair ladies."

Even Aunt Peggy managed to crack the smallest of smiles at Daddy's playfulness, although it was behind a hand cupped around her mouth.

Mother walked up to him and squeezed his muscles. "Oh my, aren't they hard?" Daddy lifted her onto the hood of the car. He bent down and gave her a long, passionate kiss, the type they used to censor in the movies.

Aunt Peggy's face took on that horror-stricken look she reserved for unseemly public displays of affection.

"Telephone me when you get home, Elizabeth!" she called as she headed for the door, shutting it tight behind her to lock out the scent of hormones in bloom.

When they finally unlocked lips, Daddy helped Mother off the car and clapped his hands together.

"Where's my Johnny?" He walked over to the carriage, picking John up like a sack of potatoes.

"There's Daddy's little man." He danced around with him, raising my brother high over his head.

Suddenly, he held him away from his body. "Lizzie, honey, I think he needs to be changed."

"Give him to Gerri. She knows how to do it."

Daddy seemed surprised. "What's the matter, Lizzie? Don't you want to get dirty?"

"Frankie, don't be a pain. I've changed more diapers in my life than you can even count. Can't I ask my own daughter to help out now and then?"

"Just remember, he's *your* baby."

Mother opened the back door to the car, got in and slammed it shut.

Daddy sighed as he handed John to me, "Sweetheart, please?"

"Of course, Daddy. I'll take care of it."

I changed his diaper as fast as I could while Mother glared at me from the back seat.

We drove back to the city in a silent truce, Daddy listening to the baseball game on the radio, Mother sulking behind a magazine, me and John trying to find peace in our dreams.

The following Sunday morning, the family got ready for John's christening. He was dressed in the white satin baptismal gown all the Moran children had been christened in. When Paddy Boy said he looked like a fairy, Daddy reminded him he had been christened in the same dress. That shut Paddy up.

We arrived at our parish shortly before eleven. As we entered the church, my parents beamed when they saw it was filled to overflowing. It was one of those occasions where people who hadn't been in a church in years showed up and tried to remember the words to the rituals.

As I sat in the pew with my brothers, I looked at Mother. She was radiant, hair lacquered to bouffant perfection, makeup applied perfectly. A ray of light shone through the stained glass window, casting a rosy glow across her face. At that moment, holding John close to her bosom, she was the image of the Madonna.

Mass was long and I began to look around for points of interest. My eyes focused on Jesus nailed to the cross behind the altar. Studying him, I had an urge to go up and fix the diaper hanging so sloppily from his skinny frame. I guessed they did not have safety pins back then.

The time came for my parents to go up to the baptismal font, and I was left alone with my brothers. I was shocked to find Paddy reading a Batman comic behind the cover of a holy book. Billy, on the other hand, seemed to be following each word the priest was saying as if his very salvation depended on it.

After Mass was finally over, we walked to the Knights of Columbus Hall. Mother put John in a cradle in the corner. She took a seat next to him, waiting for her throngs of admirers to gather around.

As the guests began to filter in, groups of women would gravitate to Mother, put their heads into John's bassinet, and make comments.

"Oh, he looks just like Francis."

"Maybe around the forehead, but he definitely has Lizzie's eyes."

"You're both wrong. He takes after Irene's Sean."

Mother basked in her role, exchanging kisses and making small talk as well as any seasoned politician.

Daddy, for his part, passed out obligatory cigars to the men as he nearly burst with pride. His good mood was momentarily disrupted when he caught Paddy Boy lighting up a cigar in the men's room and had to chase him out of the hall to give him the licking he deserved.

When the buffet table was ready Daddy went to the microphone that was set up in front of the stage. He turned it on, tapping on it with his finger.

"Can I have everyone's attention, please?" A hush fell over the crowd.

"I want to thank everyone for coming today to celebrate with us. It's been awhile since we've welcomed a new baby into the clan. I wasn't sure if I had it in me anymore, but my beautiful wife convinced me just how much of a man I am."

Mother blushed as she shook her head.

"Before we head to the chow line, I've asked Father O'Meara to say a few words."

The priest got up and shook hands with Daddy. "Bless you, Francis. This is truly a joyous occasion, a time to welcome a new soul into the communion of saints."

As if on cue, John began to cry.

"It looks like he's talking to us. Let's reply with a prayer."

We closed our eyes.

"Father, hear our prayer as we seek your heavenly blessing. We submit ourselves as children that we may be reborn anew. This we pray, in the name of the Father, the Son, and the Holy Spirit. Amen." We crossed ourselves as we said amen in unison and opened our eyes.

"Now, I don't know about you, but I'm starving. I declare the buffet officially open," he announced, and he raced to the table as if he had advance word from above that another famine was coming to plague our people.

We gorged ourselves on plate after plate as the smells of food and liquor and smoke intermingled to form a hedonistic curtain around our Celtic tribe. After dinner, an accordionist appeared at the microphone. He was short and stout, with a full beard, looking like a younger version of Burl Ives. His name was Danny "Magic Fingers" Hannigan.

When the music began, Daddy had already downed several pints. He slammed his mug down, and held his hand out to Mother. "Dance with me, sweetheart."

He led her onto the floor, and they began to twirl.

None of the other couples could match my parents' gracefulness. They were perfectly in sync, each move followed by a countermove. It was a flawless performance of two bodies that know each other so well they can anticipate where the other is going.

The music stopped for a brief intermission when cake and coffee were served. When we were done with dessert, Danny Hannigan announced there would be a "Ladies Only" jig contest.

Aunt Colleen grabbed my hand saying, "Come on, Gerri, you can win it."

"No, I'm not good enough."

"Yes, you are. You know you are."

Now, unknown to anyone else, Aunt Colleen had been teaching me her best dance moves for the past year. We both knew I was good. Still, I felt too self-conscious to dance in front of a crowd. Jiggling rolls of flesh can be so unflattering on a young girl, Mother always said. Ignoring my protests, Aunt Colleen half-dragged me to the dance floor. Four rows of dancers lined up, ready to wage battle. Mother parked herself directly in front of a giddy Aunt Colleen.

Danny explained the contest rules. "Here's how it's going to work. We're going to have a dance-off. To stop us voting for our friends, Father O'Meara will be the initial judge. If he taps you on the shoulder it means you've been eliminated and have to leave the floor. We'll eliminate dancers until we're down to the final two. The audience will decide the best dancer. Father O'Meara will put his hand over the dancers' heads, and the audience will clap the loudest for their favorite. Ladies, are you ready? Dancers line up. On your mark...get set... dance."

The music began, slowly at first, building speed with each subsequent chorus. There were hoots and whistles as contestants were sent packing by a tap of unbiased Father O'Meara's "Fingers of Doom."

Danny continued to play at a frantic pace, building to a feverish pitch. It wasn't long before there were only four of us left: a teenage girl I did not know, Aunt Colleen, Mother, and me. The priest moved down the line and tapped Aunt Colleen on her shoulder. As she walked off the floor she whispered in my ear, "You can do it, Gerri."

Next, the teenager was eliminated.

It was mother against me.

Heels clicking in rapid fire, I let the music possess me, until the rhythm hypnotized me. My feet seemed to move without my telling them to do so—one-two-three-four. I did not see or hear, just felt the beat in my blood driving me into a dizzying frenzy, until Danny wound up with a last squeeze of his accordion for the final notes and a step-step-step. The crowd kept singing along with the music that had stopped before Danny hushed them, and we stood still for final judgment.

Father O'Meara put his hand over Mother's head, and the crowd clapped enthusiastically. When he put his hand over my head, however, the applause was twice as loud.

Danny Hannigan came over and led me to the microphone. He raised my arm the way a referee lifts the arm of a prizefighter. Taking a gold plastic trophy from the table behind me, he pressed it into my hands. "Ladies and gentlemen, we have a winner."

The spectators cheered wildly. I curtsied as I let the golden aura of triumph wash over me. All I could see was the crowd clapping for me, feeding my need with their love. I didn't notice when Mother left the floor.

Paddy Boy and Billy gave me a standing ovation. They rushed over, hoisted me up on their shoulders, and paraded me around the hall.

When we arrived back at our table, I finally noticed Mother was panting, perspiration pouring down her pale face. Daddy caught her in his arms as she fainted. "Get that girl down from there, you fools! Can't you see your Mother is sick?"

My brothers lowered me, retreating to their seats. I smoothed my dress down and stood there, not knowing what to do or say.

Slowly, Mother came to and sat up. Daddy helped her to a chair and planted a kiss on her head as he stood behind her.

She raised her eyes, and I saw the anger behind them.

I tried to hand her my trophy. She pushed it away. "No, it's yours. You earned it. I'm nothing if not a good sport. Isn't that right, Frankie?"

"Yes, Lizzie, you've never been one to begrudge an opponent their victory prize."

Show over, the party broke up, leaving guests scattering until the next orgy of food and drink that marked their social calendars.

Before I turned out the bedroom lamp that evening, I examined my trophy, fingering the words "Number One Dancer," tracing the letters over and over. I put it on my dresser in a place of honor next to the crucifix Grandma had given me for my first communion and the Kewpie doll I had won at the church bazaar.

The following Friday afternoon, I went to throw a candy wrapper in the kitchen garbage. When I lifted the lid, something gleaming caught my eye. I dug it out from beneath a rotten head of cabbage. It was the top half of my trophy. I took a dish towel and wiped the filth from my prize. I found the base beneath another four inches of trash. Retreating to my bedroom, I sat down on the edge of the bed in disbelief, holding the two pieces against each other, unable to figure out how to put the broken puzzle back together again.

Paddy startled me when he suddenly appeared in the doorway. "She did it, you know."

"What're you talking about?"

"Your trophy, you dummy. Mother smashed it under her heel."

"You're making it up."

"Do you really think so, Gerri? Look me in the eyes and tell me that you think I'm making it up. Come on, do it if you can."

I looked at him. Our eyes locked, and I knew I could not call him a fibber. Tears started to roll down my cheeks as the hurtfulness of what Mother had done overwhelmed me.

Paddy pulled me to him and hugged me tight, then pushed me away while he shook his head. "I know, Gerri. But that's the way the truth is sometimes; it hurts. And this is a pretty awful truth. I think I'd have to call this a real kick in the balls."

"Paddy, Mother will wash your mouth out."

He laughed. Suddenly, he ripped the trophy from my hands, went to the window and opened it. "This is what you have to do with Mother." He reared back and threw the top half out the window.

He tried to force me to take the bottom part. "Here you go, sister. It's your turn."

I resisted for a moment, and he withdrew his offer. Rearing back, he pitched the rest of my prize into the street before vehemently shaking his finger in my face. "I told you, Gerri. You've got to let go. Just let go."

Tackling me to the floor, he began to tickle me. "Say it. Say you'll just let go."

"I give, I give."

"Say it."

"I'll let go. I swear I'll let go."

He released me from his grip, then pulled me to him and whispered in my ear. "You only hurt the ones you love." He smacked me on the top of the head with the palm of his hand.

"Well then, you must love me a whole lot, Paddy Boy." I gave him a punch in the shoulder, and he helped me to my feet.

"Come on, I'll buy you a soda at Tony's."

When we arrived downstairs, I spotted the top half of my trophy in the middle of the street, picked it up, and smashed it under my heel.

Paddy pinched my cheeks. "Good girl. Come on, I'll race you to the candy store." Of course, he tripped me so he would win, shouting as he flew past, "Never give a sucker an even break!"

Chapter 14

"Get that filthy rodent out of here!" Mother screamed.

Aunt Colleen held fast to Lizzie-the-squirrel's cage as Mother waved her knife in the air. "She's not dirty. I gave her a bath last night."

"I'm warning you."

Aunt Colleen pulled the squirrel close to her chest, whispering in its ear. "Don't let the mean old sourpuss scare you. She doesn't know what it means to love anyone."

Before Mother could respond, Grandma entered the room. "Colleen, why is that animal here? I've told you a hundred times to keep it in your room. You know the rule: If you can't take care of a living thing it will be taken away from you. It's dangerous to keep it out in a house with a baby."

Mother pointed her knife at Aunt Colleen. "See. I told you so."

In a rapid move, Grandma snatched the knife from Mother. "You're just as dangerous, waving sharp utensils around like that."

Aunt Colleen stuck her tongue out.

Mother threw a roll at her, but it missed the target and hit the wall. Aunt Colleen bent down to pick it up. Tearing a piece off, she fed it to her squirrel saying, "Thanks. Now I can feed her so she'll be very strong when I have her bite you."

Mother glared at her.

"Just take that thing upstairs, Colleen. I'm in no mood for your shenanigans, missy," Grandma said as she took a seat across from Mother.

"Okay, fine and dandy, eat some candy. No one wants to stay in this smelly apartment anyway," Aunt Colleen replied. Lifting the cage over her head the way a player on the winning team hoists a sports trophy, Aunt Colleen marched out of the apartment saying, "Come, Lizzie, let's get out of this dump."

Grandma shook her head. "Three days before Thanksgiving and my girls are fighting. I'm only glad your father isn't alive to see this." Grandma rolled her eyes toward heaven the way she always did when invoking Grandpa Sean's name. I barely remembered my grandfather, other than as a figure who insisted on forcing animal crackers on me every time he saw me. But I'd heard his name invoked so often during a lifetime of family fights that I began to picture him as a saintly spirit in white robes who hung his head in shame whenever his daughters got into a knock-down and drag-out.

"Daddy would never have approved of your letting Colleen keep that creature as a pet."

"My Sean always kept animals. I used to tease him and say he reminded me of a rum-soaked St. Francis."

"Daddy never would have brought something like that home."

"I remember one time he brought home a stray dog that had followed him back from the pub. He scrubbed it and taught it tricks."

"Yes, a dog. That's a normal pet for a normal person."

"He named it Scrappy, owing to the fact that he was a wiry little guy, always skittering back and forth. Yes, he was a fine dog, our Scrappy."

"Mother, you're not listening."

"Then there was the time he brought home that bird that'd been injured, and nursed it back to health."

"Mother, it's not the same."

"Oh, Gerri, it was the cutest thing."

"Damn it, Mother, your precious Colleen is parent to a fucking squirrel."

Quick as a flash of lightning, Grandma leaned over the table and slapped Mother. "I will not tolerate that sort of language from a child of mine."

The blood rose to Mother's cheeks as she stabbed a stick of butter with her knife. Quickly regaining composure, she got up and walked out the door without saying a word. Grandma just stared at her own hand as if it had betrayed her.

The phone rang, and I scrambled to answer it. It was Daddy.

"Gerri, I'm bringing home the biggest turkey you ever saw. I won it in the pub raffle. Where's your mother?"

"She went out, but she didn't say where she was going."

"Okay. Let's keep this our little secret then. She'll be thrilled when she sets eyes on it. It's a beauty. Promise not to say anything?"

"I promise."

"Good. I'll be home soon. See you in a bit, sweetheart."

He hung up and I turned around to find Grandma was gone. I went to my room and settled down on my bed to do my homework.

An hour later, I heard Daddy come in. He called for Mother saying, "Lizzie, my love, I have a surprise for you."

Suddenly, I heard Mother let out an ear-piercing shriek.

I ran to the living room to find Daddy holding a live turkey while Mother stood atop the sofa flailing her arms as if she was desperately trying to fly away. "Get it out!" she yelled.

"But it's for Thanksgiving dinner. I won it," Daddy replied.

"It's disgusting."

"But baby, it's a perfectly good bird."

Bending down, Mother removed a cushion and jumped off the couch. She ran behind Daddy and began to hit him with her weapon of choice.

"Out, out!"

When he lifted his hands to shield himself from her blows, the bird flew from his arms and began to run through the apartment. Mother ran to her bedroom, locking herself in, while Daddy chased the turkey.

The apartment door opened and Paddy announced, "Honey, I'm home." I watched in amazement as the bird ran past him, followed by Daddy, hot on his heels. It took a moment for Paddy to realize what he had witnessed, then he joined the festivities in mad pursuit down the steps, shouting for all the neighbors to hear, "Turkey hunt!"

The next day, Daddy came home with a regular bird, dead and plucked, dumping it on the dining room table with a resounding thud.

"Hope this will do."

Mother got up, hugging him around the waist.

"Yes, that will work nicely."

Suddenly, Aunt Colleen came running in, followed by Grandma. She went up to Mother, pointing an accusatory finger in her face.

"Where is she?"

"What're you talking about?"

"Where's Lizzie? What have you done with my squirrel?"

Grandma grabbed Aunt Colleen by the arm. "You don't know that your sister had anything to do with it."

She pried Grandma's fingers from her arm. "She took her. She kidnapped Lizzie."

Mother shook her head. "I've had enough of this."

We were all surprised when she calmly walked to her bedroom. But Aunt Colleen started to go after her, and Daddy had to restrain her, actually carrying her upstairs while Grandma led the way.

Thanksgiving morning arrived. Grandma was ready to start cooking at the crack of dawn. I was going to be her assistant that year.

As I was about to go upstairs, I remembered to get Mother's stuffing from the refrigerator. She always made the dressing, finding some way to make it special: raisins, walnuts, diced celery. That year she made it with sausage she'd bought at Gino's Butcher Shop the day before. She said it would be the best meal we'd ever had because the meat was very special.

It was a lot of work for Grandma and me to cook the dinner for all of us, but it was worth the effort when I saw how much everyone enjoyed themselves. Best of all, despite all the stressful turmoil of the past few days, we all got along, even Mother and Aunt Colleen.

On Friday afternoon, Daddy took Billy, Paddy, and me to the park to toss the football around. I wasn't usually included in their games, as Mother found such sports to be unsuitable for a young lady. But she had gone shopping that day, so I was one of the boys.

I never knew sports could be so much fun. I was usually left on the sidelines, one of the kids who got picked last. My brothers and Daddy made me part of the team, not seeming to mind that I did not know the rules and could neither catch nor throw. It was as though I had been given a free pass. I felt almost... happy.

Time passed quickly, growing close to dinnertime before we knew it. I knew it was going to be the perfect day. When it was time to leave, we exited through the south side of the park where the Italian stores were located. As we strolled down the block, a sign in the window of Gino's Butcher Shop caught my eye. I did a double take, but it still read, "Out of Business."

Daddy noticed my expression. "Gerri, what is it? You look like you've seen the bogeyman."

I pointed at the sign.

"She said she bought it here."

"Who bought what?"

"Mother bought the sausage for the stuffing there."

Paddy punched me in the arm. "You must be wrong. He closed up and went back to Sicily a couple of months ago. He made a couple of mobsters angry and had to leave real fast... or else," Paddy said as he moved his finger across his throat.

Daddy crouched down, looking at me with his most solemn face. "Are you sure that's what she said?"

"Yes, Daddy, I'm positive."

Daddy got up, scratching his head. "What a funny thing for her to lie about. Oh, well, let's go home. I'm sure it's nothing."

We'd gone another two blocks when he suddenly stopped as though he just remembered something. "Billy, come here."

Daddy opened his wallet, handing him a couple of bills. "I want you to take your brother and sister to the movies. Get some hot dogs for supper."

Paddy objected. "Hot dogs? You must be joking! What about Thanksgiving leftovers?"

Daddy glared. "When I'm talking to you, little boy, I'll let you know."

Paddy Boy shrank into himself.

"Now, go."

"Thank you, Daddy," we all said as we walked toward the movie theater.

It was getting dark as we approached our apartment building on the trip home that day. Through the encroaching shadows, I saw Aunt Colleen sitting in her lawn chair.

"That can't be what I think it is," Billy said.

"I see it, too," Paddy replied.

The three of us ran to her.

It was the first turkey!

Aunt Colleen smiled, winding the rope attached to the bird's neck around her wrist the way you might do when walking a dog.

"Isn't it great? Your Mother gave it to me."

I jumped back when the turkey that Daddy had brought home moved its head toward me in a pecking motion.

"She said it was to replace Lizzie. She said she knew how much she meant to me." Aunt Colleen picked the protesting fowl up onto her lap as if it were a beady-eyed baby. "I'm sure your father put her up to it."

Billy looked at me, and I looked at Paddy, then back to Billy.

"I've named her Lizzie the Third."

Paddy bent down, kissing Aunt Colleen on the cheek.

"She's a fine bird, Aunt Colleen."

Our aunt broke into an enormous grin. "Are you going to say goodnight to her?"

Hesitating just a moment, Paddy tried to lay a kiss on the bewildered creature, but the fickle fowl spurned his advances. "I guess she just has to get used to me first. I'm usually a hit with the ladies."

Billy patted him on the back. "Come on, Romeo. We'd better go up."

"But you didn't say goodnight to Lizzie."

Taking his handkerchief from his pocket, Billy faked a sneeze.

"I'm afraid I may be catching cold. I wouldn't want her to get sick."

Aunt Colleen nodded. "What about you, Gerri? Come show Lizzie that you're going to be friends."

I reached in my jeans pocket and pulled out the box of chocolate-covered raisins I had left over from the movies and put some in the palm of my hand. "Here you go, Lizzie."

The bird pecked at them with a ferocity that hurt. I wiped the turkey germs on my pants.

"Better not fatten her up, Gerri. Thanksgiving comes every year," Paddy said.

Aunt Colleen gasped, pulling Lizzie close to protect her from my brother's threat. "Don't worry, Lizzie. I won't let the mean boy touch you."

My brothers and I started upstairs, but at the landing, Paddy blocked our path. "She should have named it Squirrel Stew."

Billy gave him a quizzical look. "What do you mean?"

"Put it together, Sherlock. The squirrel disappears. We get sausage from a closed shop. Then Mother gives a new pet to Aunt Colleen."

"No, she couldn't have. That's just... crazy. "

"And you think Aunty Colleen is the only Looney Tune in the family? "

Billy's face took on the shocked appearance of someone who has just heard an awful truth, but isn't ready to accept it.

We went to the living room and sat in a row on the couch, but a minute later, Billy sprang to his feet. "No, you'll see. I'll prove you're wrong." He ran to the kitchen and opened the refrigerator, frantically pulling out plates and bowls in a desperate search for evidence to refute reality.

The noise attracted Daddy, and he charged from the bedroom to the kitchen. "What're you doing?" he asked.

"Where is it?" Billy replied.

"Where's what?"

"Where's the stuffing? What have you done with the stuffing?" Our poor Billy kept searching in vain for the missing dish.

Finally, Daddy pulled Billy out from the refrigerator and carried him back to the couch, where he dumped him before taking a seat on the coffee table. Daddy's eyes were menacing slits, and his voice quivered with rage when he addressed us.

"Thanksgiving is over. I don't want to hear another word about stuffing or sausage or missing squirrels again." He rose, his massive body towering over us. "Ever."

We nodded.

He got a beer from the refrigerator, went to his bedroom, and locked the door.

After he had been gone a few minutes, Paddy took a walnut from the bowl and flicked it at Billy's head.

"That hurts!" he protested.

Paddy stuck his tongue out at him, and Billy got up with clenched fists. Paddy Boy raised his arms to shield himself.

"Here comes Daddy," Paddy said to distract Billy long enough to move from the couch to the lounge chair.

"I just want to know one thing," Paddy said.

"What's that?" Billy asked.

"Doesn't this make you want to become a vegetarian?"

Billy took the bowl of mixed nuts and dumped the contents on Paddy's head.

"Nuts to you."

Billy began to walk toward their bedroom.

Grabbing a fistful of nuts from the floor, Paddy began to pelt him mercilessly with them as he shouted after him. "You just need to get down on your knees and thank God you're not a squirrel! Lizzie would skin you just as soon as look at you, little man!"

Chapter 15

We never put the tree up before Christmas Eve in our family. It had nothing to do with tradition. It was due to the fear of a fire breaking out. Mother constantly kept refilling the base with water, reminding us that just one spark could set the whole house ablaze. Grandma, too, would fill us with horror stories of families being burnt to death, just as they ought to have been celebrating the happiest day of the year.

By the day after Christmas, the tree lay out on the sidewalk, mocking us from below with how it terrified us: *Look at me, I'm the deadly evergreen tree.*

Paddy dragged it to the lot on the next block and tossed a match onto it saying, "You're not so tough now, are you?"

New Year's Eve, on the other hand, seemed to bring out feelings of tranquility in my relatives; it unleashed a vague hope that things would change for the better, destiny would be fulfilled, and the Moran clan would be crowned as kings and queens of Erin. After much pleading, I was allowed to stay up late that year, but was mystified by all the fuss. I ended up bored by the whole process and really wanted to go to sleep; however, my pride would not allow me to admit defeat.

Daddy broke out the best liquor right before midnight. He poured out real drinks for the adults and gave us kids cokes with lemon slices, totally exotic to us. At midnight, I raised my glass with the others and toasted the New Year with a healthy swig. Daddy kissed Mother, then Grandma, followed by Aunt Colleen. Paddy Boy chased me around the room until I gave up and he planted a messy raspberry on top of my head.

The next morning, Mother was still asleep when she got a phone call. Paddy had picked up. Mother was not a morning person, and the effects of a hangover could only make her mood worse. Savvy fellow that he was, Paddy asked Billy to wake her.

She looked very cross when she passed us at the breakfast table. The lingering odor of alcohol wafted through the kitchen when she grabbed the receiver from Paddy's hand.

She just kept saying, "I see, uh-huh." When she hung up I could have sworn I saw a twinkle in her eyes. She went back to bed without saying a word to us.

"What do you think that was about?" Billy asked.

"I don't know, but it must have been important for someone to call on a hangover holiday," Paddy replied.

We only had to wait until we finished dinner that evening for her to reveal the topic of her conversation. Daddy had just swallowed his last morsel when she got up and wrapped her arms around him. "Frankie, I have something to tell you."

"Yes, what is it?"

"Guess what it is. Come on, take a guess."

There was a football game on television that Daddy wanted to watch, so he was short with her.

"I don't have time to play guessing games, Lizzie. Just tell me what you have to say."

She took her arms from my father's shoulders and sat back down. "No, now I should make you wait."

Grandma shook her head. "Why do you always have to make such a production out of everything? Just tell us what the news is."

Aunt Colleen snickered. Mother stood and started to walk away. Daddy rose and grabbed her around the shoulders saying, "Please, sweetheart, can't we start off the new year in a spirit of goodwill?"

Succumbing to his charm, she decided to play nice. "I had a call this morning from upstate." She tried to hide her glee by keeping a solemn expression, but could not conceal the joy in the tone of her voice. "Aunt Peggy is dead."

Chapter 16

"All right, let me look at you," Mother said. We stood in a row, three tin soldiers ready for inspection. Mother gave me the once-over. "Your hat's a little crooked," she said as she untied and retied the strap.

Paddy was next. "Pull your tie up." He tightened the knot. "Tuck your shirt in." He shoved the tail in. "Can't you ever comb your hair?" Mother clicked her handbag open and pulled out her pink styling comb. Paddy Boy squirmed while she created a part.

"Jesus Christ, Ma, I'm not a girl," he said.

Billy shook his head.

Daddy yelled from the kitchen. "Don't you talk to your mother with that tone of voice!" He stuck his head in the doorway.

"But Daddy, I'm a man."

Daddy galloped into the room. He wrapped his massive arms around Mother's tiny shoulders, engulfing her with muscles. "How's about we let Paddy be a boy, Lizzie?"

"I just don't want my family looking like a bunch of ragamuffins."

He let go of her. "What about me, Lizzie? Am I still the man of your dreams?" He smoothed down his overcoat and slicked back his hair with the palm of his hand.

Mother eyeballed him. "You'll do, Frankie Moran. You'll do."

He clapped his hands. "Hallelujah! She still loves me." He winked. "All right, troops. Let's move out."

We buttoned up and followed Daddy out the door, marching down the tenement steps. A bitter wind slapped us in the face as we stepped outside.

71

Daddy walked briskly, crunching snow underfoot. The rest of us tried to keep up with his long strides, doubling and tripling our normal gait, only to fall behind time and again.

It was only four blocks to the funeral home, but I would have preferred it to be four miles. It was my first funeral. I was terrified at the thought of being in the same room with a dead person. Paddy had been filling me with stories about the living dead since we had heard about Aunt Peggy's death.

Daddy held the door to Sullivan Brothers Funeral Home open for us. It took a few moments to focus after coming in from the bright sunshine. A series of lamps cast a jaundiced glow against the walls.

I felt to make sure my cross was still around my neck, protection against any vampires who might be lurking within.

Mother took a seat on a dark green sofa, while Daddy stood. After several minutes, a gaunt man who looked like Boris Karloff approached my parents and shook their hands. I reached into my pocket and caressed my lucky rabbit's foot, backup in case the cross did not work. "If you'll follow me, I'll take you to Mrs. Donovan. I think you'll be pleased with the arrangements."

We entered a large room with a high ceiling. There were rows of bridge chairs leading up to two wing chairs in the front row. The fragrance of a mixed assortment of flowers penetrated my nostrils, nauseating me with their cloying sweetness.

Then, I caught sight of it. The wood was smooth and dark. Brass handles gleamed like golden coins from a pirate's treasure chest. White bedding lined the inside. In the middle, head propped up by a satin pillow, lay Aunt Peggy. Her hands were folded across her body, over her finest dress.

Daddy took a seat in the back of the room, Billy on his left, Paddy Boy on his right. Mother took me by the hand, and we walked to the wing chairs in front. Grandma was sitting on the left, clutching a balled-up tissue in her hand. She looked up. "Lizzie, you've come," she said.

"Of course I've come. Why wouldn't I come? I loved Aunt Peggy."

"I loved Aunt Peggy," a voice from the chair on the right mocked.

I turned and saw Aunt Colleen's shock of red bangs beneath the veil. She pulled the netting back revealing her blue eyes and freckled face. "The only thing you loved about Aunt Peggy was her money."

Mother's lower lip began to twitch.

Grandma jumped out of her seat and put her body in front of Aunt Colleen to shield her from Mother's wrath.

"Now, Elizabeth, you know she doesn't know what she's saying. It's not her fault."

Mother shook her head. "How many times have I heard that before?"

Aunt Colleen started to cry. "Boohoo, boohoo," Mother said. She grabbed my arm and began to drag me toward Aunt Peggy, but I resisted. I was too afraid to approach the casket. She loosened her grip and snapped at me. "Go sit with your father until you're ready to pay your respects!"

I scurried off to Daddy's side while Mother went to Aunt Peggy, wailing her heart out like it was the end of the world. When she came back, Daddy and the boys went up in turn. Mother would not look at me, choosing instead to keep weeping into her handkerchief. Periodically, mourners would come in and greet my parents with remarks such as, "She had a good life."

"She didn't suffer. That's what matters."

And most puzzling of all, "She's in a better place."

Then they would go to Grandma and Aunt Colleen to make small talk before going to visit with Aunt Peggy.

Afternoon faded to dusk, and the last of the mourners filed out. As Grandma and Aunt Colleen proceeded to the exit, Daddy called to them, "See you at the pub!".

Grandma nodded as she walked past, arm in arm with Aunt Colleen.

Mother whispered to me. "Don't you want to say goodbye to Aunt Peggy, Gerri Girl? You know that after me you were her favorite niece."

"She's a chicken," Paddy said.

"No, I'm not," I said.

Of course, he was right. I would rather have died myself than admit it to him.

The funeral director returned. "May I have a word, Mr. and Mrs. Moran?" he asked.

"Of course, Mr. Sullivan," Daddy replied.

Mother stopped to encourage me one last time. "Gerri, I can't force you to go up, but I think you'll find that it's not as bad as all that. We all need to say goodbye, to make our peace."

The gaunt man bared his teeth as he nodded. He looked like a skeleton in a suit. My parents followed him out.

I took a deep breath and started down the aisle. Beads of sweat trickled down my back. I went up to the pad, knelt down and shut my eyes. When I opened them I looked down at Aunt Peggy's rouged cheeks. She looked like a circus clown, all white powder and lipstick and rouge. Even the flower pin on her lapel looked like one of those joke flowers that squirt water. I got off the kneeling pad and stood up. That's when I thought I heard a noise. At first, it was barely perceptible, like the whisper of leaves in a gentle autumn breeze. It grew louder. It was the sound of snoring. My heart began to flutter. Paddy had told me that sometimes doctors make mistakes and people who are still alive get buried by mistake. What if they had made a mistake with Aunt Peggy?

I leaned closer to the casket. The snoring continued, but her lips were still, her chest was not heaving. My curiosity grew larger than my fear. I stood up on the cushion to get a better view. The snoring continued.

Standing up on my toes, I lost my balance. As I tumbled forward into the coffin the last thing I remember is my hand brushing against Aunt Peggy's cold, rouged cheek. It sent a shiver through me before I passed out.

"Gerri, can you hear me?" Daddy asked.

I opened my eyes to find myself on the sofa in the lobby. "Aunt Peggy! Daddy, she's alive, we have to help her!"

He pulled me up and brushed the hair out of my eyes. He pressed a damp handkerchief against the lump on my forehead where my head had hit against the side of Aunt Peggy's new home.

"Hush. Believe me, Aunt Peggy is stone cold, dead. It was just Paddy's idea of a practical joke to make those snoring noises. Billy saw him and let me know."

I looked around for Paddy, but did not see him.

"But don't you worry. He won't be able to sit for a month of Sundays. I'll see to that."

Later that evening, Paddy knocked on my door.

"Come in."

He had a sheepish grin on his face.

"I just wanted to tell you I'm sorry for what I did to you today. Can you forgive me, little sister?"

"I don't know."

"What if I promise that I will always protect you? Will you let me be your guardian angel?"

"How will you do that?"

He thought for a moment. "Anytime you think a zombie is coming to get you, call me and I'll be there."

I didn't answer him. He reached into his pocket and took out his most treasured possession, a Swiss Army knife, and offered it to me. "What if I give you this to seal the deal?"

I shook my head.

No matter how angry I was with him, I couldn't let him give up his knife. But I knew how serious he was about being sorry by the offer so I decided to forgive him.

"Why don't we just swear that no matter what, we'll always be friends? Okay?" He spit in his hand and held it out to me.

I never could resist Paddy's charm.

"What do you say? Is it a deal?"

I spit in my hand and we shook. "Deal."

The next morning our family went to Saint Timothy's church for the burial Mass. We took seats in the second row behind Grandma and Aunt Colleen.

The casket stood in the middle of the aisle where you lined up to take Holy Communion. Try as I might, I could not avoid looking at it. My eyes were drawn back to it each time I turned away. A shiver passed through me as I remembered the sensation of Aunt Peggy's flesh against mine.

I resolved to fix my gaze on something else and chose the massive crucifix on the wall above the altar. If all else fails, turn to Jesus.

The crown of thorns dug deep into his head, carved droplets of blood dripping down his face. His eyes betrayed his pain; his mouth pleaded for drink.

My eyes continued down to his torso: pierced side; ragged loincloth on a pitiful frame. Down the legs to his feet, nails holding them firmly in place, no escape. I reversed direction and raised my eyes upward to his outstretched arms. More nails, more pain. There would be no escape, but at least his Mother loved him. Thin or fat, Mary would support her child. I felt tears well up in my eyes.

A hand on the top of my head brought me back to the mortal world. "Bless you, Geraldine, don't weep for Aunt Peggy," Father O'Meara said. He brought his other hand to my cheek and wiped away the trail of tears that had flowed there. The warmth of his touch spread over my body. It felt like the hand of God touching my soul.

When he removed his hands, I felt cold.

No, put them back. Suffer not the little children.

Instead, he turned to Daddy. "I'll ride with Mrs. O'Reilly and our Colleen."

"Very good," Daddy replied.

We put our coats on and walked out into freezing sleet and gusty winds. I pulled my scarf over my mouth.

Suddenly frail, Grandma leaned on Daddy's arm for support. He led her to the limousine parked at the curb. Daddy helped her in first, then Aunt Colleen. Finally, Father O'Meara got in of his own accord.

Daddy opened the door to the second limousine for Mother and we followed him. "Scoot in, kids," he said. We piled in and he shut the door.

The driver pulled out and we drove to the cemetery. The ride was unnaturally quiet for the Moran clan. Each of us sat with our thoughts, together, yet alone.

By the time we arrived at the cemetery the sleet had turned to snow. We sloshed through the muck to the burial site. A small tent covered Aunt Peggy's casket. There were two bridge chairs on either side.

Daddy escorted Grandma and Aunt Colleen to their seats. He stood to the left of Grandma. Mother and I sat opposite them, Billy and Paddy flanking our sides.

Father O'Meara began to chant the magic words and we all joined in with our well-rehearsed responses "In the Name of the Father, and the Son, and the Holy Spirit... Amen."

About midway through the performance, I saw Daddy pull a silver flask from his coat pocket and take a healthy swig. As he started to put it away, Grandma tugged at his sleeve. He handed it to her and she took a healthy nip. She tried to give it back to him, but he shook his head. With the swift move of a seasoned pro, she slipped it into her purse.

When the service was over, we began to march away from the grave. I turned and took one last look as the workmen started to lower Aunt Peggy into the ground.

Goodbye, Aunt Peggy. Don't forget to wipe your feet.

We drove straight to Clancy's Pub, filing into Daddy's home away from home.

"Hey there, Mike," he greeted the bartender.

"Hi-ho, Frankie," Mike replied.

"Is everything ready?"

"You know it. Go on back and enjoy yourselves."

Daddy led us to a door with a sign that read "Private Party." He opened it and a thick curtain of tobacco smoke enveloped us and I began to choke from the stench. There were half a dozen banquet tables scattered about. The people sitting at them were strangers to me. Several of them greeted Daddy as we passed, standing to shake his hand.

"Thank you for inviting us. I was so sorry to hear about your loss."

"Keep your spirits up, lad. There's a better life waiting for us."

Only one of them, a wizened old man wearing a timeworn suit, spoke to anyone else in the family. He went to Grandma, putting his hands over hers. "I was so sorry to hear about Peggy. Aren't many of us from the first generation left, are there?"

"That's true. It'll be our turn soon enough."

"No, not you, my fair Irene. You're a flower that will never wither— a thing of beauty that will last forever."

Grandma blushed like a schoolgirl. "Go on with you now, Finnerty. The devil has a warm place reserved for liars of your sort."

He put his hand over his heart. "You've hurt me to the quick."

"Well, go on and have a drink. That will fix what ails you soon enough." Grandma slipped her hands from his grasp, and we continued on to a table in the corner, next to a jukebox.

Mother, Billy and I sat against the wall, Daddy and the rest of the lot on the outside.

Almost immediately, two waitresses appeared at our table with pitchers of beer. The younger one was a shapely brunette. As she poured Daddy a glass, her ample bosom overflowed out of her too-tight uniform like lava spewing from a volcano.

"Good to see you, Frankie," she said.

"Hi there, Belle," he said.

The other waitress, gray and plump, began to reach for Mother's glass, but she put her hand over the top. "Can you bring a gin and tonic for me and soda for the children?" she asked.

"Of course, dear," the waitress replied. She stood erect, snapping her fingers at Belle. "Belle, get the lady and the little ones their drinks."

Belle smiled through clenched teeth when she answered. "Yes, Miss Brady. You're always right, Miss Brady." Belle walked away with Miss Brady on her heels.

Soon Belle returned with our beverages, but she did not serve us the rest of the evening. Miss Brady came back with plate after plate of food: corned beef and cabbage, boiled potatoes, roast chicken, soda bread. The relentless procession of courses reminded me of a black-creped Thanksgiving feast.

When the food was gone and tables cleared, Daddy began to feed the jukebox, coin after coin clinking to the bottom. He pressed the buttons in a rapid-fire staccato-A1, B7, G8. Guests tapped on the tables with their fingers. It wasn't long before the tables were pushed against the walls and dancers began to fill the floor. Daddy extended his hand to Mother. "Come on, sweetheart, let's take a spin," he said.

"Not right now, Frankie. I'm not up to it," she said.

Daddy looked disappointed.

"I'll dance with you," Aunt Colleen said.

He looked at her, then at Mother, who shrugged.

Daddy led Aunt Colleen to the floor, and they began to cut loose. Despite the difference in their sizes, they fit together, moves in sync, attuned to each other's rhythm.

The boys asked to be excused and disappeared through the outer door. Mother and I watched the dancers while Grandma nodded off periodically. As each song ended, she would awaken and look around as if she had forgotten where she was.

After an hour or so, the music stopped. Daddy led Aunt Colleen back to the table. They were soaking wet with perspiration. He poured each of them a glass of beer before taking the butter knife and clinking on his glass. Daddy stood, steadying himself by holding on the back of his chair as he addressed the crowd. "Ladies and gentlemen, I propose a toast. Fill your glasses and raise them high." He waited a moment for everyone to prepare. "Here's to Peggy Donovan. May she always find a song in her heart and a drink in her hand." He raised the glass and lowered it to his lips and took a swallow.

Several in the throng chimed in, "Hear, hear!" as they knocked glasses with those around them.

"Let's get the music back on!" Daddy shouted.

He filled the jukebox with coins once again. However, as he got ready to make selections, Grandma grabbed his forearm. "It's time for my music now, Francis," she said.

"Oh, of course," he said.

Grandma leaned over the machine and depressed buttons, slowly, methodically, almost as if she were afraid that she would make a mistake and find herself listening to someone as un-Celtic as Elvis. She sat down next to Daddy, and the songs of the old sod began. They were filled with lyrics about love and war and getting the English out of the homeland. The crowd began to sing along in a drunken chorus, ready to take up arms against the oppressors.

The boys rejoined us, and we all rocked from side to side, singing at the top of our lungs. Grandma smiled in a happy stupor.

When there was a break in the music, Mother took my hand. "Come on, Gerri. Let's go to the ladies' room."

I stood next to her in front of the cracked mirror as she primped with the pink styling comb. When she was done with her own hair, she did mine as best she could manage. "You just don't have hair anyone can work with. It's like a rat's nest."

As we exited the bathroom, we were greeted by a swing tune. Trumpets blared, snare drums rat-a-tatted. Paddy and Aunt Colleen were in the middle of the floor doing their best jive steps.

Mother and I walked along the outer edges of the room. As we approached the table, I saw that Grandma was asleep in the corner. Daddy rose and placed his hands on Mother's shoulders. "Come on, sweetheart. Don't you want to dance with me?" he asked.

She shrugged his hands away. "No. I'm not in the mood."

At that moment, Belle happened to be passing by with an empty tray in her hands. "Come on, Belle, let's have a dance."

She took one look at Mother's expression and spurned Daddy's advances by ducking under his bear paws. Mother sat down while Daddy stood until the song stopped.

When the next song began he went to Aunt Colleen and Paddy to cut in. My brother ran back to the table. "Aunt Colleen is really good."

I watched as the pair moved to a ballad. They were close enough for me to hear the rustle of Aunt Colleen's dress. Daddy twirled them to the middle of the floor, and at a deep note, dipped Aunt Colleen so low that the back of her head brushed the ground. Suddenly, Mother ran over to them, grabbing Daddy by the forearm. He stopped dancing mid-turn, releasing Aunt Colleen. It was too noisy to hear what they were saying, but you could tell both my parents were getting angry by the blood rushing to their cheeks. The song stopped and I saw Daddy put his arms around Mother's shoulders as he led her back to the table.

Over the din of the partygoers I heard Aunt Colleen call out after them. "You never could get a man of your own, Lizzie Moran! You always did have to steal them!"

Mother stopped in her tracks and in two giant strides attacked Aunt Colleen like a rabid flying squirrel. She wrestled her to the ground and began to pummel her about the face. I watched in horror as she took her head and began to slam it against the floor. Daddy tried to pry her off my aunt's helpless body, but as big as he was, he couldn't separate them. The bartender came and helped Daddy pull Aunt Colleen out from Mother's grasp. Daddy carried Mother over his shoulder, kicking and screaming into the ladies' room.

Aunt Colleen sat up as blood streamed from her nostrils. Her dress was torn, hanging off her shoulder. The bartender helped her to her feet and back to our table.

Grandma woke up with a start. "What is it?" She looked at Aunt Colleen. "What happened to you?"

"Mommy socked her. She was as good as Graziano," Paddy Boy said with a note of pride in his voice.

Billy wagged a finger at him. "Shut up, you moron. Don't you have any shame?"

Grandma took it all in stride, as if public brawls were just another fact of life. "Now, let's all take it easy. Billy, go with Mike and bring back a wet rag."

He did as ordered and they cleaned Aunt Colleen's bloodied face.

Ten minutes later, Daddy came back to the table alone. "I'm so sorry, Irene."

"Hush. What's done is done. Just go to Lizzie and take care of her. She needs you. We all do." Daddy bent down and kissed her on the cheek. "Go to her, Frankie."

After he left to go back to Mother in the bathroom, Grandma took us home. She made sure we were tucked in before retreating upstairs.

That night I had a nightmare. I was sitting on the ground in a large meadow, surrounded by sunflowers. I looked up and was greeted by Aunt Colleen's smiling face. Her bright red hair shimmered in the brilliant sunshine. She did not speak, but took me by the hand and led me to a clearing. It seemed vaguely familiar, as though I had been there before. A moment later, I saw the casket. The rest of the family was gathered around it. They were all looking into the hole in the ground. As we approached, they continued to stare down. I leaned over the grave and peered in. Suddenly, I felt myself being pushed from behind. I landed at the bottom of the pit, palms sullied with a mix of blood and dirt. Turning around, I tried to get out by clawing at the sides. There was nothing to grab hold of to support myself.

"Help me! I can't get out!"

No one answered. They began to shovel dirt, throwing it on top of me, so I shielded my eyes with my hands.

"What are you doing? Are you crazy?"

I sensed a presence. Someone else was there.

I uncovered my eyes and saw a ghostly vision of Paddy Boy.

"Help me, Paddy! I can't get out! Please, stop them!"

"I tried to warn you."

"What are you talking about?"

"I told you they buried people alive. But you wouldn't listen to me. You just wanted to close your eyes and hope it would all go away."

Dirt rained down on me as he continued. "You can take my hand and I can help you out. But you have to break away by your own power. Will you take my hand?"

I started to reach for it, but he withdrew it, and the apparition disappeared. Dirt rose around my legs, torso, neck, finally filling my mouth, and I began to gag. Everything grew dark. I woke up gasping for breath, clawing at the sheets. I did not close my eyes again that night.

Chapter 17

"We got the house," Daddy said.

"Congratulations. Here's one on me," the bartender said as he handed Daddy a beer.

"Well, of course, we got the house. Why wouldn't we?" Mother said. "I thought the old bat would live forever, just to spite me."

"Now, Frankie, don't be mean. Aunt Peggy never meant any harm. She just wasn't used to being around rough men."

"Is that what I am? Rough?"

Mother went over and stroked the five o'clock shadow that Daddy could never keep under control. "Yes. But I happen to like them rough."

"All right, you two, the little ones are here," the bartender said, motioning toward my brothers and me with his towel.

Much to their embarrassment, Mother took her "little ones," Billy by the left hand and Paddy the right, and led them into the back room. "Coming, Francis?" she said.

Daddy lifted me up in his arms and over the threshold. "Come, princess, let's go to the castle."

As we ate our victory meal that afternoon, the conversation revolved around what our new life would be like in Ferrytown. I listened as Daddy and the boys discussed joining the little league. Mother said she was going to plant roses in the front yard. She had always wanted to be able to cut her own flowers. After all, she said, if she waited on Daddy to bring her flowers, she'd be waiting a month of Sundays. Daddy said he would be sure to get a dog, a big one, so he could have it run loose and fertilize Mother's flowers. "Never let it be said a Moran man shirked his responsibilities," he said.

We had been sitting there the better part of an hour before Grandma arrived. "Sorry to be late. Colleen isn't feeling well so I wanted to try and get her to eat some soup," she said.

Mother rolled her eyes.

"Come sit next to me, Irene," Daddy said.

Grandma sank into the booth cushions with a whooshing sound. She groaned as she adjusted her bony limbs. "I can't stay long, Francis. Colleen really doesn't seem well."

Mother smiled.

"I just wanted to let you know that Finnerty will let us borrow his truck for the move."

Mother put her sandwich down mid-bite. "Oh? And what makes you think we would want to put our stuff in that smelly old van?"

"Well, it's not as though any of us has all that much worth taking."

"Speak for yourself. I have enough decent things that I don't want ruined in a truck that your rummy friend uses to transport fish."

"Finnerty is not a fish monger. He delivers caviar to some of the finest establishments in the city."

"Fish, fish eggs, it's all the same. I won't have my living room set ruined by the stench."

"Now, ladies, let's not fight," Daddy said.

Both Grandma and Mother sent him icy looks.

"I have a question," Billy said. All eyes turned to him. "Nothing has to be decided right now, does it?" he asked.

"Well, no, it doesn't," Daddy said.

"Then can't we just toast our good fortune and enjoy ourselves?" Billy raised his glass and the rest of us followed suit.

"To better days ahead," he said.

"To better days," we responded.

Chapter 18

On a warm Saturday in June, almost a year to the day after our visit, we moved to Aunt Peggy's house. Grandma and Aunt Colleen would be living in the smaller house to the west of the main house. The large cottage to the east was still occupied by Aunt Peggy's tenant, Sarge Flanagan. Once I overheard Daddy joking with Grandma that he thought Aunt Peggy kept Sarge as a specimen in the cottage the way a child keeps fireflies in a jar. Personally, I had nothing except warm feelings for the man. He was the one who had rescued me on the day that John was born.

It had been agreed that we would use Finnerty's fish truck to deliver Grandma and Aunt Colleen's stuff. Mother insisted that Daddy rent a van for our precious possessions.

"Go along to get along," I had heard him whisper in the hallway to Grandma.

This arrangement seemed to have satisfied Mother, but it meant Daddy would have to make two trips from Brooklyn to Ferrytown.

When we arrived upstate that morning, Daddy pulled into the driveway, going as far back as he could. The plan was to move everything into the backyard first so we could start moving things into the house while he drove back to the city for the second run.

Daddy, Billy, and Paddy moved the larger pieces as a team. I carried some lighter boxes, filled with odds and ends that Mother would save on closet shelves and in cabinet drawers. "You never know if we may need it later on," she would say anytime you suggested throwing out a key to an unknown lock or a button to a long lost shirt. Of course, she managed to develop one of her incapacitating migraines when it came time to help unload the boxes. As soon as we got there, she took John and headed toward the back door saying, "I'm sure you'll manage without me. My head's about to explode." As she was about to shut the screen door, she stopped. "Frankie!" she called, startling Daddy so badly he barely held onto his end of the sofa he and Billy were carrying down the van ramp.

"Jesus, Lizzie! You scared the crap out of me." He set his end of the couch down, causing Billy to fall to his knees under its weight. "What is it?" he asked.

"I just wanted to remind you to be careful not to scratch anything when you go through the doorway. I know how clumsy giants can be." She went inside with a shriek of the door hinges. That's when the vein, blue and throbbing, appeared in the middle of Daddy's forehead. He pointed at the sofa. "Come on. Let's put it by the tree," he said. When they set it down, Daddy held his palm up. "Take a seat, kids. I'll be moving the next box."

He walked up the ramp and disappeared into the back of the truck. He came out carrying a carton that rattled as he passed us. We turned and watched as he walked to the dock and threw it down. The sound of breaking china echoed across the lake.

The three of us climbed up on the couch to get a better view just as Daddy used the box cutter to rip open the carton. He took out a plate and put it in the crook of his arm like an Olympic discus thrower. It was from Mother's good china set, the one you never touched under penalty of death!

He spun around and flung it across the surface of the water with a smooth, fluid move. Not satisfied, he did it with one plate after another until he made the bottom of Lake Owl's Head into a china minefield. When he grew tired of his game, he sat down on the edge of the dock and lit a cigarette.

My heart fluttered when I heard the sound of a rusty screen window being opened. Simultaneously, we turned our heads toward the house. We could not see her through the trees, but Mother must have been watching the scene. The screen window shut again with a screech.

Daddy jumped to his feet, walking past us at a brisk pace. "I'm going down to the city now for your grandmother and aunt. See if you can't get the rest of the stuff inside by the time I get back." He climbed up in the cab, revved the engine, and escaped in a whirl of driveway dust.

As soon as he was out of sight, Paddy ran to the dock and reached inside the carton. Billy went after him. Not wanting to be left out, I followed at a distance.

"What are you doing?" Billy asked.

"Just looking," Paddy replied. He pulled out a plate and began to prepare for a replay of Daddy's performance.

"Paddy, put it back."

Billy held his hand out, but Paddy ignored him.

Hugging the plate tight to his chest, he walked to the very end of the pier.

"Don't do anything stupid."

Paddy threw the plate, just as Billy tried to grab it out of his hands.

"Patrick Moran, what are you doing with my wedding china?" Mother screamed as she ran onto the dock.

Paddy jumped into the water. Billy grabbed Mother by the waist just as she was about to fall in.

"You'd better run, you hooligan! You won't be able to sit for the rest of the summer when I get through with you!"

Paddy swam to the other side of the lake. He climbed ashore and we watched him run into the woods.

"Sometimes I think he's not right in the head," Billy said.

Mother glared. "I always did think he took after Colleen," she replied. Picking up the remaining china, she walked back to the house while Billy and I continued to sort out boxes.

Ten minutes later, a sharp whistle drew our attention to the other shore, and we saw Paddy on top of a jagged rock that jutted out into the lake. He had his back to us, but I could see his arms flailing as if he were a bird in flight. Suddenly, he dropped his pants and bared his butt cheeks in our direction.

Billy blushed as his jaw dropped. I could not stop myself from laughing at his show. Maybe Mother was right. Maybe he did take after crazy Aunt Colleen.

Chapter 19

We watched with fascination as Daddy stacked the charcoal according to his scientific method, making a neat pyramid. He doused the coals with starter fluid and warned us all to stand back while he flipped a match onto the top of the pile. A flame shot up, high over the confines of the metal grill.

Unfortunately, a simultaneous clap of thunder echoed across the sky. Within five minutes a torrential downpour had put out the fire. We scrambled to gather everything from the picnic table and bring it inside, while Daddy stood there, spatula in hand, insisting it was only a passing shower. Not until he was soaked to the skin did he admit defeat and join the rest of us. Still, he refused to give up on his dream of a barbecue. "We'll use the fireplace," he announced.

We set the picnic condiments up on the coffee table. Daddy grilled hot dogs, one at a time, on the end of his barbecue fork. By the time he had finished making enough for all of us, we had devoured all the other food. Despite being full by that time, we all ate the hot dogs from end to end while Daddy watched. We did not dare insult his cooking skills.

After we cleaned up, another thunderstorm, more violent than the first, erupted. Lightning flashed through the drawn shades, illuminating the corners of the room. Suddenly, the lights went out.

Daddy lit the candles on the mantel while Mother retrieved a couple of flashlights. Throughout all the commotion, Grandma sat sleeping in the wing chair, oblivious to the turmoil around her.

We all gathered around the coffee table, candles and flashlights casting eerie shadows everywhere. I watched the embers from Daddy's pipe floating red in the darkened room.

Suddenly, there was a furious rapping at the back door, and we jumped in our seats. Daddy took a lantern to answer it. When he opened it, a hooded four-legged figure stood there. I felt for my cross, but remembered I had taken it off before my shower and had not put it back on.

Daddy brought the lantern forward to reveal the phantom. It was Sarge. What I had mistaken for an extra set of legs turned out to be the metal arm crutches he used. I breathed a sigh of relief.

"Are you folks okay?" he asked.

"Fine," Daddy replied.

"I was worried when you didn't come down to get me, Frankie. This is the day you invited me to the barbecue, isn't it?"

"Damn it! In all the excitement I totally forgot I'd said I would come down and get you when dinner was ready. I'm so sorry, Sarge."

"Don't worry about it. I was just concerned that something might have happened, what with the power out and all."

"Please, come in."

"Thanks. Don't mind if I do. It's blowing something fierce out there."

Daddy helped Sarge into the rocker.

"I think you know everyone here except my mother-in-law, sleeping in the chair, and my sister-in-law, Colleen," Daddy said.

Aunt Colleen got up and they shook hands.

"Pleased to meet you, Colleen. My friends call me Sarge."

"Pleased to meet you, Sarge. My friends call me Colleen."

Mother muttered, "Oh, brother." She took a flashlight and got up. "I'm going upstairs to check on John," she said.

"Be careful, my love," Daddy said as he blew a kiss in her direction.

"I always am, sweetheart," she replied as she caught the kiss and put it in her shirt pocket.

Daddy took her place on the couch and pointed at us. "So, does anybody want to play a game?"

"How about twenty questions?" Billy suggested.

"That's boring," Paddy said.

"Let's tell ghost stories," Aunt Colleen suggested.

"All right, but nothing too gory. I don't want to be woken by anyone's nightmare screams," Daddy said.

"I know one, a true one," Paddy said.

"Okay, you're up," Daddy said.

Of course, Paddy Boy couldn't resist seeing how much Daddy would put up with. He launched into a gruesome tale of human sacrifice among the Aztecs.

Daddy, in spite of his warning, seemed to enjoy the story, especially when the young girl who had her heart ripped out by the priest came back to haunt him.

"That's my story, and every word of it is true," Paddy said when he got to the end. We all clapped for him, and his teeth shone white in the dark as he broke into a smile.

We sat in silence until Aunt Colleen piped up. "Well, that was very chilling, Paddy," she said. We turned our attention toward her. "But it doesn't compare to my story, which like yours, is true."

She began her tale:

"My story begins many years ago with two young sisters. The older sister had been used to being the center of attention. One day her Mother told her there would be a new baby in the house. Things would change, her Mother told her, but she said there would always be enough love for everyone, because love is limitless.

"Well, the new baby arrived, and soon she took up all her Mother's time. As a matter of fact, anyone who came into contact with the baby would ignore the older sister, as though she had become the invisible child.

"One day, when the girl had won first place in a spelling bee, she tried to show the ribbon to her mother. Instead of praising her, the mother told her to shut up before she woke the baby. That was when she knew her mother had lied to her. There wasn't enough love to go around.

"This made the firstborn very angry.

"That's when the thought first appeared in her mind: If the new baby were to go away, she would have her mother all to herself again.

"She pretended to love her baby sister, of course, so as not to arouse suspicion. She played with her and fed her and changed her. She took her for walks to the playground, a block away from Miller's Hill. That's where she got the idea.

"When the younger sister became old enough to get her first two-wheel bike, the older sister volunteered to teach her to ride. They practiced on the sidewalks until the younger girl became confident enough to ask her father to remove the training wheels. After weeks of pleading, the father gave in and unscrewed the nuts and bolts.

"Everywhere they went, the two sisters would ride their bikes, waving to porch-sitters and shopkeepers as they breezed past. The entire neighborhood thought they were the best of friends.

"One afternoon, as the sun was setting, the older sister issued a challenge to the younger one. 'I dare you to go down Miller's Hill and let go of the handlebars,' she said.

"'Are you crazy? That's dangerous.'"

"Miller's Hill led into a dead end street, but you had to pass through an intersection with traffic in both directions to get to the wall."

"'Oh, if you're too much of a baby, I'll go by myself. You'll never be as good as me. I heard Mommy say that the firstborn gets all the talent, and any kids that follow get the leftovers.'"

"This angered the younger sister so much that any rational fears she may have had about the foolhardy stunt disappeared. 'All right, let's go,' she said.

"The two sisters pedaled furiously toward Miller's Hill.

"The younger girl would go first. Her sister would stand at the bottom of the hill and signal when the coast was clear. She would hold her handkerchief in the air, and when it was safe, she would drop it to signal the other to start down.

"The older sister pretended to look both ways before she dropped the cloth to signal the younger one that it was safe to go.

"She pumped the pedals with all her might, building up speed in the descent. In a rush of exhilaration, she let go of the handlebars, waving her arms above her head. Suddenly, a truck appeared in front of her, too late for her to regain control. Up into the air she went, flying higher and higher until she landed with a crunching thud fifty feet away.

"At first, they did not believe the little girl was going to pull through. She was in a coma for many days. When all seemed lost, there was what the doctors described as a miracle. She opened her eyes and began to respond.

"One day, the mother and sister came to visit her. She had a tube inserted down her throat. Her left leg and both arms were in casts, dangling above her like some abstract sculpture. She was helpless as a newborn. The mother stroked her head. 'My precious baby,' she said.

"The doctor came in and took their mother into the hall for a consultation. As soon as she left the room, the older sister wedged a chair under the doorknob. She got up on the bed and straddled the younger girl's body with her legs, her knees on either side of her torso. She leaned down over her sister and began to speak to her in a voice filled with venomous hatred. 'They think you're so special. Well, you're not.' She pulled on the traction ropes and made them dance. "We have to do everything to help you get well.' She poked her in the chest. 'We can't come to your recital. Your sister has the croup. You can't have a new dress, the baby needs clothes. Well, I'm sick of it, and I'm sick of you. Why couldn't you just die like I planned? Oh, you don't think you ran into that truck on your own, did you? Let me see if I can't get it right this time.'

"She jumped off the bed and tugged on the tube going down her sister's throat. She fingered the tubing to the respirator down to the plug in the electrical outlet. She had her hand on the plug when the doorknob began to turn. It moved halfway. She froze for just a moment, then calmly got up and removed the chair. Going into the bathroom, she shut the door. She heard her mother and the doctor come in. The older sister splashed water under her eyes before rejoining them.

"The mother looked at her and asked, 'Is everything all right? Have you been crying?'

"'Yes, Mother. It makes me so sad seeing my baby sister lying there so helpless.'

'I know. We all have to pray and be strong for her.'

'Just a few more minutes,' the doctor said as he left.

"When they were ready to go, the mother kissed the little girl on the forehead. 'We'll be back tomorrow,' she said.

"They were about to get in the elevator when the older girl made an excuse to go back. 'Oh, Mother, I forgot my purse. I must have been very upset to do so.' She appeared in the doorway and went to the bathroom where she had left the bag... accidentally on purpose. She wrapped it around her wrist and twirled it in the air. She went to the bed and leaned over her sister as she continued to spin the purse in the air. 'Next time I won't make the same mistake. Next time I'll get it right.'

"She slammed the door behind her, leaving her sister to think about the threat.

"When she was able to talk, the younger sister told everyone what had happened. But they did not believe her. They said her brain had been damaged in the accident, and she must have imagined the incident. The mind can play awful tricks on a person, they would say. Others said it must have been a dream.

"After that, the younger sister got the reputation of being the 'Crazy One' or the one who had been in 'The Accident' and word of mouth spread the news about her eccentricities. But she knew in her heart she hadn't dreamed it or made it up. It was real; it had happened.

"She knew she had to be on vigilant guard at all times. She couldn't afford to be alone with her sister or listen to any warning she might give her, because it could all be a trick to finish her off. Every accident that happened aroused suspicion in her mind that her sister was trying to kill her. The more the girl tried to keep up her vigilance, the crazier her family thought she was. They sent her to doctors who prescribed pills and suggested she be put away for her own good. Her mother would not hear of it. Instead, she decided she would watch her and shield her from harm. 'It's not her fault,' she said.

"So the child became one of those family secrets that get locked away in attics, whispered about behind closed doors.

"But what the girl said had happened did happen. She knew it was true, and the sister knew it was true. In her heart, she believed her mother knew it was true. And they all hid the truth from the world and each other and pretended that the one who was sick was well and the one who was well was sick." Aunt Colleen nodded as if to agree with herself. "But I know the truth. And now, so do you."

Like a spirit in the dark, Mother appeared in the doorway. "John's sleeping. What have you guys been talking about?"

"Oh, just ancient history," replied Aunt Colleen.

"Fairy tales," said Daddy.

"Well, I think it's time we all went to bed," said Mother.

We let Grandma stay where she was. Aunt Colleen shared my bed. Daddy insisted that Sarge stay on the sofa until morning.

When I woke the next morning, Aunt Colleen was gone. The sun was shining, bright and beautiful, almost if the previous evening had been a dream. But I knew in my heart it hadn't been a dream or a made-up story. It had happened. All of it had really happened.

Chapter 20

The hazy late afternoons of August were filled with a nothing-to do-boredom that left my brothers and me searching for adventure. On one of those days, Paddy came up with one of his most ingenious plans to date.

He had found a box of sparklers left over from the Fourth of July. At least, he said he found them. More likely, he had bought them from one of his con artist buddies from the old neighborhood.

"Let's make a Viking funeral ship," he said.

Billy arched his left eyebrow, the way he always did when Paddy was proposing a typically harebrained scheme. Knowing it would be futile to try to talk him out of it, he took on his familiar watchdog role to minimize any damage.

We collected the green plastic soldiers that were scattered throughout the yard from past combat missions. One by one, Paddy painstakingly glued them to the model clipper ship Daddy had given him for his birthday. When he finished, he said, "Wait right there" and ran into the house. He returned with something behind his back. He pulled the object out to reveal he had amputated all the limbs on my doll.

"Barbie!" I screamed. I grabbed for the poor victim, but Paddy held her just out of my reach.

"Do you want to be a part of this expedition or not?" he asked.

"But she's my favorite!" I protested.

"We all have to make sacrifices for the common good sometimes, Gerri. I'm counting on you to help us out."

He sounded just like Mother.

"Well, are you in or out?"

"In."

"Good. She's going on front. She'll bring us luck on our maiden voyage." So Paddy nailed the doll to the bow of the ship, creating a quadruple amputee beauty queen figurehead. He inserted the sparklers in the cannon holes on both sides of the vessel, fastening them in place with Daddy's special glue, the stuff you were not supposed to touch. Daddy had warned us it was made from dangerous chemicals and tried to hide it from us. We all knew it was in his top bureau drawer beneath his magazines with the naked women.

"We sail at sundown," Paddy said.

At the designated hour, the three of us met at the half-rotted pier by the haunted cabin at the opposite side of the lake. Paddy stripped to his swim trunks and waded in, pushing the boat in front of him with one hand while holding a book of matches above the water in the other. When he was in up to his chest, he began to light the sparklers.

Billy and I stood in awe as the flames shimmered in the growing darkness, brighter and brighter. Against the backdrop of the setting sun, the vessel cast an orange glow on the surface of the water.

Paddy turned toward us with his arms outstretched toward the sky. He bowed, beaming at his glorious achievement.

"Isn't she great?" he called.

Less than a minute later, a horrific explosion echoed across the lake as Paddy let out an anguished scream. I looked in horror as flames engulfed his hair. Pieces of wood were scattered across the lake in all directions.

I stood there, unable to move or speak.

Billy swam out to Paddy and pushed him under to douse the flames. Grabbing him under the arms, he dragged him back ashore.

Bits of wood were embedded in Paddy's flesh like chocolate chips in a cookie. I watched him writhe in agony as he began to moan. I saw Billy's lips moving, but could not understand what he was saying. He took his shirt off and wrapped it around Paddy.

I stared as Barbie's head floated in to shore until I felt a stinging sensation on my face, swatting at it before it stung again.

Finally, Billy's third slap woke me from my trance. "Snap out of it, Gerri! Go get help!"

I ran to Sarge's cottage, and he rang for an ambulance.

Paddy spent the night in the hospital. His injuries weren't life threatening, but he missed the entire first week of school, recuperating at home.

I remember an ongoing series of recriminations and lectures over who had been responsible for the accident. Mother blamed Daddy for keeping such dangerous chemicals in the house. Daddy blamed Paddy Boy for being so foolhardy as to mix it with fire. Paddy blamed Billy, saying he was older and should have stopped him. Billy, the martyr, accepted the blame and promised he would never let anything bad happen to us again.

The thing I remember most about the incident wasn't how everyone wanted to lay blame for what had happened at everyone else's feet. What I can never forget is that it wasn't the first time I had frozen in a moment of crisis. And sadly for all of us, it wouldn't be the last.

Chapter 21

The surface of my shiny red vinyl briefcase felt smooth as I caressed it. I had spent the entire week arranging and rearranging the contents: composition books, pencil case, Snoopy memo pad.

Grandma had given it to me along with a speech. "I won't have my grandchildren looked down on by the uppity Ferrytown snobs. They're as bad as the English with their snooty ways." She paused for a moment. "We're property owners, now. Don't let them tell you you're not as good as any of them. Don't let them treat you badly. Promise me you'll make us proud, Geraldine."

"I promise to make you proud, Grandma."

She hugged me. "If anyone in our sorry lot can, it's you."

I nodded as Daddy entered the room.

"Gerri, hurry up. You don't want to be late your first day," Daddy said. He was going to drop me off before driving down to the city.

"Lizzie, honey, we're going now."

She didn't answer from behind her closed bedroom door, probably still in bed sulking. Despite his protests, she kept insisting I didn't need anyone to take me to school. Billy would be taking the bus to the high school, so he couldn't do it, and Paddy was still recovering from his wounds. They had fought about it at the dinner table the night before.

"Gerri's old enough to go by herself. Besides, if you're that concerned, why don't you go with her?" she said.

"I will, since you seem to be so lazy that you won't even walk your own daughter to school," Daddy answered.

Mother sprang from her seat and tipped Daddy's dinner plate onto his lap. Before he could say anything, she fled, barricading herself in their bedroom. He turned as red as I had ever seen him, but did not go after her, just gathered his food in a napkin and dumped it on the table. "Dinner's over. Clean up this table and go to bed."

Daddy put his coat on and walked out the back door, not to be seen again until breakfast.

When he dropped me off that first morning of school, something made me look back at the car. He was sitting there, watching me to make sure I was safely inside. He caught me looking at him and pretended to be adjusting the rear view mirror. But I had seen him, watching out for me, making sure I was safe. It made me feel warm.

My teacher that first year upstate was Miss Baxter. She was young and shapely, with a blonde ponytail tied back with a polka-dot scarf. As I entered the classroom, I was shocked to see her exposed legs. After going to a school with habit-shrouded nuns for so long, it would take awhile for me to get used to seeing so much ungodly flesh.

"Come in. What is your name?"

"Geraldine Moran, ma'am."

"Well, Geraldine, why don't you take the seat next to the pencil sharpener?"

Before long, all the seats were taken, and Miss Baxter began to teach with all the earnestness and enthusiasm of a freshly-minted graduate. Her love for her students was evident from the outset, and she made me feel comfortable enough to raise my hand every chance I got. I never would have done that when the nuns were teaching me. They worked for God, so you had to be careful not to make any mistakes with them. One false answer and you could find yourself on the road to hell.

After lunch, however, I began to notice something I had not realized before. I was the only pupil responding to her questions without prompting.

Miss Baxter began to call on other students. Unfortunately, she made a statement that would seal my fate with my classmates. "Doesn't anyone else want to answer? Surely Geraldine isn't the only smart student I have."

The rest of the class turned their narrowed eyes in my direction. I lowered my hand and hid it beneath the desk.

I sighed with relief when the bell rang that afternoon. Dragging my book-heavy briefcase at my side, I left by the back entrance so I could take the shortcut through the hole in the playground fence. As I was about to climb through, I felt something hit me in the back of my head.

Looking down, I saw a pebble on the ground. I turned around and saw three girls gathered around the swings.

"Hey, hippo!" the ringleader shouted.

The other girls snickered.

"You better keep that hand down if you know what's good for you."

As I climbed through the hole in the fence, I heard my skirt rip as it caught on the ragged edge of metal. A shower of pebbles rained down on me as I struggled to free the cloth. I ripped the skirt to release myself, holding my briefcase over my head as I ran home.

I lay on my bed and cried myself to sleep. When I woke up, I went to the bathroom and splashed water around my puffy red eyes.

As I looked at myself in the mirror, Grandma's voice came into my head. "Make us proud, Geraldine. If anyone can, it's you."

She had been so sure I could do it, that I would succeed. I gritted my teeth and made a pledge to myself that I would not let them bully me. I would not be afraid. I had made a promise to Grandma, and I would keep it, no matter what.

The next day, I raised my hand again and again. I was not always chosen by the teacher, and I did not always have the correct answer. Most difficult of all, my tormentors glared at me in anger each time I played the game. But I did not let it stop me. I was going to succeed.

Still, not being so foolhardy as to leave myself vulnerable for reprisal, I tried to hide in with the younger students during lunchtime, finding and sitting as close to the cafeteria monitor as I could manage.

At the end of the day, I decided to leave by the front entrance to avoid a repeat performance of the previous afternoon. It would take me longer to get home, but it wasn't as though my social calendar was full.

As I walked the long way to the path leading to Lake Owl's Head, I sensed a presence behind me. Gathering my nerve, I continued on. Suddenly, they materialized from a thicket to block my path. Just like before, the head bully taunted me. "Where do you think you're going, hippo? This isn't the way to the zoo."

Her two buddies elbowed each other.

I tried to walk around her, but she mirrored my steps. Suddenly, her henchmen grabbed my arms and pinned me to the ground. The leader began to kick me. Her lackeys joined in. She got down on all fours, wagging her finger in my face. "When I tell you something, you better listen."

Summoning strength from that place where rage goes to fester and grow, I leaned up and bit down on the digit until she fell backward. The cohorts were so stunned, they loosened their grip, and I was able to break free.

I ran without looking back to see if they were in pursuit. I kept going, running as fast as I could, until I reached the shore of Lake Owl's Head. Sitting down on a tree stump, I tried to catch my breath.

I don't know how long I had been sitting there when they pulled me to the ground, burying me in a pile of wet leaves. I did not resist this time. If I just let them beat me, eventually they would get tired. Closing my eyes, I took my licking, a condemned prisoner resigned to her fate.

When they finished, the leader took my briefcase and threw it in a mud puddle, stomping on it until it was no longer red and shiny and smooth. "This is your last warning, hippo," she said as she gave me one final kick in the side for good measure.

I don't remember walking home after the beating. The next thing I remember is Mother startling me as I tried to clean my wounds at the bathroom sink.

"Who did this to you?" she asked. She began to shake me by the shoulders. I burst into tears.

"Never mind," she said as she left me to wallow by myself.

The next day I pretended to be sick, and much to my amazement, Mother allowed me to stay home. Of course, she did make me wait on her hand and foot.

When I went back to school on Thursday, Miss Baxter made an announcement at the beginning of class. "Boys and girls, I have some sad news. Paulette broke her leg last night. She won't be back to school this term. I think it would be nice if during arts and crafts we all made her get well cards."

I looked to my right and realized that Paulette was the bully. I did not know her name, but knew where she sat. Her pals turned their heads away when I looked at them.

They weren't the only ones who seemed to avoid me. When I sat down to lunch, no one would sit near me; I had the whole table to myself. As I walked down the hallway, kids purposefully parted for me, as if I had a contagious disease they did not want to catch.

I went home and lay down on my bed and tried to make sense of it, to reach a logical explanation for the turn of events. Why did I get the feeling that they thought I had done something wrong? I was being treated like a criminal instead of a victim.

There was a knock at the door.

"Come in."

It was Mother.

She was cradling John on her hip like a baby tumor growing out of her side. "I need you to look after John for awhile. I'm going to town to get my hair done. I know it looks really good, but a little touchup can't hurt. I heard even Jackie Kennedy gets touchups done between full-blown treatments."

I nodded.

She put John on the bed, and he proceeded to dive under the covers to initiate our familiar game of where's-the-baby.

"I think a little playtime with John is just the cure after what you've been through."

"What I've been through?"

"Well, yes, with those girls. But I guess you don't have to worry about them bothering you anymore. I heard everything's been taken care of."

I hadn't told her anything about what had happened to me, or to Paulette. How did she know? What had she done?

As she shut the door, she whispered in a voice that sent a shiver down my spine, "No one lays a hand on a Moran child and gets away with it. It's all for one, one for all."

I suppose she thought she was a Musketeer, defender of the innocent, righter of miscarriages of justice. But I knew better. Whatever role she might have played, I knew that even while performing the most chivalrous of acts, she never thought of anyone except herself.

Touché, Lizzie, touché.

Chapter 22

One Sunday afternoon in late September, I decided to take John for a walk around the lake. Mother was having her "woman time" and, as was her habit, lay curled up under the covers, shades down and curtains drawn.

Daddy was down in the city, a place where he was spending more and more of his time. My brothers were in town playing baseball.

As I went past Sarge's place, I saw him sitting in his Adirondack chair. He was reading a newspaper and did not see me. The back door of his house flew open. I was surprised to see Aunt Colleen emerge with a tray holding two bottles and mugs. She put the tray down on the little wooden table next to Sarge's chair. My interest engaged, I watched as she opened a bottle and handed it to Sarge.

He pulled her down to him and kissed her. It wasn't the kind of kiss I would give Grandma. I had heard from Paddy that it was the type that grownups called "French."

I turned my head away in embarrassment and began to walk away, hoping no one would see me. Unfortunately, I heard Aunt Colleen call my name.

"Gerri!" she shouted.

I kept walking, pretending not to hear her.

"Gerri, come here!" she called.

She picked up a stick and flung it in front of me. Before I turned around, I splashed my cheeks with water from John's bottle in an attempt to wash away the crimson hue I felt burning through my flesh. Trying to act nonchalant, I turned around and walked over to the couple with a feigned air of innocence.

"Hi, I didn't hear you at first," I said.

"Pull up one of those lawn chairs against the house and have a seat," Sarge said.

I did as he requested and plopped into the sticky mesh.

Aunt Colleen peered into John's carriage and began to make those ridiculous noises adults think babies like. John ignored her and remained sound asleep.

"He's getting so big," she said.

"Just like Miss Geraldine," Sarge added.

Aunt Colleen looked me up and down.

"Yes, I'd have to agree."

"Can you stay for dinner, Gerri?" Sarge asked.

"Oh, yes, please do," pleaded Aunt Colleen.

"Colleen's made a special meal, and we have plenty of food to go around."

"Mother won't know where I am."

"Where is she?" Sarge asked.

"She's in bed. She's not feeling well."

"I'm sorry to hear that."

"Don't worry about her," Aunt Colleen said.

"But Gerri said she's ill," Sarge protested.

"It's just her time of the month. No one gets cramps as bad as my sister. Cramps are her specialty. If there were an Olympics for menstrual pain, Lizzie would win the gold medal hands down. She even calls herself the Queen of the Cramps."

"You're so wicked," Sarge said.

"No, I just tell the truth. I can't help it. It's a compulsion with me."

Sarge scratched his chin. "You know, I think that must be a fact."

I couldn't come up with another reason to keep me from being the third wheel at their dinner table.

It turned out to be a wonderful meal. There was roast beef, baked potatoes, baby peas, soda bread, and strawberry shortcake, a meal fit for royalty. Too bad Queen Lizzie wasn't around to enjoy it.

After dinner, Aunt Colleen decided she would walk me back home and return to her own house. I waited outside while she said goodbye to Sarge. The sun was setting on Lake Owl's Head, doing a light dance over the water, an evening version of the show I had witnessed many times before. I focused on it so I would not see the two of them acting like teenagers at a drive-in.

When we arrived home, Aunt Colleen put her hand on my shoulder. "I guess you're wondering what I was doing at Sarge's place," she said.

I shrugged.

"You're a smart girl. You've probably guessed by now that Sarge and I have become more than friends over the past few months. We've found we have a lot in common, and we've developed special feelings for each other. The thing is, Gerri, we want to keep our friendship a secret. There are some people who wouldn't understand our love. I'm going to ask you to do me a huge favor. I want you to promise not to tell anyone about us. Can you do that for me? Can you promise you'll keep our secret?"

I put my hands on her shoulders. "I promise."

"Thank you. I knew we could count on you. I told Sarge that Gerri Girl would never break a promise." She took my chin between her thumb and index finger. "Someday you'll have a true love, and then you'll know. Love is a force of nature that can't be stopped. It's like a waterfall."

A vision of Niagara Falls popped into my head, the sights and sounds filling my mind as clear as day. As the waters rushed over the edge, I pictured Aunt Colleen plunging over in a wooden barrel.

I did not tell her what I saw. Aunt Colleen had a fear of heights.

"See you later, alligator," she said before she skipped away singing, "He loves me, yeah, yeah, yeah" at the top of her lungs.

Chapter 23

As I was walking home from school on a mid-October afternoon, I heard Aunt Colleen calling to me from Sarge's place. "Gerri, come here, I have some news!"

I ran over and gave her a kiss on the cheek. "I have to get home. I'm supposed to help Mother bake cupcakes for her PTA meeting tomorrow afternoon."

"Promise me you'll come over when she goes to the meeting."

"I don't know."

"Please, I have something important I want to discuss with you."

She made that pouting face she always made when she wanted you to do something for her.

"Please?"

"Oh, all right, I'll come. But I can't stay long."

"Be here as soon as you can. Don't tell anyone you're coming. It's just between us girls. Okay?"

"Okay."

I have to admit she had piqued my curiosity. You could never guess what Aunt Colleen was going to tell you, and the surprise made it all the more exciting.

The following afternoon, I checked the house from top to bottom to make sure Mother had gone. She had called up to me to say goodbye, making sure to order me to vacuum. Sometimes she'd return unexpectedly in the hope that she would catch me eating forbidden foods.

She took John with her that afternoon. Her practice was to take him to any public gathering that would give her a chance to show off her precious star child. She was the lady in the circus who made the ponies perform tricks for the crowd, and John was her prize pony.

I didn't have to worry about the rest of my family missing me. My brothers were playing football down at Ferrytown Park. Daddy never seemed to get home before dinner was over during those days. As for Grandma, she was glued to the television set.

I went out by the back door, dashing through the yard like a skittish doe. If I ran fast enough, maybe my guilt at leaving my vacuuming chore undone wouldn't catch up to me.

When I knocked at the cottage door, Aunt Colleen came and told me to follow her. She led me to the living room and we sat on the couch. Sarge didn't appear to be home. She must have noticed me looking around for him. "We're alone," she said.

Aunt Colleen had prepared tea and oatmeal raisin cookies, my favorite snack. Such a special treat usually meant a request from her involving work for me. I was sitting on the edge of my seat, ready to burst from anticipation, when she began her speech. She poured out the tea, making sure to put an extra lump of sugar in my cup.

"You know Sarge and I are very fond of each other," she began.

I nodded.

"Our feelings go deeper than that. Gerri, Sarge and I are in love. We want to be together for the rest of our lives. We're tired of sneaking around just because some busybodies might not believe we're right for each other. We know we were meant to be together. It's our destiny. How else do you explain Aunt Peggy willing us a house? How else do you explain Sarge coming in from the rain that night and capturing my heart? It's fate, Gerri, pure and simple." She stopped speaking for a moment to take a bite of her cookie, washing it down with a healthy gulp of tea. "I love him and he loves me, and that's all that matters. And where there's love, there needs to be a marriage. So that's what we're doing, Gerri; we're getting married. What do you think about that?"

I didn't know what to think. But I remembered the standard reply I had seen in the movies.

"Congratulations. I'm sure you'll be very happy together."

"I knew you'd approve. I told Sarge that out of everyone in the family, you'd understand. Oh, Gerri, I want you to be my maid of honor. Lizzie will be so jealous. Oh, I just thought of something. Don't move. I'll be right back." She ran to the bedroom. When she came back she had a small velvet box in her hands. "Open it," she said.

When I did, I saw a shiny ring, a gold band with three chips set on either side of a large fake diamond. Even a child could tell it wasn't real. I lifted it out of the box and held it up. The sunlight coming through the window caught the glass and made a rainbow on the wall as I rotated the "precious gem" in my hand.

"It's my engagement ring."

Aunt Colleen spent the rest of the afternoon telling me about her plans for the future. She had wanted a large church wedding. Sarge had objected, but she won him over when she told him Father O'Meara was a regular guy and wouldn't make them sit through a whole bunch of boring religious training. They would live in Sarge's house, unless Grandma preferred that they all live together in the other house.

On and on she talked, going into more and more detail. They were going to wait until Thanksgiving to announce the wedding to the rest of the family. They wanted to get married in late spring so they wouldn't have to worry about Sarge walking through the snow with his crutches.

Finally, when the sun started to fade from the sky, I left Aunt Colleen alone to ponder her dreams. I would not be the one to shatter her illusions of wedded bliss. Sometimes dreams are all we have.

Chapter 24

I watched Mother as she looked at herself in the hall mirror. She applied her lipstick and pouted in her best Lana Turner imitation. She took the necklace from the table and put it around her neck, making sure the gold crucifix dangled in the crevice between her breasts. When she had completed the ritual, she broke into a self-satisfied grin. "Frankie, come on, we need to leave."

Daddy came leaping down the steps, shaking the house. "I'm here, my love," he said as he kissed the top of her head. He took mother's coat from the closet and slipped it on her.

"Let me look at you," she said.

He stood still while the inspector general adjusted his tie and then fluffed up his handkerchief.

"Okay. You're good-looking enough to be seen with me."

"Thank you, Your Royal Highness." He held the door open for her, bowing as she passed through. I had to suppress my laughter as I saw him stick his tongue out behind her back.

When they were gone, I went up to their bedroom and locked the door. I loved to play dress-up when the opportunity arose. They'd be at their dance for several hours, so this was my chance.

Opening her closet, I began to go through her outfits. I chose a scarlet crepe dress and lay it on the bed. After removing my nightgown, I pulled the dress over my head. It was flouncy and light, and I danced around the room, spinning until I made myself dizzy.

Next, I went to her jewelry box and pulled out Mother's favorite strand of pearls. They glistened under the soft night table lamp.

As I began to caress their shiny smoothness beneath my fingertips, disaster struck. The rope broke and pearls began to roll across the rug in all directions. I gathered them up and tried to string them back together, but it was no use. Taking a towel from the bathroom, I lay the pearls down and rolled them inside.

After I changed back to my nightgown, I went to my bedroom to try and come up with a plan. In the meantime, I decided to hide them in my pillowcase. Beads of perspiration poured down my back as I envisioned the look on Mother's face if she found out what I had done.

It seemed like mere minutes when I heard my parent's footsteps. I pulled the covers over my head. My heart pounded as my bedroom door opened just a crack. The lightness of the tread let me know it was Mother. I screwed my eyelids shut tight until the door was gently closed.

The following morning, I took Paddy aside and showed him my handiwork.

"Give them to me."

I hesitated for a moment, so he snatched the baubles from my hands.

"Let Paddy take care of it." He turned his head in my direction before departing with the contraband. "We'll work out a payment plan later."

The next two days were torture as I prayed that Mother would not discover her missing necklace. Finally, Paddy returned them to me as good as new.

I waited until Mother left to go shopping before going to her room to sneak the necklace back into the jewelry box. As I was shutting the cover, I noticed a pearl I had missed on the floor near the window.

I picked it up, putting it in my pocket. I knew from all the crime shows on television that I had to get rid of the evidence. The bottom of the lake seemed the best place to bury it.

Looking around to see if anyone was watching, I casually strolled out to Lake Owl's Head. As I was about to fling it into the water, a seagull began cackling above me, startling me with a shrill, piercing cry. The pearl slipped from my hand and rolled to the edge of the dock. Suddenly, the bird swooped down, snatched the pearl in its beak, and began hovering over my head, mocking me with a taunting refrain of sing-song laughter.

As he disappeared into the trees, a disturbing thought came into my head: *What if he worked for Mother?* After all, didn't witches keep animals as their spies? But then I remembered they always seemed to have cats at their side. I'd never heard of a seagull as a familiar.

Chapter 25

On the Saturday two weeks before Thanksgiving, our family received an invitation in the mail from Aunt Colleen. She had invited us to our own house for Thanksgiving dinner. Daddy put it on the mantel. He joked that no one should move it in case we lose the address. He then telephoned Aunt Colleen to confirm that we would be honored to attend her gathering. She informed him that dress would be casual.

For the first time I could remember, neither Mother nor Grandma would be preparing the traditional feast, and Mother was clearly unhappy with Aunt Colleen for stealing the job from under her feet.

"It's not that I object to the idea of Colleen preparing dinner, but I don't remember her cooking very much when we were little. I was the one Mother always relied on to help out in the kitchen. Colleen takes after Aunt Peggy in the cooking department."

Trying to lighten the mood, Daddy laughed, saying, "No one could be that bad."

Mother was not amused.

The following Monday, Aunt Colleen met me in the road as I was coming home from school and asked me if I would be her assistant chef. I agreed, and over the ensuing weeks we spent many hours planning the menu and stocking the pantry.

Unfortunately, the dinner became a project that took me away from watching John. Mother was not pleased with the situation. She cornered me as I passed her in the kitchen on Saturday morning. "I want you to watch John for a bit while I take a nap."

"I promised Aunt Colleen I would work on her dinner today."

She pointed her spatula at me. "I suppose your promise to be Mother's Little Helper meant nothing to you, Miss Moran."

"No, it's just that I already told Aunt Colleen I would come."

Mother turned her back to me. "All right, go to your precious aunt."

I tried to put my hand on her elbow. She pulled away as she continued to fry the bacon, hissing her displeasure at me in harmony with the unclean pork.

But I couldn't back down. Aunt Colleen was counting on me. So I left her sizzling at the stove before she could engage me in further combat and went to help my aunt prepare for the big event.

I went to Aunt Colleen's house promptly at five o'clock on Thanksgiving morning. Dinner would be served at four o'clock sharp, whether Mother was there or not.

Over Daddy's objections, Mother had decided she had to take John down to the Macy's parade. "I want him to see the clowns and balloons. It will be his first time," she said.

"I don't see what he'll get out of it at his age. Just make sure you get back on time. For once, I'd like to see you and your sister getting along on a holiday," Daddy said.

"Don't worry. I wouldn't dream of spoiling Colleen's special day."

We waited until Mother departed before moving operations over to our house. Daddy set up the bridge table and chairs to accommodate the overflow. When done, he and the boys settled into the couch to pray to the football gods. Grandma stayed in her bedroom and watched old movies until dinnertime, when she emerged with four empty beer cans tucked in her sweater pockets.

At noon, Sarge arrived with a bottle of champagne protruding from his overcoat. Daddy put it in the refrigerator to chill. We took the turkey out of the oven at two forty-five and set it on the counter to cool. As dinnertime grew closer, we took the candied yams out of the oven and lit the gas under the peas and corn. The pies were lined up on the kitchen counter: apple, pumpkin, cherry. Everything was working out perfectly.

Daddy carved the bird at halftime.

At exactly four o'clock, Aunt Colleen tinkled a golden bell she had bought for the occasion and announced in a voice befitting a butler in a fancy mansion, "Dinner is served."

"What about Ma?" Paddy asked.

"She knew what time dinner was. If she can't get here on time, we're not waiting for her."

Daddy and Sarge exchanged glances. They hesitated for a moment before going to the dining room. The rest of us followed.

"Oh, Colleen, that looks magnificent," Grandma said.

"Please, sit down at the chair where your place card is," Aunt Colleen said.

We were like children playing a game of musical chairs.

When we were finally seated, Aunt Colleen squeezed my hand under the table. I squeezed back and started to let go, but she didn't loosen her grip. "I think we should all join hands and say grace," she said.

"Don't you think we could wait a few more minutes for Lizzie?" Sarge asked.

"I think not," my aunt replied.

"All right, who'll say grace?" Daddy asked.

"I'll do it," Billy volunteered.

We all clasped hands and bowed our heads.

"Dear Lord, thank you for this beautiful food and this fine house. Keep us all together and happy and in good health. Help us to remember the starving people who have no food."

"I'm starving now. Hurry up," Paddy said.

Billy shook his head as he continued, "In Jesus' name we pray. Amen."

"Alleluia!" Paddy screamed.

We had been eating for less than two minutes when Mother came in. "Couldn't you gluttons wait for me to get home? I'm not really late, not by normal standards," she rocked John against her bosom.

"We were just praying for your safe return," Paddy said. Daddy smacked him on the back of his head.

"We held out as long as we could, my love," he said.

"I'll bet you did," Mother replied.

"Please, sit down. Your sister has worked very hard to make a lovely meal. Let's not spoil it for her," Grandma said.

Mother glared at her, but quickly broke into an impish grin. There was something about her crooked smile that unsettled me. It seemed almost... evil.

"Of course, this is a special day. It's going to be a day for celebrating. Let me put John down, and I'll be right back."

When she came back, she kissed Daddy on the top of his head, and he pulled her down into the seat next to him. He tucked her place card into his pocket with a wink.

The rest of the meal was marked by uncharacteristically warm cheerfulness with good-natured small talk among family members. We had second helpings, followed by third. By the time we finished the pies, I thought we would all explode.

We retired to the living room to digest, not even bothering to stop to clear the dishes. None of us could move once we settled into our positions in front of the television. There was no fighting over what we would watch because we all knew we would be asleep within minutes of turning the set on.

At precisely six o'clock, Sarge got up and went to the kitchen. Aunt Colleen followed him without saying a word. When they came back, she had a tray with glasses and the bottle of champagne in her hands.

"Listen everybody, we have an announcement to make," Aunt Colleen said.

I looked at Mother, and her expression made it quite plain that she knew what was about to be said; she had a look brimming with glee at her sister's impending doom.

"Will all the grownups take a glass, please?" Aunt Colleen said as she passed them out.

I looked at Daddy, then Grandma. Neither seemed to have a clue as to what was happening.

"Frankie, will you do the honors?" Sarge asked.

"Sure thing, buddy," Daddy replied.

He lifted himself off the couch and took the bottle from Aunt Colleen. He pulled the cork out and champagne began to foam over the top, spilling down the sides. Daddy quickly began to pour so as not to waste a drop of the magical elixir.

Sarge cleared his throat and began his speech. "It may come as a surprise to most of you, but Colleen and I have been seeing each other for quite some time," he said.

Everyone looked at Sarge and Aunt Colleen, first at one, then at the other, then back again. Everyone except Mother. She just sat there with the grin on her face getting bigger and bigger.

Sarge continued. "We've grown very close. As a matter of fact, we're in love, and we're going to get married. We hope you'll all attend our wedding and join us now in a toast to a happy union. I can tell you, for my part, that I have never been happier, and that I will do everything in my power to see that Colleen is happy for the rest of her life. Won't you please lift your glasses in a toast to our happiness?"

No one moved or said a word until Daddy stood and raised his glass high. "To eternal love and happiness," he said.

Paddy stood, raised an imaginary glass and said, "Ditto."

Mother's eyes were twinkling with sheer delight.

As my glance turned toward Grandma, I saw nothing except rage in her ancient eyes. Suddenly, she charged at Sarge and threw her champagne in his face. "You dirty old bastard," she said before she ran out of the house, slamming the door shut behind her.

Mother swigged her champagne, refilled her glass, downed another drink, and ran off after Grandma.

Daddy went over to where an in-shock Sarge stood. He took his handkerchief out of his pocket and wiped the befuddled man's face for him. "Welcome to the family," Daddy said, whereupon Paddy got up on his chair, pointed his fork at Sarge, and made the sign of the cross saying, "And may God have mercy on your soul!"

Chapter 26

Aunt Colleen went home with Sarge that night.

A week after the announcement, we received a postcard from the happy couple. The day after Thanksgiving they had packed their bags and eloped to Niagara Falls. Sarge had written that he hoped Grandma wouldn't come looking for him to push him over the falls in a barrel. He had drawn a cartoon on the back showing himself flying over the edge, complete with a set of crutches spread like wings to break his fall.

Grandma refused to believe that Sarge loved Aunt Colleen and would take care of her. Whenever the subject came up, she said that all Sarge was interested in was getting his hands on her body. She called him the "dirty lecher." I didn't know what a lecher was, but it sounded close enough to leech that I knew she thought he was slimy.

Mother, on the other hand, couldn't have been happier with the situation. She had Grandma to herself. They went shopping together, took walks, cooked meals. Lizzie was the replacement daughter, relishing the role like an eager understudy taking over the lead. It was the nearest to normal that I would ever see their relationship.

But their newfound closeness was short-lived.

Two weeks later, I went to see the Christmas show at Radio City Music Hall with Grandma and Mother. When the show ended, we went to a delicatessen for lunch. The restaurant smelled of dill pickles and corned beef and waitresses who used too much hairspray. We sat in a corner booth and ordered overstuffed sandwiches and egg creams. Mother didn't even seem to care how much I ate. She hadn't made a nasty comment about my weight in weeks. I was beginning to think she didn't care anymore. Her good fortune was my good fortune. As we sat gorging ourselves on the best of New York deli fare, we discussed the show.

We talked about the little old lady seated in front of us who sang along in the worst off-key voice I'd ever heard whenever the organist played a Christmas song. We discussed the living Nativity and the Rockettes and the beautiful ladies' lounge. Opinions were freely exchanged and debated. It was almost as though we were civilized guests on a talk show engaging in witty banter, a Noel Coward and Oscar Levant routine.

Toward the end of the meal, as I sat finishing the remains of my hot fudge sundae, the conversation turned to family.

"We should take John next year," Mother said.

"Every child should go at least once. They should make it a law," Grandma said.

"It's something you remember forever. I remember when you took Colleen and me. You made me promise not to tell her ahead of time because it was going to be a surprise for her birthday."

"Oh, yeah, I remember that."

"Then I caught her sneaking a peek at the tickets you had hidden in your bureau drawer."

"You never told me that."

"Why would I? There's a lot about that sister of mine that you seemed to think was okay, so long as she could hide behind her excuse of not being right in the head."

"Now, Lizzie, don't be spiteful. It's not Christian. Besides, it is Christmas."

"No, Mother, I want you to hear this. She was a sneak and a liar as a child, and she never changed."

"Now, Lizzie, that's a very unkind thing to say."

"But it's true. That's what she was doing with Sarge, sneaking through the backyards every chance she got. But I knew what she was up to. I saw her trying to escape notice as she walked along the shoreline to that creepy old gimp's place for their secret rendezvous. You'd have to be blind not to know what was going on between those two."

Grandma put her teaspoon down mid-stir.

"You knew about her and Sarge?" she asked.

"Of course, I did. It was so obvious. She's not exactly a wizard at covering things up, now is she?"

Grandma's cheeks became crimson.

"You knew about it and you didn't tell me?"

122

"Why would I tell you? Colleen's a grown woman, for Christ's sake. She knew what she was doing."

Grandma's hands began to shake. "She knew what she was doing? Are you listening to yourself? This is Colleen we're talking about here. You know she's not right in the head."

I cringed and tried to sink into the booth, away from the two of them.

"You just don't get it. No matter how many times I remind you, you refuse to remember what happened to her. She had a brain injury. She was in a coma for months. When she finally came out of it she was like a newborn baby. And all because of a foolhardy game of chicken with bicycles."

Mother slammed her fist down so hard the utensils jumped off the table and landed back with a resounding metallic clang. "Now the truth's coming out, old lady. You blame me for what happened to Colleen. You've always blamed me. You think it was my fault."

"No, I didn't say that. I'm just saying that you should have protected her from Sarge. You should have come to me, and we could have nipped it in the bud. You let me down, Lizzie. As always, you let me down."

Mother slumped back in her seat. Tears started rolling down her cheeks. As I turned my head, I realized the people in the booths around us were staring in amazement at the freak show. I prayed to God to make me shrink to Lilliputian size so I could climb into the sugar bowl and pull the cover over me. Even if I drowned in sugar granules, it could not have been a worse fate than being mortified by my family's inability to act normal in public.

Grandma pulled a tissue out of her purse and offered it to Mother. She ignored it as she continued crying.

The waitress appeared at our table. "Is everything all right?"

"Check, please," Grandma replied.

Mother and Grandma did not speak to one another during the rest of the trip, choosing to use me as a go-between to relay messages.

"Please tell your grandmother we need to catch the train on track nineteen."

"Inform your mother that I am well aware of what track we need to go to."

And so it continued, all the way back upstate.

123

I counted telephone poles in an effort to distance myself from them and the wounds that would never heal. There weren't enough telephone poles in the country to shield me from the palpable presence of their emotions: anger, hurt, bitterness.

After that day, Grandma and Mother's newfound friendship crumbled. Soon, it was as if the intervening weeks had never happened. As their relationship melted back to what it had been, Grandma reached out to Aunt Colleen. She offered her an olive branch in the form of a dinner invitation, and my aunt responded eagerly, although Sarge was not included. The rift was sealed, and they easily slipped back to their old roles: Mother-Protector and Child-Innocent.

I don't think Grandma ever truly forgave Sarge for taking Colleen away from her. But I think she respected his ability to make Colleen happy. She could only hope he would protect Colleen when she was no longer there to take care of her baby girl.

On her side, Mother turned to Daddy, clinging to him during every waking moment. When he got up, she made him breakfast. When he went to the hardware store to buy nails, she insisted on tagging along. If he tried to escape to the garage to work on the station wagon, she would come out and hover over him, asking questions about lug nuts and oil changes in an attempt to draw him out. She was like a baby who refuses to let Mommy leave. This went on day and night, January to February, for weeks on end until he could no longer stand it. One day, he was trying to shut the bathroom door when he noticed she was ready to follow him into his last bastion of privacy.

"Damn it, Lizzie, you're suffocating me."

When he emerged from his lair, he put his coat on and walked out into the frigid February air and did not return for two days. When he finally came home with a drunken crying jag on, Mother put him to bed and shut their bedroom door.

Slowly, family life settled back to normal. Or at least as normal as the Moran clan could hope to be. As bad as things had been, in only another month our lives would be changed forever by Daddy's next departure.

Chapter 27

On a Saturday early in March, Daddy did not come home from the city. Before Daddy left that morning, he said he was going to take care of some business at the apartment building and expected to be back in time for dinner. At six o'clock the rest of us sat down to eat. By six-fifteen, Mother began to tap her fingernails on the table. Still, we waited. At six-thirty, Paddy had the audacity to grab for the bowl of boiled potatoes in front of him. Mother reached across the table and stabbed him on the back of his hand with the tines of her fork. Four dots of blood appeared where she had pierced his flesh, stigmata of his selfishness. "Did I say you could eat?" Mother asked.

We sat looking at the food until the chimes on the grandfather clock struck seven. Mother lifted her knife and fork and began to dissect her pork chop with the precision of a skilled surgeon. "I guess we'd better start. There must be train delays," she said. We waited for her to take the first bite and then began to devour our cold, congealed food, the sooner to leave the table. When she excused us, my brothers and I marched straight upstairs like good little soldiers.

I couldn't get to sleep that night. I kept thinking about train derailments and automobile accidents and all the other gruesome things that could have happened to Daddy. One thought, more hideous than all the others, kept popping into my head: What if Daddy never came home and we were left alone with Mother forever?

The rest of the evening she stayed downstairs waiting, watching. Every time headlights appeared on the wall of my room, I heard her go to the front door and unlock it. But the cars never stopped. They kept driving past to other children's houses, to other angry mothers. So she'd come back and wait as the cars grew fewer and the night grew darker.

Finally, the telephone rang. I switched on my bedside lamp and looked at the clock: Ten minutes to five. Slithering downstairs, I hid myself on the bottom step. Mother was on the kitchen phone. I could hear her voice but was unable to make out any of the words. I knew when she was done with the call; she slammed the receiver down so hard the sound of the ringer reverberated through the house. It grew quiet again, save for ticking clocks and the eerie sounds of an old house settling into its foundation. I crawled back up to bed and pulled the covers over my head.

Dawn was breaking when I woke to the sound of knocking at my bedroom door.

"I have news," Paddy said. He came in, sat on the edge of the bed and ripped the covers from me. "The old man's okay, but there's going to be trouble when he gets home."

Billy appeared in the doorway.

"What kind of trouble?"

"A complete fireworks show. You know that flirty waitress down at Clancy's Pub? You know her, the one all the guys say is built like a brick outhouse. Well, apparently, Daddy and her have been on friendly terms for quite some time."

"How do you know?"

"I listened in on the upstairs extension."

"That's an invasion of privacy."

"Your old man's been invading that tart's privacy for years, so he has no right to complain."

"I wasn't thinking of him."

He scratched his chin.

"Oh, yeah, right. You mean Lizzie the Loon. She has no right to gripe about that. Our dear sweet mother rifles through everyone's personal effects, just like a KGB agent."

Maybe that was why I always found my stuff in different places when I got home from school. He was making me more nervous with each revelation, but I still had to ask the next question that came into my head: "What do you think will happen when Daddy comes home?"

"You mean if he comes home. I don't know. Mother's reactions are difficult to predict. She can go either way—immediate warfare or plot for future revenge. There is one thing I am sure of."

"What's that?"

"We'd better hide the knives."

The next morning, my brothers and I ate breakfast alone. None of us said a word about what had happened. We ate our meal with an artificial politeness usually reserved for visitors.

Mother stayed in self-imposed exile in her bedroom until we went to sleep. The rest of us went about our business, not bringing up the subject of Daddy, except by the look in our eyes.

Monday morning came. We left for school, haunted by the specter of one ghost parent missing in the world, another passing us in the hallway as if she did not see or hear us, in a dimension of time and space that we could not enter and that she could not leave.

When school let out that afternoon, I was surprised to find Aunt Colleen waiting for me by the playground fence. I shuddered when I spotted her, fearful she might have news of a disaster. I took a deep breath and put on my bravest face as I went to greet her.

"How are you, Gerri Girl?"

"I'm fine. Is everything all right?"

"All right? As far as I know it is. I just wanted to talk to you. It's so hard to get to visit with you nowadays. Lizzie doesn't exactly make me feel welcome at your place, and you never seem to drop by anymore. Can you come to the diner with me? I'll buy you a soda."

I hesitated for a moment. She didn't seem aware of our situation. I didn't want to let anything slip about Daddy and the state of affairs we found ourselves in. After all, we had enough trouble without getting her involved. "Okay, but just for a little while. I have a lot of homework."

"Great."

The crowd in the Ferrytown diner at that time of day consisted of one waitress and a quartet of grizzled elderly men in their usual hangout, hunched over cups of coffee. I talked about school events until the waitress brought our drinks. That's when private investigator Colleen began her probing.

"So, tell me, Gerri, how is everyone?"

"Okay."

"The only reason I'm asking is that your father was supposed to drive Sarge to the doctor and he never showed up. Sarge called the house, but your Mother kept hanging up on him. It's not like Frankie to just forget about an appointment that way. Is he feeling well? Is he home?"

"He stayed in the city Saturday night, so it probably slipped his mind."

"That's certainly odd. Did he call?"

"Yes, he called."

"So, what happened?"

I quickly grew annoyed at her attempts to pump me for information.

"Look, Aunt Colleen, I don't know any more than what I've just told you. If you really care, talk to Mother. I'm not your little spy."

Aunt Colleen's spoon and jaw dropped simultaneously. She needed a minute to compose herself, but when she spoke again there was a smirk on her face. "No, you're right," she said.

A moment later, her eyes welled up and tears began to flow down her cheeks.

"I'm sorry, Gerri. It's just that I've always felt extremely close to your father. We share a special bond. If it weren't for Lizzie..."

I jumped at her words, accidentally knocking my soda over. I got up, fumbling to clean the mess with a napkin.

"I have to go now."

She clamped her fingers around my wrist. "Gerri, you know I'd never hurt you."

I brought my face close to hers. "Let go."

She released me from her grip, and I walked away, fast, nearly breaking into a run by the time I reached the door. I heard her call "I love you, Gerri" as I fled, not stopping to return the sentiment.

I kicked up wet leaves and crunched twigs beneath my feet as I ran; thoughts popped into my head, one after another. *What did she mean by extremely close? What kind of a bond did she have with Daddy? What would have happened if it weren't for Lizzie?* My side began to ache, and was burning by the time I reached the house.

As I sat down on a tree stump to rest, the answer to all my questions came to me: She's crazy Aunt Colleen, the one they warned you about. She doesn't know what she's saying. Hadn't I heard Grandma say that she wasn't right in the head a thousand times? I felt stupid for even allowing myself to listen to her strange statements. They were stuff and nonsense, the gibberish of a child looking for attention. I was still grinning at my own stupidity when I went inside my house.

A radio was playing. The music led me to Mother in the kitchen. She was draining a pot of boiled potatoes. She dropped the pot in the sink with a resounding clang and turned around to greet me, face full of bitterness, voice tinged with barely-contained rage. "Where have you been?"

"I had to stop at the library. I forgot to tell you I'd be late."

She wrinkled her nose, looking like a mad hare. "That seems to be a growing habit with the Moran clan, not telling me when you're going to be late. Why do you all insist on making me frantic with worry?"

"I'm sorry, Mother. I promise I won't let it happen again."

She raised her arms over her head, eyes rolling toward the heavens. "That's another thing you're all famous for, making promises and then breaking them at the drop of a hat. Well, I'm having none of it anymore. Things are going to change around here, believe you me. Now, go clean up and tell your brothers to do the same. Dinner will be at exactly six o'clock."

I flew up the stairs, fleeing the range of her verbal jabs. As I was passing the boys' room, Paddy signaled me with a whistle.

I heard furniture being moved.

"Is Mother there?" Paddy asked.

"No. What's going on in there? Let me in." The door opened a crack, and I saw him check out the hall. Suddenly, Paddy grabbed my arm and pulled me into the room. He shut the door and pushed the dresser against it. That's when I noticed Billy sitting in the corner, knees pulled up to his chest. He was holding a bloodied handkerchief up to his face.

"Hi, sis, join the party," Paddy said.

"What happened to Billy?"

He didn't answer.

I sat down next to Billy.

"Tell me."

Billy began the tale:

"I was in the kitchen having milk and chocolate chip cookies. Mother came in and put the kettle on. She went back to the living room. When the whistle blew, she came back and poured herself a cup of tea. The telephone rang and she picked it up. I could tell by the look on her face that it was Daddy on the other end. She just kept repeating "I see" to everything. When she hung up, she picked up her cup and began to walk away. But instead of going to the living room, she went to the pantry and locked herself in.

Just then, Paddy came in and started to munch an apple. I had no time to warn him she was hiding there. So Paddy, being the loudmouthed jackass that he is, started in with the wisecracks. He said, 'So, where's the old man? Is he down in Brooklyn screwing that whore?'

Mother sprang from the pantry and threw her teacup at Paddy. She missed, and it hit me square on the chin. When Mother saw she had missed Paddy, she went nuts. She jumped on his back and began to choke him. Paddy tried to get loose, but nothing worked. I tried to pry her fingers from around his throat, but it was no use, and he was gasping for air. So I grabbed the kettle and hit her in the back of the head. I had to do it; I had no choice. He could have died. I had to. But I didn't hit her hard enough. She started to move, so I helped Paddy upstairs. Just as we reached the top, we heard a noise below us. Mother was crawling up the steps, pulling herself up by the rungs on the banister. She had a carving knife in her hand. Suddenly, she fell backward and landed at the bottom of the stairs. God, I thought she was dead for sure that time. We locked ourselves in, but she managed to get up here and started banging on the door. She loosened the knob, so we pushed the dresser over and made a barricade. After ten minutes, she gave up and went back downstairs."

Story over, Billy blinked his eyes several times before focusing on me. "Where were you?"

"Does it matter?"

"No, I guess not."

"She expects us for dinner at six," I said.

"Should I wear my tuxedo?" Paddy said.

"Haven't you caused enough trouble with your mouth for one day?" Billy said.

"Don't put this in my lap!"

"And why shouldn't I?"

Paddy squatted down and explained to us. "I'll tell you why. Because no matter how good or quiet or helpful any of us could have been, sooner or later she was going to go off. I love her as much as anyone could, but the woman's got some serious mental health issues. She's crazy as a bedbug." He pulled the bedspread off and peered under the sheets. "You in there, Lizzie?"

I looked at Billy's shocked expression, and knew my own mirrored it. Paddy had said it out loud, the ugly truth you do not utter, the secret you do not reveal. If Aunt Colleen was not right in the head, did that mean Mother and she were birds of a feather?

"We have to get out of here," Billy said.

"Relax," Paddy said.

"No, I have to get out of this house, away from her." He began to shake. "I can't take this anymore."

Paddy wrapped his arms around him and tried to squeeze the fear out. "So long as we stick together, we'll be all right," he said.

"But what do we do now?"

"Well, I don't want to go through another scene with Mother."

"One of us has to go for help."

"You've played hero enough for one day. It's my turn now."

"But where?"

"To Sarge's place. He'll know what to do."

Paddy went to the window and climbed onto the back porch roof. He shimmied down the drainpipe and disappeared into the trees. He had only been gone a couple of minutes when Mother called us. "Kids, dinner's ready. Come down and eat."

Billy took me by the hand and led me to the table. Mother was sitting in Daddy's place. She did not mention Paddy's absence as we took our seats. "Would someone like to say grace?" she asked.

"I will," Billy said.

We bowed our heads. "Dear Lord, please help us through our daily sorrows. Keep us safe from harm and protect our loved ones. Heal our sicknesses and the sicknesses of those who are hurting. In Jesus' name we pray. Amen."

The meal began with a flurry of dinnertime niceties:

That looks good.

Please pass the butter.

May I have some more?

Everything was going smoothly until she brought up the subject of our missing sibling.

"Where's Paddy?"

I swallowed a chunk of potato that landed in my stomach with a thud.

"I asked where your brother is."

"He's upstairs. He's not feeling well," Billy said.

"What's wrong with him?'

"He's nauseous."

"I'd better go up and have a look at him."

"No, no, he'll be okay. You know how he gets when he eats too many potato chips before dinner."

"Still, a boy needs his mother when he's sick." She went upstairs.

Panic began to seep out of Billy's pores. "Oh, God, she'll see he's not there. What'll she do? We have to get out of here."

I grabbed him by the shoulders. "Calm down. Like Paddy said, we have each other."

Mother returned and stretched her arms across the doorway like Samson when he knocked the temple columns down. "Where is he?"

My right leg began to shake.

"I asked a question, and I expect an answer," she said.

She leapt out of the doorway and put her face so close to mine I could feel her breath on my cheeks.

"Gerri, do you know where your brother is?"

"He went to Sarge's place. He was afraid."

"Afraid of what?"

"Of you."

She let out a half-snort, half-laugh, like a combined warthog-hyena. She backed up and pointed to herself.

"Of me?"

Suddenly, she banged her fists on the table so hard the dishes jumped. Pointing an accusatory finger, she continued her tirade. "You're liars, the lot of you. I see what's happening here. They're turning you against me. That old woman and her crazy daughter and that gimp, they're all in on it. Well, I won't stand for it, I tell you. I will not tolerate disloyalty from my own children. Isn't it enough that I've been humiliated by my husband?"

Billy went and tried to put his arms around her, but she rejected his gesture with a turn of her body. "No, I'll have none of your pity. I just want it to end. Just leave me alone, all of you." She jumped, knocking her chair over in the process, and ran to her bedroom. She began to sob, hard and deep, like an ancient Celt drowning in a fog-shrouded bog, deep in the murky waters where no one could save her from the depths of her despair. It felt like hours had passed when there was a furious rapping at the back door.

Billy opened it and Grandma came charging in, pink curlers bobbing on her head as she moved.

"Where's your mother?" she asked.

"Upstairs," Billy said.

"Paddy called me from Sarge's. Are you kids all right?"

"Grandma, I'm scared," Billy said.

She went over to him and examined the cut on his chin by the light of the lamp.

"Good Lord, child, did she do that to you?"

He nodded.

"Well, Grandma's here now. Don't you worry about a thing, baby. I'm going up to her."

"Grandma?" I said.

"Yes, Gerri?"

"Be careful."

"Hold your tongue, child. I'm in no danger. She's my baby."

But aren't we her babies?

She went to Mother and stayed by her side all night.

Mother did not stop crying for several hours. Still, I could not get to sleep and kept looking out the window, half of me hoping Daddy would come home, half of me praying that he wouldn't.

Next morning, Grandma made us breakfast. She asked us to come home directly from school. She promised us she'd set things right.

When we arrived home that afternoon, she took us to the living room. Aunt Colleen was sitting on the couch. There were empty beer cans and bowls of chips scattered about the room, as if there had been a party.

We had been sitting there a few minutes when we heard the sound of footsteps descending the stairs. My brothers and I turned toward the doorway. It was Daddy. "Hello," he said in a soft voice, almost a whisper.

He plopped his hulking body on the floor in front of the coffee table. A smell of unwashed body mixed with beer wafted across the room. "I have something I want to say to you. I want you all to listen. Can you do that for me?"

We nodded.

"Good. I'm very sorry that you had to go through what you've had to. I'm making no excuses for my actions because there is no way I shouldn't be held responsible for them. I will tell you this. Sometimes

133

married couples grow apart. Sometimes there are reasons beyond their control. It doesn't matter why. What matters is the marriage vows, because they're made before the eyes of God. When you promise to stay together in sickness and in health, it's a promise for life. A promise is a promise."

Grandma nodded.

His voice began to crack as he continued. "I'm very sorry about what's happened. I never meant to hurt any of you. All I can do is ask for your forgiveness and promise you that things will change, that I'll change. If you'll have me, I'm home for good."

His helpless puppy dog look seduced us. We could not help ourselves. "What about it? Will you give me another chance?"

Paddy slapped him on the back. "So long as you've dropped that tart, you're square with me," he said.

Daddy turned a deep crimson. "Uh, uh, of course," he replied.

Daddy leapt up from the floor and clapped his hands together. "C'mon team, let's clean up this house. Billy, you get the vacuum. Paddy, my lad, I want you to wash the floors."

Paddy put his hands on his hips. "But that's woman's work."

"Not today, little man. Not today."

Aunt Colleen went over to Daddy. She put her index finger on his chest and began to draw a circle. "And what do you want me to do, Frankie?"

He snatched her hand and put it at her side. "I want you to go home and take care of your husband."

She stomped her foot like a child who doesn't get her way, then ran out.

Grandma got up and began to follow her, but stopped in the doorway and blew a kiss to Daddy. "Love you, Francis."

He caught it and put it in his pocket. "Ditto, Irene."

Applying ourselves to the goal of making our house spotless, we worked as one unit, scrubbing away the sinful past to create a purified chapel. Perhaps we made a mistake using ordinary household cleansers. Perhaps we should have used industrial strength chemicals to eradicate the contagion of layer upon layer of lies.

Germs are persistent devils. You never know if they're really gone. Sometimes they come back. And sometimes when they do, the consequences are deadly.

Chapter 28

Paddy found out more of the story and relayed it to Billy and me. They had taken Mother away while we were in school. She was committed to the Good Samaritan Psychiatric Hospital. Whether she went voluntarily or by force, I never found out. All we were told is that we wouldn't be able to see her for at least several months. Oddly enough, that didn't bother me.

Daddy stayed upstate except for his monthly visit to collect the rent money from his tenants. He had hired one of them as building superintendent in exchange for a reduction in rent. In short order, he became the model of a good suburban parent. When Paddy joined the soccer team, Daddy signed on as a coach. He became a volunteer fireman. When he received his uniform, we all went down to the firehouse to celebrate the event. Daddy posed in front of the fire engine and broke into a huge grin as Chief Wilson snapped his picture. A few weeks later, he put the photograph in a silver frame and hung it next to Mother's picture of Kennedy. Whenever he passed it, he would pull out his handkerchief and wipe it clean. Sometimes he made a special trip expressly for that purpose.

We resumed our Sunday afternoon habit of gathering for family dinner. Although no one mentioned her, the presence of our missing parent could be felt. As I stared at her empty chair, I found it difficult to hide my glee at being rid of my tormentor.

One day, toward the end of May, Daddy shouted for us kids to come to the living room. He was sitting in Aunt Peggy's wing chair, legs wide apart. A beer can was balanced atop his left thigh.

"Your mother is going to be allowed to have visitors," he said. He took a swig of beer and put the can back on his leg. "The only question is which of us should go this time."

We looked at each other.

"I think I should go," Paddy said.

Daddy scratched his chin. "No, you tend to open your mouth before you think. We don't want any crude remarks upsetting her."

Paddy's expression revealed that he felt insulted, but he held his tongue.

"What about you, Billy? I think she'd like to see you," Daddy said.

Billy hesitated, and we all stared at the scar where the teacup had hit him. "It's not as though anything bad can happen there."

Billy nodded as he said, "Of course I'll go, Daddy. The family has to stick together."

Paddy muttered, "Oh, brother."

Daddy took a gulp of beer, laid the can down on the coffee table, and rose to his feet. "What's that, Patrick Moran?"

Paddy shrank back into the sofa. "Nothing, sir."

"I didn't think so." Daddy sat.

"What about you, Gerri Girl? I'm sure your mother wants to see her only girl."

I looked into his eyes, and although I was afraid, I didn't want to let him down. "I'll go," I said.

"Are you sure? A hospital can be a scary place."

"I'm not afraid."

"All right, it's decided. Come Saturday, the three of us will go." He got up and held his hand out to Paddy. "Come on, boy. Let's go out and get some pizza."

Paddy did not reciprocate, so Daddy withdrew his hand. "That just means more food for me. Billy, Gerri, get in the car."

I looked back at the house as we pulled out of the driveway and saw Paddy standing at the window, finishing off Daddy's beer. He held it high in a toast to us. I watched Daddy and Billy, but neither of them noticed Paddy's cockiness.

I never told anyone what I had witnessed at the window that day. Later on, when I thought about the chain of events that followed, it made me wonder just how angry Paddy Boy might have been.

The following night I had a nightmare.

It was pitch black except for the stars in the sky. I was sitting on a tree limb that hung over a barbwire-topped brick wall surrounding the grounds to what I knew was Mother's hospital. Guards led a pack of snarling German Shepherds, patrolling the lawn. Others stood in watchtowers, rifles ready to gun down any escapees.

Suddenly, a siren broke the silence of the night, and a figure in a white hospital gown began running toward the wall. Searchlights scanned the grounds to find the prisoner. The phantom was within twenty feet of me when one of the lights focused on the ghostly figure, and it dropped to the ground. "Help me!" the creature pleaded.

I climbed to the edge of the branch. It cracked under my weight. Falling to earth with a thud, I found myself lying on my back inside the grounds. The figure leaned over me just as the searchlights once again found their prey. I raised my head and shuddered in horror as my own face stared back at me.

I woke up, soaked with perspiration, body trembling.

"Time to get up, lazybones!" Daddy called.

We arrived at the hospital a little before ten. There were brick walls, but they were small and covered with ivy, not barbwire. There was a guard in a booth, but he was armed with a clipboard, and the only animals were a couple of sparrows flitting down the walk.

Daddy went to the admissions desk and spoke to the nurse on duty. She told him to have a seat. We sat in the lounge and browsed through old magazines. We had been sitting there for a few minutes when an olive-skinned young woman with raven hair and gold-rimmed half-glasses approached. Daddy stood up.

She extended her hand and they shook. "Good to see you, Mr. Moran," she said.

"Thank you. These are my children, William and Geraldine," he said as he made a sweeping gesture in our direction.

She bent down to be on eye level with me. "I'm Doctor Romano. I want us to chat before I take you to see your mother." She led us to her office. "Please have a seat," she said. We sat on orange plastic chairs arranged in a semi-circle around the room.

"Mrs. Moran is making marvelous progress in her therapy. If things keep up the way they've been going, we'll be able to let her go home and will continue to treat her on an outpatient basis. I just want you to be prepared. You've been through a crisis together and sometimes it's

137

awkward getting to know each other again. Just do one thing for her. Let her know you're there for her."

I didn't believe it: She was asking me to be Mother's Little Helper!

Doctor Romano leaned forward, gently placing her hand on my shoulder. "Just let her know you love her."

I nodded.

"Very well. Let me take you to her. I'm sure she'll be delighted to see you."

We stood as one, but as we started to walk down the corridor, Daddy stopped. "I'll meet you back at the lounge," he said.

Doctor Romano took her glasses off and slipped them in her breast pocket. "I was rather hoping you'd be there, Mr. Moran."

"I'd rather not just yet. I'm partly to blame for her being here, and I don't think I can talk to her about it. Not yet."

She looked into his face. "Fine, I won't pressure you into anything you don't feel comfortable doing. You do know her better than anyone else, I suppose."

He touched Billy on the shoulder. "You'll be all right." Leaving us to face Mother alone, he quietly walked away.

Doctor Romano escorted Billy and me to a plant-filled atrium. Plastic circular tables were scattered about, seats securely bolted to the floor. I spotted Mother sitting alone at one in the corner. Our eyes connected, and she waved. As we got closer, I noticed the glassy look in her vacant eyes. Billy kissed her as she stared straight ahead.

"Well, I'll leave you three to talk," Doctor Romano said.

I followed Billy's lead and wrapped my arms around her shoulders and kissed her on the cheek. She did not respond. It felt like I was kissing a cold, lifeless mannequin.

"I'm so glad to see you. Where's the rest of the family?"

"Daddy didn't think it would be a good idea for everyone to visit at once," I said.

"I see."

She tilted her head at an unnatural angle. "Is everyone okay? It's so hard not seeing my little ones every day." She reached to pat Billy on the top of his head, and he was so startled he jumped back a foot.

"Everyone's fine. How are you? Doctor Romano said you might be able to come home soon."

"That's what they tell me. I can't wait to get back into my kitchen. Who's been cooking your meals?"

"Gerri and..."

"And?"

"Sometimes Grandma helps out. And sometimes Aunt Colleen pitches in."

Mother paused for a moment before she replied. "I'll have to thank Colleen when I get home. I'm glad she's been there for you. You know, sometimes I think she gets along better with my kids than I do. I only wish I could have been as close with her over the years. For some odd reason, we never connected." She scratched her forehead. "But that's all in the past. That's one of the things they teach you here. It's extremely important to know how to let go of the past."

I didn't know how to respond to that.

She turned her head in Billy's direction. "And how's my little man? You haven't been missing me too much, I hope."

"No, I mean, yes. I mean..."

"Stop stammering, Billy. It doesn't suit you."

"Daddy's a soccer coach for Paddy's team," I said.

"Well, that's wonderful. He can find time for that with his active social schedule, can he?" Her expression turned solemn. "Is your father staying home now?"

Billy answered. "Oh, yes, he's always there. He's turned fixing the apartment building over to a tenant. He rarely goes to the city, only when he collects the rent money. He's even become a volunteer fireman so he has to stay home to answer the call of duty."

"You mean he's not down at the firehouse drinking all their beer?"

Billy managed to force a weak smile. She was right, of course.

We sat making small talk for another ten minutes before Mother walked us back to the visitor's lounge. Daddy jumped up from his seat to greet us.

"Hi, Lizzie. You're looking well."

"Thank you, Francis. Weren't you in a friendly mood today?"

"I wanted you to have a chance to see the kids alone."

"Oh, that's most thoughtful of you. Thank you so much. Are you coming next week? We have a lot to discuss."

"Yes, of course. I'll call you during the week."

"Speaking of kids, where is my Paddy Boy?"

"He would have come, but he has soccer practice today."

"Oh. We wouldn't want him to miss that to visit his mother."

Daddy cringed.

"They have a limit on the number of visitors, too, sweetheart."

"Oh, I see. We mustn't break the rules, right dear? We always play by the rules."

Daddy lowered his eyes.

She wrapped her arms around Billy, pulling him close. "I love you."

"We love you, too."

"Take care of John for me, Gerri. We have a deal, don't forget."

She smoothed down my hair.

"You really need to groom yourself a little better, Gerri. Neatness counts."

"I will. I love you."

She did not reply. Turning away, she looked at Daddy.

"Goodbye, Francis."

"Goodbye, Lizzie." They did not touch.

Later that evening, I sat on the back porch with my brothers, eating sunflower seeds.

"How did she act with Daddy?" Paddy asked.

"Polite, as if he were a stranger," Billy said.

"Guess that's normal, all things considered."

Paddy spit a sunflower seed at me.

"Hey, cut it out," I protested.

He grinned. "Don't be such a baby, Gerri. You're the woman of the house now."

"Don't be silly. When Mother comes home, she'll be in charge again."

Billy shook his head.

"You don't think she can live together with Daddy after what he did, do you?"

"You mean what he's doing," Paddy said.

"Doing?" Billy asked.

"My God, you're such a child. I'm telling you he's still humping that waitress."

"Watch your mouth, Patrick Moran."

140

"It's true. You know my pal Willie Six Toes, from the old neighborhood? Well, his uncle's brother-in-law is Daddy's super. Willie tells me that every month Daddy goes to collect that slut's rent. Thing is, she doesn't pay in money. It's the ultimate in landlord-tenant relations."

"You mean she lives in the building?"

"Of course she does, moron. How do you think they got together in the first place?"

I thought about Daddy and how he had promised us he would change his ways. He had never meant it. He had lied to us. I felt the anger begin to surge within me. My cheeks grew hot as I started to feel dizzy with rage. How could he have sat there and lied to us? Maybe Mother was right. Maybe we were all a pack of liars, our promises like empty shells, ready to crumble to dust under the slightest pressure. Worst of all, I began to believe you could trust no one at their word, not even your own flesh and blood. Perhaps them least of all.

Chapter 29

After that day, every time Daddy left the house I prayed that he was not going to visit that woman down in Brooklyn. Despite what Billy had said, I still harbored hope that our parents would get back together again and life would return to normal. Or at least as close to normalcy as the Moran family could achieve.

For my part, I tried to maintain order as best I could. I did as much of the housework as possible after school. Daddy and the boys did not seem to notice how much effort I was putting into making sure their world did not collapse in a pile of filth. Even Grandma seemed to take my role as maid for granted. Still, I did not mind. Playing house was fun.

One evening, as I was getting up from the dinner table, I dropped my fork. As I bent down to pick it up, the seam to my pants ripped, and I could feel my panties exposed through the hole.

Paddy pointed at me as he sang, "I see London, I see France, I see Gerri's underpants."

"Shut up, you knucklehead!" Daddy shouted as he threw a biscuit at Paddy's head.

I ran upstairs to my bedroom and locked myself in. Throwing myself on the bed, I burst into tears. A few minutes later, there was a gentle knock at the door.

"Gerri, may I come in?" Daddy asked. I wiped my tears away on my pillowcase before letting him in. "Can we talk?"

He took a seat on the end of the bed and indicated for me to join him. "I'm so sorry that Paddy made fun of you. He will be punished, have no doubt about that. He has no right to tease you that way."

I nodded.

"Listen, I know how it is to be different. I was a giant for my size at your age."

"Did other kids pick on you?"

"No, but that was only because they knew I could crush them with one hand."

"Oh."

"Yes, but I still felt like the odd man out." He put his hands on my shoulders. "You have to learn to ignore the bullies, Gerri. There's always going to be someone out there who thinks they're better than you."

"That's because they are."

Daddy's face grew stern. "Don't ever let me hear you say that. You're a wonderful girl, Gerri. I wouldn't trade you for anything." He took my chin between his index finger and thumb. "I've told you before, and I'll keep on saying it. The day you were born, the angels wept for hours and hours to lose your soul from heaven." He stroked my cheek with his massive hand. "What do you think about going to the diner for a double scoop of ice cream?"

I stood, but quickly remembered the hole in my pants.

"I have to change clothes first."

"Oh, right. You do that, and we'll meet at the car."

He pulled his wallet out and handed me a wad of bills. "Tomorrow, I want you to buy yourself a whole new wardrobe. I won't have any girl of mine looking like a ragamuffin."

"Thank you, Daddy."

I hugged him before he moved to the doorway, stopping to add the remark that struck me with the full force of a freight train.

"Yes, all my women are smart dressers."

All his women? All... his... women?

He went downstairs, and I squeezed the money in my hands as Paddy's words echoed in my head, "I'm telling you he's still humping that waitress."

I pounded my pillow with my fists repeatedly until I grew tired. For a moment, I considered flushing the filthy bills down the toilet. Instead, I put them in my jewelry box, payment currently due for promises broken and in advance for lies yet to come.

Chapter 30

The next time Daddy went to see Mother, he took Paddy and baby John with him. Billy asked me if I wanted to go to the movies with him. I agreed, and the two of us went to a matinee and to the diner afterward.

"Get whatever you want. It's my treat," he said.

The waitress came over and flipped her pad open.

"What can I get you?"

"I'll have a deluxe burger platter and a large root beer, please," Billy replied.

I did not want to take advantage of his generous offer. He did not have a job, just an allowance.

"I'll have a grilled cheese and a coke, please."

"I'll be back in a jiffy," the waitress said before taking off for the kitchen.

"Are you sure that's all you want? Wouldn't you like some French fries?"

"No, I'm not very hungry."

"You're not feeling ill, I hope?"

"No, sometimes you just don't have an appetite. Don't you ever feel like cutting back?"

He thought for a moment.

"Well, you do know that many of the saints went on fasts to purify their souls. I've often thought that I'd like to try it sometime."

If Paddy were there, he would have made a cutting remark about Billy's quest for religious elevation. Or perhaps he would have made a snide comment on how I would sooner go to hell than skip a meal. I was glad it was just the two of us that day; I was in no mood to tolerate Paddy's hurtful tongue.

"You always have such interesting ideas. I wish I were as clever as you are. Sometimes I think you're the only person who isn't..."

"Isn't what, Gerri?"

"I don't know."

He smiled as he reached across the table to take my hand. "You know, Gerri, I've always believed that out of anyone in our family, you're the most likely to survive."

"Survive?"

"I mean... succeed."

"Why?"

He put his index finger on his cheek while he thought. "I've always thought we were alike in many ways. We know how to walk on water while everyone else is drowning."

A vision of Billy gliding over the surface of Lake Owl's Head popped into my head. I looked across the table at him and did not know if I believed he could really do it. But I knew he believed it, and a shiver of fear took hold of me.

"Here's your food," the waitress announced as she set our order down.

Billy took his fork and began to shovel fries onto my plate. "Now, eat up," he said.

"Can I get you anything else?" the waitress asked.

"We'll have the largest banana split you can make. Bring two spoons."

"Excellent. I'll bring it to you lickety-split. Get it, lickety-split?" She was grinning at her own corny joke as she walked away.

"Why did you order that?"

"We have to keep our strength up for the fight."

"What fight is that?"

He took the Saint Christopher medal hanging around his neck and kissed it saying, "The fight to stay afloat while those around you are sinking."

Chapter 31

The entire family was having Sunday dinner at our house when the telephone rang. Paddy sprang to his feet and ran to the kitchen to answer it.

"Daddy, it's for you," he said.

A hush fell over the table. Daddy wiped his mouth off with his shirt sleeve and went to the telephone. Paddy handed him the receiver and went back to his seat.

"Hi, this is Frankie," he said.

After a few minutes, he pulled a chair over and sat down, straddling it in a backward position to face the wall. From where I was seated, I could see Daddy twisting and untwisting the phone cord around his index finger. He lowered his voice as he continued the conversation for a full ten minutes before hanging up.

He came back to the dining room and stood in the doorway, placing his hands on his hips before he began to speak.

"That was my super. I have to go to the city. One of my tenants just passed away, and I have to help get things in order for the authorities."

"When will you be back?" Grandma asked.

"Tomorrow evening. Can you keep an eye on things for me?"

"You know I'm there for you, Francis."

Arrangements made, he packed a bag and left the house.

The following morning, I decided to ask Grandma to call the school to tell them I was sick. I wanted a holiday from everyone, and this was an opportunity I did not want to pass up. Grandma did not question me very much. I think she knew I was faking my illness, but understood my need to be alone.

A little before ten, I decided to take a shower. Uninterrupted bathroom time was one of the luxuries you could take advantage of when you had the house to yourself. I remember squishing the golden shampoo between my fingers as I worked it into my scalp.

I moved under the flowing stream of steaming, hot water. Suds ran down my body. Grabbing the scrub brush from the corner of the tub, I began attacking my face. I worked my way down the length of my body, shedding layer after layer of skin cells until I had rinsed myself to a squeaky clean state.

As was my ritual, I immediately shut the faucets off and wrapped myself in a towel as fast as possible. I felt revived in my newborn skin, tingling with freshness.

The mirror was fogged over. I wiped a circle with a piece of tissue and studied myself. Maybe there was hope for me; no one could argue with clean. I began to comb my hair out.

As I stood there, I thought I heard voices. No one was supposed to be home so early. Daddy had said he wouldn't be back until evening.

I went to the door and strained to listen, but couldn't hear anything. Opening the door slowly, I turned the knob gently so as not to make an old house noise. Tiptoeing into the hallway, I crept to the banister and peered over.

I saw the back of Daddy's massive frame facing the door. Someone was behind him, but I could not tell who it was. The figure had a windbreaker on, hood up. Arms reached and wrapped themselves around his waist. He pushed them away. "No, stop it."

"No, stop it," she mimicked.

She pulled the hood down. Even before I saw the shock of red hair, I recognized Aunt Colleen's voice.

"Go home. Sarge is waiting for you."

"Sarge is an old, gimpy skeleton. Why would I want him when I can have a real man who has a real body?"

"Colleen..."

"No, I want you."

She tried to hug him. Again, he rejected her advances.

She moved backward a step. "Oh, so that's how it is." She pummeled him on the chest with both fists. He grabbed her wrists and gently placed them at her sides.

She shook her finger at him. "You weren't so proud once upon a time, were you? You weren't too good to come to my bed then."

Daddy raised his hand and slapped her across the face.

She backed up to the door, opened it behind her, and slammed it as she stomped out in defeat.

Just as she shut the door, the comb slipped from my hands and fell over the banister. I saw it land next to the cellar steps, but did not know if Daddy had seen it. He turned his head to the left, then right.

I went to my room and lay down on the bed. It was just a few minutes before I heard him walk up the steps.

"Hello?" he asked as he stopped in front of my door. My heart was pounding when he knocked. "Gerri? Are you in there?"

"Daddy? What are you doing here? I thought you were in the city."

"I finished up earlier than expected. Why aren't you in school?"

"I... I... I'm having my woman's time so I called in sick."

He did not answer. It was a lie he would not question. In the 1960s, fathers did not discuss menstruation with their little girls.

"Well, let Grandma know if you need any help. I'm going down to the firehouse now."

"Goodbye, Daddy."

"Goodbye, sweetie. I love you."

"I love you, too."

I heard his heavy footsteps go out the front door.

Feeling overwhelmed by the morning's events, I lay on my bed and stared up at the ceiling. As I continued looking up, I felt as though the ceiling were descending down to meet me, moving closer and closer, ready to crush my bones to dust.

I had to get out of there or I would die.

I sprang up, quickly getting dressed.

The next thing I remember is running down the trail to Ferrytown Park. A driving rain began to fall as I ran down the wooded path, stinging my face like a mob of angry mosquitoes.

Running in the direction of the gazebo, I collapsed onto the middle of the deck, closing my eyes. My chest heaved as I struggled to catch my breath. A shiver passed through my body as the dampness penetrated my clothing and made my blood grow cold. I fell into a dreamlike state, remembering Aunt Colleen's insistent clawing at Daddy, his slap across her face, so hard it made my teeth ache.

A clap of thunder brought me back to the present. Watching the lightning streaks across the sky, I felt a tingling on my skin that made me feel as though I had never showered. It was like ants marching up and down my arms and legs, pricking my flesh, hundreds of tormentors discharging electrical sparks with their antennae. When the rain let up, I rose and made my way home with a feeling of dread.

When I opened the door, I stood still in the place where my aunt and father had played out their warped version of Romeo and Juliet. I had a sense that something seemed out of place. I looked around, searching for the missing piece to the scene that made it feel just slightly off center.

Turning in all directions, I realized what it was as I glanced down at the spot where my comb had landed.

It was gone!

No one else was home yet, and I had not stopped to pick it up before I had run from the house. Daddy must have picked it up. There was no other possible explanation. He must have known I was there watching, listening to his encounter with Aunt Colleen. He knew I was in on the secret, and I became filled with fear.

Paddy had told me secrets are dangerous. You never knew what people would do to keep them.

Sometimes they would lie.

Sometimes they would cheat.

And sometimes... if the secret was big enough... they would kill.

Chapter 32

"Why are you so pale? You look like Gerri the Friendly Ghost," Paddy said.

I couldn't tell him what I had seen Aunt Colleen doing with Daddy or what she had said. It was too awful, too evil.

"Daddy scared the heck out of me. Neither one of us knew the other was home. He thought I was a burglar."

"Imagine that, the thief of hearts thinking his little girl was a burglar. What was he doing here, anyway? He wasn't supposed to come back until tonight."

"He said he was done earlier than he expected to be."

Paddy stood for a moment staring into space until he collected his thoughts. "Come down to the kitchen, and I'll fix you a milkshake. I have some juicy news I want to share with you."

Although I didn't think I could handle any more surprises that day, I followed him downstairs.

My mouth watered as I watched him mix milk, strawberry ice cream, and chocolate syrup in the blender. He banged the cover into place and punched the high-speed button. The whirring of the machine comforted me, a soothing refrain preparing to deliver the friend that never let me down: food.

I watched in eager anticipation as he filled our glasses to the rim with the frothy concoction.

"Let's make a toast," he said.

"What kind of toast?" I asked.

He broke into a wide, goofy, full-toothed grin. He raised his glass and we met across the table with a clink.

"To the death of whores," he said.

"Paddy Moran! That's a very bad word and only bad people use it."

He brought his glass to his lips and polished off half the shake in one long, gluttonous swig. He banged the table with his fist and wiped his mouth with the back of his hand.

"But she's dead," he said.

"Who's dead?"

"Daddy's little tart, the waitress. She's gone to that big slut farm in the sky."

"Paddy, you're going to go to H, E, double hockey sticks if you don't watch your potty mouth."

He snorted sarcastically. "I'm not the one who committed adultery. She got what she had coming to her, the little home wrecker."

"How do you know she's dead?"

He rapped his knuckles against my forehead.

"Hello, is anybody home? Don't you remember my buddy Willie's uncle is the super in Daddy's building? No landlord rushes to an apartment building on a Sunday afternoon just because any old tenant has died. I had it figured out the minute I heard the words come out of the old man's mouth. All I had to do was call my sources to confirm it."

Although I didn't really understand the network of connections between Paddy and his sources, I knew that if he told me it was true, I could rely on it.

"Oh."

"There's a bright girl. I can almost see the light coming on."

"What will Daddy do now?"

"Daddy? That dirty old bastard will just get himself another girlfriend. No, I take that back. He probably has another one already, just like a reserve catcher. A man like him can't get enough."

"Enough what?"

He smiled as he got up, interlaced his fingers behind his head, and rhythmically began to grind his pelvis like a leprechaun belly dancer.

"The sweet taste of love."

The image of Daddy and Aunt Colleen in the hallway passed across my mind. I had to get away from there, away from the truth that was threatening to crush me once again. "Thanks for the drink," I said as I pushed myself away from the table. I ran to the coat rack and put my jacket on.

"Where are you going?" Paddy asked.

"Out."

"Well, don't be late. Daddy will be home soon."

"Uh-huh," I mumbled as I flew through the door.

Yes, we must not let Daddy down. He was always doing so much for his beloved family. I couldn't begin to guess how we'd ever repay the debts we owed him.

Chapter 33

A week later, Aunt Colleen invited my family to dinner.

Daddy declined and said he would stay home with John, as his youngest had a cold and he thought he should monitor him. My brothers and I were only too glad to be able to escape the confinement of being stuck in the house with Daddy. He had been in a foul mood for days, and there was no predicting who would face his wrath next.

Aunt Colleen had a gleam of excitement in her eyes when she opened the door that evening. "I'm so glad you could make it. Come inside and sit by the fire," she said. We followed her into the living room. Sarge was sitting in a rocker in front of the fireplace. He stabbed the blazing logs with the poker and made the flames dance a sparking jig.

Grandma was in the recliner, eyes closed. She had a beer can in one hand and a fistful of peanuts in the other. There were half a dozen half-crushed cans scattered around her feet. It looked like a boozy pileup on an alcoholic freeway.

"Sit down and relax. Dinner will be ready soon," Aunt Colleen announced.

The boys sat on the sofa and almost immediately began to tussle for control of the television remote.

"Gentlemen, if you don't mind," Sarge said as he held his hand out to Paddy. My brother gave it up with a hint of spite in his thrust as Sarge said, "It's my house, so it's my remote, huh?" He grinned as he snatched it away and turned on a baseball game, and the three of them settled into an uneasy truce.

Wanting to escape the tension, I tugged on Aunt Colleen's sleeve "Do you need any help with the dinner?" I asked.

She smiled. "Gerri, you're always reading my mind. I think you have a psychic gift."

As we entered the kitchen, I saw a roast chicken resting on a platter; a pot of corn was boiling on the stove.

"Can you get the potatoes out of the oven while I start to carve the hen?" Aunt Colleen asked.

She handed me a long fork, and I attacked the potatoes like a hunter spearing game and tossed them into a bowl.

"The corn should be done," she said.

I found a pair of tongs and plucked the ears from their watery grave, putting them in a bright yellow serving dish.

"Why don't you go inside and have a seat? You're my guest. You shouldn't be doing all the work."

"I don't mind."

"So long as you don't have to sit next to your pickled grandmother."

"Well..."

"I can't say as I blame her for getting stewed today. She's had a bit of a shock. It isn't every day that you find out you're going to be a grandmother for the fifth time."

I was stunned.

"I thought Mother was just getting fat," I said.

"Is she?" Aunt Colleen asked. She looked puzzled.

"Gerri, it's not her we're talking about."

"What do you mean?"

"It's me. I mean it's us, Sarge and me."

"You?"

I looked at her stomach. It didn't seem any bigger.

She shook her head.

"No, no, there are other ways. Sarge and I are adopting a child. The mother can't take care of the boy." She bent down as she whispered, "The poor thing isn't married." Straightening up, she continued. "She knew Sarge and I wanted a child of our own. One thing led to another, and soon you'll have a cousin."

"Does Daddy know?"

"Oh, yes. As a matter of fact, he helped arrange it. You know your father has some amazing connections."

She gave me a quick hug.

"Your father's a saint. He's finally making my dream of motherhood come true."

"I see."

There was a momentary lull before Aunt Colleen broke the silence. "There's just one thing, Gerri. Do you think you could help me with the baby?"

"Help you?"

"It's just that you're a lot more experienced with taking care of babies than I am. This is the first time I'm going to be a mother. They wouldn't let me before." Her face had the innocence of a newborn, helpless, pleading to be fed.

"Don't worry. I'll show you what to do. Just don't forget that I have to help out with John, too."

She kissed me on the cheek and took me by the hands, twirling me around in an impromptu dance around the kitchen. We finished preparing the dinner with smiles on our faces. It was the happiest I remembered being in a long time.

But as we walked to the dining room, plates in hand, she couldn't resist spoiling the moment.

"I can't wait to tell Lizzie. She'll just die with jealousy when she hears about it. She had to go through excruciating labor pains every time she shot a baby out. All I have to do is sign some papers, and I'm an instant mother."

I examined the joy etched into every crevice of her face and a wave of revulsion overtook me. Only one of my family members could twist the happiness over the arrival of a child into a means to take pleasure in someone else's pain. Only one of them could relish another's suffering and make an innocent child a pawn in their game of human chess. All I could keep thinking over and over the rest of the day was this one thought: *Why couldn't I have been born into another family?*

Chapter 34

Despite my loathing of her gloating, I helped Aunt Colleen prepare for the arrival of my new cousin as I had promised I would.

I taught her how to bathe him by using a doll at first, gradually working my way up to letting her watch me do it for my baby brother John. Fearful she would not handle the job herself without hurting him, I repeatedly kept putting her off when she asked to do it on her own. As we fed him, she grew used to caring for something other than herself or her pet turkey.

We made lists of everything we would need for the baby: diapers, crib, pacifiers, all the thousand-and-one items no mother could do without. If there had been time, I might have tried to arrange a baby shower for Aunt Colleen.

But it was only a week later when Aunt Colleen and Sarge were scheduled to bring their baby home. Never having experienced the adoption process, I had no idea that the speed with which events were unfolding was highly unusual.

No one seemed to remember that the same Saturday was my birthday. Although I was hurt that they had forgotten about it, I did not say anything. This was Aunt Colleen's special day, and I would not spoil it for her, even though I felt bitter about the timing.

Daddy drove the four of us the morning we went to pick up Michael. We arrived at the foundling home a little before ten. It was a large brick building set back on a well-manicured lawn. Goose bumps rose on my neck. It reminded me of the institution Mother was in.

The woman at the reception desk directed us to the third floor. Daddy and I waited in a lounge while Sarge and Aunt Colleen went to fill out the final papers. We had been waiting half an hour when Aunt Colleen returned.

"Come with me," she said.

She brought us to a room at the end of the hall where we found Sarge sitting on the floor, stacking colored blocks in size order. When he leaned back, I caught sight of my cousin.

He was dressed in overalls and a tee shirt, slightly more than baby-fat chubby. He reminded me of a darker-haired Dennis the Menace. I watched with amusement when he took the lime green beach pail he had in his hands and placed it on Sarge's head like a crown. The thing about him I found most surprising was that he wasn't the newborn I'd assumed he would be. He was a toddler, I guessed somewhere around John's age.

Daddy cleared his throat.

"Here they are," Sarge told his new son Michael.

"I like your hat," Aunt Colleen said.

Sarge started to take it off, but the baby pushed it back on. Each time Sarge attempted to remove the pail, my cousin would insist on replacing it. Finally, Sarge gave up and left it where it was. Suddenly, the little imp slapped it off his head and giggled with delight. Sarge did the "for shame" sign with his fingers to the boy. Michael laughed the way babies do when you play their made-up games.

"Frankie, Gerri, this is our son, Michael, Jr.," Sarge said.

Daddy stood in place. I went over to my cousin and extended my hand. He grabbed my index finger and squeezed it.

"Pleased to meet you. I'm your cousin Geraldine. You can call me Gerri."

Aunt Colleen picked Michael up and brought him over to Daddy.

"Michael, this is your Uncle Frankie," she said.

She tried to hand him to Daddy, but he held his arms at his sides and took a step back.

"I've never been very good with babies."

"Don't be silly; just hold him."

"No, I'd rather not."

"He won't hurt you. He's not a time bomb."

"Colleen, if he doesn't want to hold him you can't force him to," Sarge said.

My aunt's face became taut. Her voice quivered with rage when she answered him.

"Don't ever tell me what I can and cannot do. I'm not a child," she said.

"Please don't fight over me," Daddy pleaded.

Just then a stout woman in a white lab coat came by. "Is everything all right?" she asked.

Daddy smiled the smile he used when he was about to tell a fib. "Oh, yes, we were just discussing who would get to hold my nephew next. I believe it's my turn. Pass him to me, if you please."

Aunt Colleen handed him over. Michael looked into Daddy's face and clung to him like an old pal he had known forever, no evident fear of a stranger.

"I don't know why you made such a fuss. He really seems to like you," Aunt Colleen said.

She took him back, and Michael began to cry.

"Don't feel bad," the woman said. The stout woman patted Aunt Colleen on the forearm. "Don't worry. You just need to find your way with him." She looked at Daddy.

"How many children do you have, sir?" the woman said.

"Four," he said as he held up his fingers.

"God bless you. I'll leave you with your son, now."

"No, no, he's not mine. This gentleman is the father."

She took one look at Sarge's crutches and blushed. "Oh, I'm so sorry, sir. I just assumed you were the grandfather. Good luck with your new family."

Sarge shook his head. "No, just an old cripple who couldn't perform like a real man."

The woman turned a deep crimson as she fluttered away from my vulgar relatives.

"Maybe we should leave before she comes back with a couple of security guards to throw us out," Daddy suggested.

He helped Sarge up. We gathered Michael's belongings and got ready to leave. A small group of social workers and attendants walked us to the door. They waved to us as we drove away.

Michael fell asleep on Aunt Colleen's shoulder as she beamed with pride. Sarge took out his wallet and pointed to an empty plastic space between a photo of the Statue of Liberty and one of Aunt Colleen. "That's where my boy's picture is going," he said.

It was nearly noon when we pulled into the Denny's parking lot. We were seated in a booth near the restrooms.

The waitress came to take our order. "Can I get you guys something to drink?" she asked.

"Cokes all around," Sarge answered.

"No," Aunt Colleen interrupted.

The waitress turned to her. "Would you prefer another beverage?"

"I'll have an iced tea with lemon."

"But you always get soda ," Sarge said.

"I'm in an iced tea mood."

"Suit yourself."

"I'll be back in a jiffy," the waitress replied.

Daddy wrinkled his nose.

"Something smells bad," he said.

"Yeah, what is that odor?" Sarge asked.

We all turned our heads toward the culprit.

"Did baby make a boom-boom?" Aunt Colleen asked. She looked inside his diaper and held her nose. "Gerri, can you change him for me?"

"No, you have to start sometime, and it might as well be now. Let's go to the ladies' room."

We spread a blanket out on the sink counter, and I guided her as she changed him. Michael was fully awake by now and kept trying to kick his diaper off. When we finally got it to stay on, he began to cry again. Aunt Colleen reached into her bag and fished out a bottle. She gave it to him, and he began to drink like a drunken sailor on a three day pass.

When we got back to the table our three sodas and one iced tea had arrived.

"Come sit next to me, sweetheart," Sarge said.

"No, thank you," Aunt Colleen replied. She slid in next to Daddy while I sat to the left of Sarge.

"I'd rather have Gerri Girl by my side, anyway," he said.

The waitress reappeared.

"May I take your orders?" she asked.

"Just a minute," Aunt Colleen said.

She dug into the innermost recesses of her purse, pulled out and unfolded a document. She pressed the paper into the waitress's hand. The woman broke into a smile as she looked it over.

"I believe this birth certificate proves my niece is entitled to a free birthday meal," Aunt Colleen said.

She had remembered!

"Of course. May I wish her a happy birthday and take her order?"

"Burger and fries, please."

The waitress took the rest of the orders before rushing off to the kitchen. As she walked away, tears rolled down my cheeks.

"What's wrong, sweetie?" Daddy asked. He reached over the table and took my hands in his.

"I thought everyone forgot about my birthday."

He leaned over the table and kissed the top of my head.

"Honey, I told you before that the angels in heaven wept to lose your soul. I would never forget the day my little girl was born."

Aunt Colleen took my birth certificate and waved it in his face. "But I'm the one who has the birth certificate. Don't ever forget that, Frankie."

He scowled as he pushed her hand away, but they said nothing more as she folded the document and shoved it in her pocketbook. There was something about the exchange that made me uneasy, but I did not think about it again until later... much later.

We were almost through with our meal when Michael threw his bottle across the room. It landed at the feet of a group of four middle-aged Hispanic women who were just getting up to leave. The one closest to the bottle picked it up, and all four of them marched over to our table like a flock of pigeons.

"I think you lost this," the leader said.

"Sorry, thanks," Aunt Colleen said as she snatched the bottle from her.

"That's how babies are. Is he your first?"

"Yes."

The woman looked at Michael, then at Daddy.

"He's precious. He looks just like your husband." Daddy stared down at the table.

"He's not the father... he is!" I blurted out, pointing at Sarge.

"*Dios mio!*"

The other three warbled in Spanish amongst themselves. The head bird made the sign of the cross. "God bless you, sir. The Lord surely does perform miracles. We will pray for you and your family."

With that, the group moved on. When the last one passed by, she dropped several pamphlets on our table. There was a picture of Jesus hanging on a cross on the cover. The caption below read, "Have You Been Saved?"

I looked up just as our waitress came down the aisle with my birthday cake.

My family burst into song.

"Happy birthday to you! Happy birthday to you! Happy birthday, dear Gerri! Happy birthday to you!"

The other customers broke into a round of applause as she set the cake down in front of me. I counted thirteen candles—twelve and one to grow on.

"Blow out the candles and make a wish," she urged.

I blew them out in one breath, and there was another wave of applause.

"What did you wish for?" Sarge asked.

"You know she can't tell or it won't come true," Aunt Colleen said.

"Yes, of course, you're right as usual."

Even though I had kept my wish to myself, it still didn't come true. You can't get a new family by wishing.

Chapter 35

Paddy Boy did not know Daddy as well as he believed he did: he didn't seem to mind when I didn't arrive home on time after I began to tutor Tracy Newhouse during the afternoon. I guess it was because he was late himself most of the time. I tried not to think about why that might be.

Tracy Newhouse was one of those golden girls who don't seem to have a care in the world. She had all three P's going for her: perky, popular, pretty. She always wore the right clothes. Her teeth were so white they hurt your eyes to look at them. You didn't talk to a perfect creature like Tracy or any of her kind. The best you could hope for was not to get caught standing next to them so the obvious comparisons could not be made.

This is why I was shocked when she sought me out in the library during study period. She was in my science class, but hadn't said a word to me the entire semester.

"Hi."

I looked up from my encyclopedia and glanced around to see who she could be talking to.

"Mind if I sit down?"

She pulled out a chair.

"I'm Tracy. It's Gerri, right?"

I nodded.

"Listen, I want to ask you a favor."

What could she want from me?

Leaning closer, she straightened her perfectly pressed skirt over her white tights.

"Listen, I know you're really smart. You won that award, right?"

She was referring to the blue ribbon I had received for my science fair project.

"Well, anyway, I need someone to tutor me for my science final. It's not that I couldn't do the work. It's just that with my busy social schedule I haven't had a lot of time to study."

"I'm kind of busy myself. I know how it can be."

She looked at me, and we both knew it was a lie.

"I could pay, of course."

"I don't know."

"Please."

There was something in the way she said it that almost sounded sincere.

Well, why not? I had always been curious to see how other families lived, especially ones that seemed, if not glamorous, at least normal.

"Okay. I'll do it."

She clapped her hands, and the passing librarian shushed her.

"Just one thing. This has to be our secret."

I nodded.

"Great. I'll call you tonight. I'm sure your family must be listed."

Oh, yes, only the elite had unlisted numbers.

She got up, her ponytail bobbing like a fishing lure as she walked away.

We agreed we would meet for our first session at her house the following afternoon. Of course, she couldn't be seen walking home with someone like me, fat and unpopular, definitely not one of her crowd. Instead, I would meet her there later, when the coast was clear.

Tracy didn't live in our part of Ferrytown. Her family owned one of the big new homes where the executives who commuted to the city kept their fancy cars and perfect wives and children behind gates. Should an unwelcome visitor intrude, the cast-iron lawn jockeys with their mocking grins stood ready to swing their lanterns at the vermin.

I knew before I rang the bell what would greet me.

Tracy's mother was exactly the right height, dressed precisely the way an upper-crust housewife from Ferrytown was expected to: khaki pants with penny loafers and a pinstriped Oxford shirt beneath a navy blazer with crest embroidered above the breast pocket.

"You must be Tracy's tutor. Follow me through."

Not *you must be Tracy's friend*. She knew better than that just by looking me over. She showed me to the den the way she must have showed her maid the layout of the house on her first day of work.

Tracy was sitting on the sofa in front of the coffee table, surrounded by books that looked as if they had barely been touched since the beginning of the semester. Next to them there was a mound of snack food piled high, and several bottles of pop.

"Gerri, come sit here."

She waved her hands over the snacks the way a game show hostess points out the prizes a contestant has the chance to win. "I bought you some goodies. I know how you love to eat. Help yourself."

I didn't get angry. After all, it was the truth. If eating were an Olympic sport, I would have won the gold medal. Maybe bronze if I had to eat broccoli.

I began to munch on a bag of chips, washing it down with some orange soda.

When I offered Tracy some chips she refused.

"You know I can't. Cheerleaders have to fit into their uniforms, or we get kicked off the squad."

"Well, you also have to pass your exam or get kicked off the squad, right? Let's get started."

It wasn't long before I came to realize what a daunting task I had before me. Tracy was like a flowerpot with a crack in it. The more information I poured in, the more data leaked out. She couldn't seem to retain anything, and I had no potting soil.

Still, I had agreed to do it, and I wasn't going to break a promise. I had been taught that you do not go back on your word.

The second day, we began to settle into a routine: snacks first, work second, intermittently broken up by backhanded compliments aimed at me. For example, "Gerri, you're so smart. I would give up a little bit of prettiness if I could have a chunk of your brains." It was almost like having Mother home.

By our third session, I began to resort to using flash cards. They didn't seem to help. To her credit, she was trying to learn. I could hear the frustration in her voice and see it in her eyes.

"I'll never get this. There's just too much to memorize."

Time was growing short, so I came to an independent decision. If I couldn't teach her honestly, maybe I could come up with a plan for her to cheat. It seemed our only chance for her to pass.

There was only one person to turn to for a scheme so daring, a genuine venture into the realm of the criminal mastermind. Paddy Boy would know what to do.

I found him sitting on Sarge's back porch. He put down the fishing line he was untangling and listened intently as I explained the situation.

"Gerri Girl, I didn't know you had such wicked thoughts," he said.

"Well, can you think of anything else?"

He scratched his chin and stared up at the sky as if the sun would shine down a solution.

"This is Tracy Newhouse? The one with the ponytail and body two grades ahead of her mind?"

"Yes."

"It'll be tough, but I'll do it as a personal favor to you. She needs to make sure no one ever finds out about it. Can you get her to agree to that?"

"I'm sure she will."

"Oh, and there's one other thing she has to agree to. It's the price she has to pay."

"What's that?"

He pressed his lips together in a full pout. "I want her to kiss me."

"Kiss you? I don't know if she'll go for that."

"If she doesn't kiss me, I won't do it." Although I had no idea how she would react, I nodded and went to phone Tracy to ask her to meet me at our house the following day.

When I opened the door that afternoon, I was met by a Tracy I had never seen before. Her kerchief-covered hair was in curlers, and she had on jeans and a sweatshirt.

"I have to be home in time to get ready for the dance tonight," she said.

"This won't take long."

"I hope not. Bobby Ryan is picking me up in his father's new convertible."

She was supposed to be studying that night. I guess if you're in junior high and a high school boy asks you out, sacrifices have to be made. We went to the living room and sat on the sofa.

"I'll come right to the point. I don't think you'll pass the final exam without some extra help."

"What kind of extra help?"

"Well, my brother has come up with a plan to cheat."

"Cheat?"

"I know it's not right, but I don't see how we can do it any other way."

She tilted her head. "Okay. I'll do it."

"There's just one thing. My brother has a price."

She reached into her shoulder bag and pulled out her wallet.

"No, it's not money."

She looked down at her wallet as though she couldn't comprehend being unable to buy her way out of a situation.

"He wants you to kiss him." She laughed.

"You're kidding?"

I shook my head.

"Kiss your brother? We're talking about Patrick? He's the one who always looks like he just crawled out from under a car, all greasy like a mechanic." She hesitated for just a moment.

"I'll call you and let you know where he can meet me. This can go no further than the three of us. My reputation would be ruined if anyone in my set knew I made out with a grease monkey."

As she stood, a curler popped off her head. It flew to the doorway, and I was surprised to see Paddy bend down and hand it to Tracy.

"For you, my love," he said.

She snatched it from him.

As she bolted for the door she said, "Just be sure to wash and use deodorant. I don't like smelly things near me."

As soon as she was gone, he banged his fist on the coffee table.

"That bitch! Who does she think she is calling me a smelly grease monkey?"

I had never seen Paddy so angry. A vein in the middle of his forehead bulged in a monstrous blue-green color as his left eye began to twitch like a worm on a hook.

"I'll help you, Gerri. But I'm only doing it for you. I could care less if that prissy little snob lived or died." His voice grew more venomous. "But I'd prefer it if she died."

"Do you want me to tell her you decided to call the deal off?"

He smacked me on the top of my head. "Oh, no, little sister, don't you dare. I'm going to kiss her like she's never been kissed before."

He took me by the wrist and led me to the kitchen. Gathering up spice jars in his hands, he lined them up on the counter: garlic powder, hot sauce, red pepper flakes.

"Yes, I think Tracy is going to be surprised at just how spicy my kisses can be."

They met the following day and kissed in the darkest woods of Ferrytown. Despite having to endure the sickening mixture Paddy donated to her mouth, Tracy still went along with the plan. I guess her desire to stay on the cheerleading squad and remain popular outweighed her disgust with the vulgarity of the Moran family.

When I asked Paddy how he enjoyed the kiss, he just grinned and put his fingers to his lips and began to lick them like he had just eaten a piece of fried chicken.

The plan moved forward. Paddy Boy got his hands on a copy of the test. Fortunately, it was a multiple-choice quiz. We had Tracy memorize the answers by coming up with a cheer for every four questions.

"Cheerleaders are always cheerful" translated into c, a, a, c, and so forth.

So as not to arouse suspicion, however, we gave Tracy some incorrect answers as well.

When test day arrived, I watched her as she mouthed the words to her cheers and had to restrain myself from laughing.

The following Monday, the teacher handed back the tests with a solemn expression on his face.

"I'm sorry to say a number of you did not pass," he said.

He handed me my test, and even though I knew my grade, I still smiled at the 100.

"Good work," he said.

When he arrived at Tracy's desk, he tapped her on the shoulder.

"Stand up."

He handed her the paper and took her hand, shaking it vigorously.

"Students, I want you to give a round of applause to Tracy. She studied hard and did what I always knew she could. It just shows that if you apply yourself, you can succeed." He began to clap and the class joined in. When she sat down, I glanced over at her test. She had done it according to plan and scored an 80.

It wasn't until I was walking home from school that day that I learned it wasn't enough. I was on the back road, halfway home, when I heard her call me.

"Moran," she said.

When I turned around, I saw a face full of anger.

"Tracy."

She whipped out her test and began waving it in my face.

"What's the meaning of this? This is a lousy 80. Why didn't I get a 100?"

"You couldn't all of a sudden get a perfect score when you've done poorly all semester. It wouldn't have looked right."

"Bull. If you had been a better teacher I could have passed without cheating. But I guess that's the best someone with your background can do."

I began to walk away.

"Don't turn your back to me. We're not done talking, lard butt."

I kept going, building up speed.

"Yeah, run away. Why don't you run to your crazy mother in the loony bin?"

Something snapped in me, and I pounced on her like a savage wildcat as a surge of adrenaline gave me the strength to pin her to the ground with the full force of my weight. Picking up a rock, I held it over her head. My urge to smash her skull was stronger than any desire I had ever known. Luckily, she let out a shrill scream that brought me to my senses. Dropping the rock, I ran until I reached the pier, collapsing face forward onto the deck. A few minutes later, I felt a kick in my backside.

"Hey, what's wrong?" Paddy asked.

"I tried to kill Tracy with a rock," I said.

He pulled me up to a sitting position and hugged me.

"That's great."

"No, it isn't. It's horrible. How can you say that?"

"Don't you know what she's about? She doesn't care about anyone except herself. She doesn't care who she hurts, the little bitch."

"But that doesn't mean I can just hit her."

He stared at me with disbelief.

"Yes, it does. You have to get them before they get you."

"That's not very Christian. If you follow that rule you'll never get to heaven."

He sighed.

"Oh brother, I keep forgetting I have a saint for a sister. I had such high hopes for you after that cheating scheme you came up with. I suppose I'll have to keep carrying you until you learn how to carry yourself." Squatting down, he offered me his back. "Climb on."

"I don't think you can lift me."

"Little sister, I've been carrying heavier loads than you since before you were born. Come on, hop aboard the Paddy Express."

I climbed aboard my piggyback train and he wobbled, but managed to bring us to the back door. He carried me up the stairs, pulled the door open and we tumbled into the house. I pulled myself up. He held his hand out, and I helped him to his feet.

"Gerri, make me a promise, please."

"What?"

"If I ever get the idea to do that again, stop me."

He grabbed his belly above his crotch, bending over as if in horrible pain. "Hernias are no joking matter."

"Oh, Paddy, I'm so sorry. I should have known I weigh too much."

He let go of himself and smacked me on the top of my head. "You're such a sucker. Do you really think you could give me a hernia?"

I had to resist an urge to wrap my hands around his throat.

"Come on, Gerri, be a good sport. Let me make it up to you."

I was hesitant to forgive him so quickly.

"I'll let you decide my punishment."

I thought for a moment.

"You have to wear my new dress while I pin up the hem."

"Wear a dress?"

"And you have to do it in the living room when Daddy and Billy are home."

He nodded.

"I'll do it. After all, I know I'm a man. No matter what they say, I'll always be able to remember my kiss with Tracy, and how I made her quiver from the spiciness of my mouth." He held his hand out. "Do you forgive me?"

I started to reach for his hand to shake, but he suddenly pulled it back. "You really are a sucker. I will do it, but only in the hope that it will teach you a lesson."

"What lesson is that?"

"Never give a sucker an even break."

Chapter 36

The following week, Daddy and my brothers went to see Mother. Doctor Romano said she would be released for outpatient treatment by the second week in July.

Billy had been right about my parents living in the same house. It was agreed that Mother would move in with Grandma and Daddy would continue to live with us. There was never a word mentioned about either divorce or an attempt at reconciliation. It seemed as though it had been decided to leave their marriage at the status quo.

Relationship limbo, that's what we were all in. As the days to her homecoming grew closer, a tidal wave of fear over our uncertain future washed over me. Anxiety took control, manifesting itself in a series of physical symptoms ranging from sweaty palms to nausea to relentless insomnia. Catching a glimpse of myself in the mirror, I was repulsed by the dark circles around my eyes. It was the look of a beady-eyed raccoon prowling the night, searching for nourishment.

The evening before Mother was due home, Daddy called my brothers and me to the living room. He was sitting on the edge of the wing chair, empty beer cans positioned on the floor around him like flares at an automobile wreck. We sat in a line on the sofa like hockey players waiting for inspirational words from their coach before taking the ice.

"We're all going to have to help your mother adjust to a normal routine when she gets home," he began.

Rah, rah team.

"She needs to know we're there for her. She has to see she's an important part of our lives," he said.

"How do we do that?" Paddy asked.

"Just be here for her," Daddy said.

Paddy responded in his deepest voice. "I've always been here. Where were you?"

Sitting back in his seat, Daddy stroked his chin. He leaned his mammoth frame forward again, perched his elbows on his knees and interlaced his fingers.

"I never left. Through thick and thin, I never left. That's one thing I would never do. I love your mother more than life itself. If I lost her..." He sat back again and closed his eyes.

Paddy held his right hand up and made a fist. Slowly, he raised his middle finger and pointed it at Daddy. Billy reached down to the coffee table and picked up a copy of *Better Homes & Gardens*. He put it in front of Paddy's accusing digit to cover it before Daddy noticed the obscene gesture. Grabbing the magazine out of Billy's hands, Paddy smacked him over the head with it. The noise roused the giant from his slumber.

"What's that?" Daddy asked.

He looked around before clearing his throat to continue giving his players their last minute instructions.

"As I was saying, let's make tomorrow a special day." He reached into his back pocket and pulled his wallet out. Opening it, he began to count bills. "Billy, come here."

My brother raced to his side.

"I want you to buy a dozen red roses and present them to your Mother," Daddy said as he placed a stack of bills in my brother's hand.

Billy folded them, put them in his shirt pocket, and sat down.

"Paddy, come here." Paddy climbed over Billy's legs, giving him a little 'accidental' kick in the shin as he went. Bending down, he took a knee in front of Daddy.

"I want you and Gerri to get some balloons and streamers and decorate the place." Daddy pulled more money out and handed it to Paddy, who wadded it in his jeans pocket. "Oh, and make a "Welcome Home" sign for over the door."

"Is that all?"

"That should cover it, unless you can think of anything else."

We looked at each other, but remained silent.

"All right then, let's get some rest. We have a big day ahead of us."

He shut his eyes by way of dismissal, and we went upstairs. When we arrived at the top, Paddy touched my elbow. "Do we have any stain remover?"

"Why?"

He reached into his pants pocket and pulled the wad of crumpled bills out, holding them in his outstretched palm. "I want to try and get the bullshit stains out."

Billy shook his head as he went to their bedroom, shutting the door behind him.

Paddy stood there with his best self-satisfied cocky grin.

"Don't forget, we have to buy the decorations tomorrow morning. Maybe we should do an orange-and-black color scheme."

I gave him a puzzled look, so he answered my unasked question. "Well, we *are* welcoming home a witch."

It was my turn to shake my head before going to my room and putting my pillow over my head. It did no good. I could not drown out the sound of hatred in his voice.

On a warm Saturday afternoon, Mother came home.

We had moved her personal possessions into Grandma's house in preparation for her arrival.

We were standing together on the front steps when Daddy pulled the station wagon into the driveway. He went to the passenger side and opened the door.

A beautiful, slim Mother stepped into the bright sunshine. She had on a beige pantsuit with matching kerchief and dark wraparound sunglasses. She reminded me of Princess Grace—beautiful and vibrant and regal.

Daddy followed in her footsteps at a suitable distance for a commoner.

Billy was first in the receiving line. He presented her with the roses and kissed her on the cheek.

"It's great to have you home, Ma," he said.

She nodded.

Paddy was next.

"I love you, Ma," he said. He took her hand and kissed the back of it.

Finally, she stood in front of me. I hugged her. She whispered in my ear, "How's Mother's Little Helper?"

"I'm good. We're glad to have you back."

She pulled me away and eyed me up and down. "Have you lost some weight?"

I couldn't believe it. It was almost a compliment. She proceeded up the steps. "Well, aren't the rest of you coming in?" she asked.

We followed her inside, being careful not to tread on her royal robes. Grandma was sitting at the head of the dining room table. "Elizabeth, come sit next to me," she said.

I watched as Grandma patted her on the back of her hand.

"Welcome home."

"Thank you. It's good to be here."

Mother studied the food on the table.

"That sure smells good."

"It should. We all spent a lot of time preparing it."

Grandma made a sweeping gesture with her arms.

"Come on now, everyone, dig in. There's plenty more in the kitchen."

We all sat in our usual places, gathered to celebrate the return of the prodigal, treading delicately in her path.

Pass me this.

Have a little more.

This is delicious.

After we had been eating for a few minutes, two separate conversations broke out. Mother and Grandma were talking about some old movie star I had never heard of. Billy and Paddy were discussing who they thought was the greatest baseball player of all time. Having no interest in either discussion, I turned my attention to Daddy. He was eating like a condemned prisoner devouring his last meal, savoring each morsel.

Mother and Grandma were at a lull in their conversation when the words ripped across the table.

"Are you a mental case?" Paddy asked.

"Paddy," Billy whispered.

But it was too late. We had all heard it.

Like spectators at a tennis match, our heads turned to Paddy, then to Mother, then back to Paddy. It took a moment for Paddy to realize his faux pas. When it dawned on him, he got up and wrapped his arms around her. "Ma, I'm sorry, I wasn't thinking," he said.

"There's no reason for you to apologize. Mental is not a swear word. As a matter of fact, you can call me mental if you want, but I think the greatest baseball player of all time has to be Ted Williams."

Paddy bent down, kissing her on the top of the head. She patted him on the rear end. We all breathed a sigh of relief. "Go on with you, now," she said.

"Patrick, why don't you help me carry the dessert in?" Grandma asked.

"Sure, I can do that."

They went to the kitchen.

Daddy picked up his fork and resumed eating while the rest of us cleared the table in preparation for the dessert. A few minutes later, Paddy came in with an ice cream cake and put it in the middle of the table. "It's a little late, Ma, but Daddy said you wouldn't mind celebrating your birthday."

"I suppose I could force myself to eat a piece... or two," Mother said.

Daddy lit the candles and we began to sing, "Happy Birthday to you." Mother joined in and sang for herself. "Happy Birthday to you."

We grew louder. "Happy Birthday, dear Lizzie. Happy Birthday to you." Mother blew the candles out and we all burst into applause.

"What did you wish for?" Daddy asked.

She pushed him away, wagging her finger at him. "Frankie Moran, you know that if you reveal your wish it won't come true."

Something about the playful way she said it filled me with a glimmer of hope. Maybe things wouldn't be the same. Maybe things would be better.

Mother cut the cake and began passing out slices. When she got to the last piece, she made it a third the size of the rest.

"Here, Gerri, just a sliver for you. We have to keep that weight off."

"No, thanks, I don't want any."

Her jaw dropped, and the table fell silent.

Suddenly, Paddy snatched the plate away. "Well, if you're not going to eat it." He was just about to dig in when Daddy took the plate.

"I don't think so, little boy. As head of the family, I have control of all property in this house. You can watch." He shoved the entire piece into his mouth, devouring it with two swallows. Maybe my glimmer of hope for a new and improved life together was premature. Maybe the saying was true. The more things change...

Chapter 37

It was apparent from the outset that Mother was going to try to become someone she could never be. We were going to be the mother-daughter duo that works on projects together in a spirit of fellowship and teamwork.

In an attempt to attract tourists to town, the local politicians decided to hold a summer festival the first week in August. There would be music, horse-drawn carriage rides, and booths selling homemade goods. It would be capped off by nightly fireworks. The festivities would conclude with the crowning of the Midsummer's Eve Queen on Saturday night.

"Gerri, we're getting a booth to work on," Mother announced at breakfast.

I tried to muster some enthusiasm in my tone of voice. "That's great. I can't wait to get started."

They put us in charge of the candle booth. It was not a prime choice. Mother, as she was prone to do, had managed to alienate the wrong person with her antics. This time it was Virginia Whitcomb, Ladies Club President.

She had caught the woman's grandson throwing rocks at a stray dog and had screamed at him to stop. She had been right to do it, to stand up for a defenseless creature. That is, she had been right up until the point when she called the boy a "retarded jackass." After all, the boy did have Down syndrome.

I knew we were destined to get the worst spot after that incident and resigned myself to our fate. Looking back, I guess I was alone in that.

After weeks of planning and construction, opening day finally arrived. We set out our display of candles by size and color and lit a bayberry-scented one in an effort to draw customers; however, the scent of the candles couldn't compete with the intoxicating aroma of fried chicken wafting across the field. It also paled with the enticement of the cracker and jam samples being given away at the booth next to that. Our candles were even outmatched by the repulsive shrunken apple head dolls. They had a level of interest generated by the bizarre. Candles were merely the kind of gift you gave someone you did not know very well, or care enough about to put any effort into choosing.

By the end of the first afternoon, we had sold three candles. A hippie couple, who, despite the scorching heat, wore matching serapes, bought the first two. Several hours later, we sold the third one to a woman who said the color reminded her of her French poodle. It must have been an extremely weird-looking dog as the candle was pink.

I could see that a week of boredom didn't figure into Mother's plans. The next day she bought a battery-operated portable television to the booth. Setting up a tray of snacks, Mother positioned herself in a lawn chair behind the booth.

During that afternoon, Mrs. Whitcomb strolled past and caught her watching television. When she saw the set, a big, blue vein began to bulge in her neck above the white starched collar of her matronly suit.

"Mrs. Moran, just what do you think you are doing with that television set?"

Mother, startled by the woman staring down at her, jumped up, nearly dropping the set in the process. Balancing on the balls of her feet, she jammed her face within a foot of a surprised Mrs. Whitcomb.

"What am I doing? Why I would think it would be obvious to the feeblest of minds that I'm watching Monty Hall give a bunch of horny housewives their jollies."

Now, I didn't know what the word horny meant, but judging by the woman's expression, I knew it was not a polite one.

Mrs. Whitcomb stood there for half a minute, her jaw nearly touching the ground, before regaining her haughty demeanor. She tugged on her stiff white shirt collar as if it were a talisman of good breeding.

"I don't expect to see a television set at this booth again. The mayor and town council will be dropping by to pay their respects on Saturday. If you couldn't handle the responsibility of manning a booth without another adult present, you should have asked for help. There's no shame in being ill. As you know, I have a grandson with mental health issues."

Without waiting for a response, she walked away, crushing dandelions beneath her heels.

I looked at Mother.

At first, I thought she was going to cry as her eyes began to well up with tears. They quickly narrowed to slits, and she reached for a candle, picking up the largest one she could find, and began to aim.

"You snobby, bitch! Here's what I think of you and your kind!"

Mrs. Whitcomb turned to see Mother's rage and fled in terror down the midway, her heels sinking into the muddy field.

As I wrapped my arms around Mother, I could feel her body trembling with rage. It frightened me, but I held fast. She struggled, and we fell to the ground. Slowly, she relaxed, and I cautiously released my grip.

"You can't do things like that, Mother."

We sat up and she broke into the mischievous grin of a child who has been caught being naughty.

"No, you're right. That would be... inappropriate. I guess it's one of the areas I need to work on."

When I helped her up, we saw that a crowd had gathered.

Mother scowled. "Well, what are you looking at? Show's over." The onlookers scattered as Mother began to tidy up the stand. "Let's close up shop. I've been dying to try some of that fried chicken."

"Can we get some corn on the cob, too?"

"Okay. Just try to control yourself. I don't want your gluttony embarrassing me."

The next day I was initially puzzled by the sudden appearance of customers at our booth. They came and picked up the candles, then put them back, casting a sideways glance at Mother. Hushed voices would whisper as they walked away.

Word had obviously spread about the previous day's events, and everyone wanted to catch a glimpse of the crazy woman. Our booth turned into a freak show with Mother as the star attraction. The odd thing was, Mother didn't seem to mind.

"So they want to see another show, do they? Well, they say you should always give the customers what they want," she said.

She turned on the charm like a skilled snake oil peddler. As a customer approached, she would begin her act. Picking up a candle, she said, "Do you know this candle was made by starving orphans in India to support themselves so they can eat? Won't you please buy one?"

The poor customer would try to make an excuse, and she would continue. "Their bones show through their pitiful brown flesh. Please, sir, won't you buy one?"

If they hesitated she would pretend to get angry. "How could you sleep at night knowing that those poor orphans were beaten by their masters just to make this candle?"

Some would flee from her haranguing sales pitch. Yet others would buy the candles to allay their fear of being guilty of allowing orphans to die because they were cheap. It was a small price to pay to exorcise their sins.

Every day for the rest of the week, Mother would change her line of palaver. One day the candles were endowed with magical powers that could be unleashed by saying the words, "Help me to help you," three times while standing in a tub of hot water. The next, she changed it to a story about how they were made from the last known whale blubber brought from the mysterious sailing ship, *Nantucket*, lost off the coast of Maine in a raging nor'easter.

By the end of the week we only had a handful of candles left. Mother had managed to sell almost the entire stock with her powers of persuasion, mixed in with a healthy dose of sideshow.

A little before noon on Saturday, the mayor and town council, accompanied by a proud Mrs. Whitcomb, began their rounds. The mayor presented each booth with a certificate of appreciation as hearty rounds of congratulations were exchanged.

Finally, the entourage stopped at our booth.

"As a token of thanks for all you've done for Ferrytown and the festival, please accept this certificate of appreciation from the Ladies Club."

Mother took the document, shaking her head.

"All the credit should go to Mrs. Whitcomb. Without her moral leadership none of this would have been possible. I want to present her with something as well. Come here, Virginia."

The woman's face took on the appearance of someone about to be handed a pile of dung.

"No, I can't accept anything. I do this work out of my love for Ferrytown, not for reward."

The mayor nudged her in the side.

"Go on, Virginia. Be a good sport."

Mrs. Whitcomb extended her hand.

Mother reached under the counter and unrolled a poster with Mrs. Whitcomb's head on a bare torso shaped more like Raquel Welch than the stout matron.

Mrs. Whitcomb turned a deep crimson as she snatched the poster from Mother and threw it to the ground. She proceeded to stomp on it with her pointy-toed shoes.

"How dare you!"

Mother burst into laughter.

Mrs. Whitcomb picked up the picture, handing it to the mayor. She pulled a lighter out of her handbag and lit the edge. The paper rapidly caught fire, and the mayor dropped it before stomping on it like he was doing the Mexican hat dance.

Mother shook her fist. "That'll teach you to treat us like dirt."

Mrs. Whitcomb cowered behind the mayor.

"You can't touch me! I have witnesses!" the hysterical woman screamed.

But then Mother revealed part two of her plan as she calmly took a shopping bag and began walking away. She had only gone a few yards when she reached into the bag and began flinging sheets of paper across the field. The crowd picked them up and began to laugh.

I picked one up and saw they were copies of the poster of the nude Mrs. Whitcomb. When Mrs. Whitcomb realized what was happening, she scrambled to pick up the papers as fast as she could. But she couldn't keep up with Mother, who kept moving, tossing fliers as she went.

I was too shocked to move. The sound of whistling boys snapped me out of my trance. Gathering up our candles, I threw them in a box. I had to find Mother.

Following the trail of naughty pictures, I spotted her walking across from the village green.

"Mother!"

She turned around and waved. At that moment, I spotted the horse-drawn carriage turning the corner. My heart skipped a beat when I saw Tracy Newhouse sitting in front. Instinctively, I ducked behind the statue of George Washington until the carriage disappeared down the road.

Mother crossed the street.

"Friend of yours?"

"Just some girl from school."

She lowered her head.

"Was it really necessary to pretend you didn't know me? I saw you hide." She actually sounded hurt. I followed her home in silence, unable to explain away my cowardly act. When she turned down the lane toward her house, she called back to me, "Don't forget the dinner tonight."

When I arrived home, Daddy was in the kitchen hanging up the phone.

"How did it go today? Were there any problems?"

The way he asked made me suspicious that he knew what had happened.

"Fine."

"Good. I heard there was an incident, but I guess it was blown out of proportion."

"Yes, it was nothing."

"Gerri, I need you to make sure your mother gets here on time tonight."

"Why?"

"Oh, I've pulled a few strings and arranged a surprise for her at the dinner."

"What kind of surprise?"

"You'll see. It's just going to be an extra special homecoming gift."

The crowning of the Midsummer's Eve Queen was being held at the Legion Hall. Sarge was president that year and would have the honor of announcing the winner.

As we entered the hall, I was awestruck by the number and variety of American flags on display throughout the auditorium. We were escorted to our table and occupied ourselves with small talk until the ceremonies began.

First, there was the singing of the National Anthem with the presentation of colors by the Boy Scout honor guard. Next, we had to listen to a recitation of the Preamble to the Declaration of Independence by Debbie Lynn Fowler, the mayor's precocious seven-year-old daughter. A report by the Festival Commissioner took another five minutes away from our lives. Finally, we arrived at the crowning of the Festival Queen. Sarge climbed up on the stage with help from Daddy.

"Ladies and gentlemen, it is my honor to announce that the first annual Midsummer's Eve Queen is Mrs. Elizabeth Moran. Lizzie, come on up here, old girl."

Everyone turned toward Mother. The expression on her face went quickly from disbelief to sheer joy. The audience didn't seem to know how to react. Rising to his feet, Daddy began to applaud. I got up, followed by Paddy and Billy. Finally, Grandma pulled Aunt Colleen up, and they rose as one. Soon everyone was giving Mother a standing ovation.

The mayor presented her with a silver wand and helped fasten a tiara on her head. Daddy thrust a bouquet of roses and baby's breath into her arms.

Mother stood. She stroked her fingers across my cheek as she passed on her way to the stage. Her touch sent a shiver down my spine. Daddy winked at me. This was his handiwork. Mother stood at the podium as she surveyed her subjects. I never saw her more radiant than on that glorious summer night when, for one brief glorious moment, she became the object of everyone's adoration.

She was Queen Lizzie. She basked in the glow of stardom until we took our seats, before beginning her acceptance speech.

"I want to thank those of you who chose me as your queen. It's something I never expected. I will do my best to carry out my duties. Do I have any duties?"

She glanced at Sarge and he shrugged.

"Well, anyway, I want to thank you from the bottom of my heart. I have one very special thank you, however."

She waved her wand in a circle.

"To my husband, Frankie. Thank you for your love and support." The audience burst into applause, and Mother stepped down into the admiring throng, accepting kisses and accolades as she made her way back to our table and Daddy's waiting arms. He kissed her, and the hall broke out into catcalls and whistles.

After the ceremonies concluded, Mother and I went to the ladies' room before the drive home. As we stood in front of the mirror, she questioned me. "What is it, Gerri Girl? You look like you have something serious on your mind. "

"Where did you get the idea about making the poster of Mrs. Whitcomb?"

She gave me a wink, "Let's just say I have my sources." Paddy's face flew into my head, and I knew they were birds of a feather.

Chapter 38

The slow pace of summer soon gave way to that pre-school season of new clothes and notebooks and pencils. During the last week before school, Mother decided we would go to the city on a shopping expedition.

We went to Gimbel's department store and hit the racks, ending up in the lingerie section at the end of the day. Mother stopped in front of a mirror to reapply her makeup. I stood behind her, weighted down with our shopping bags. She saw my reflection as she put her lipstick back in her purse. Turning around, she grabbed my shoulders and pushed me in front of the mirror.

"I just noticed something. Little Gerri isn't so little anymore. You need to be fitted for a bra. I just hope they have something suitable for someone with your heft."

As if by magic, a white-haired sales clerk appeared. A measuring tape dangled from her neck like a holy crucifix.

"May I help you?"

Mother put her body between us.

"This young lady needs a brassiere. It will be her first."

"Of course. It will be my pleasure. If you'll follow me I'll show you our full line of training bras for young misses."

We followed her into the fitting room and she measured me with the worn yellow tape measure that must have been used on a thousand other girls.

"32C," she said.

"Take off your top," Mother said.

I unbuttoned my blouse and hung it on the hook.

"Why don't I get some styles for you to choose from?" the clerk asked.

She began to pull the curtain across, but Mother ripped it right back to an open position and put her body in the doorway.

"Take off your undershirt," Mother ordered.

I looked to the saleslady, but she averted her eyes and kept her mannequin-like expression plastered on her heavily-powdered face.

"I'll be right back," she said.

My eyes fixed on a pair of teenage girls staring at us from the opposite side of the room. The taller one giggled as her friend shook her head and whispered in her ear. They walked out, and as they passed, Mother grabbed the bottom of my shirt and pulled it up over my head revealing my flesh. I covered my nipples with my hands and tried to find a direction to turn where I would not be exposed. It was no use.

Mother stood there with a smirk on her face.

"Geez, Gerri, it's not as though you're Jayne Mansfield. A couple of mosquito bites is what you have there."

I decided to play her game and uncovered my bosom, thrusting my chest out like a cocky rooster strutting across a barnyard.

Mother frowned in disapproval, folded her arms and said, "Show a little decorum, Geraldine. A young lady does not flaunt her body."

She began rummaging through her handbag and unrolled a Pep-O-Mint Lifesaver. Tossing it in her mouth, she crunched down hard on it, making a horrible cracking noise that made my flesh crawl. She just stood there looking at my breasts, biting down on the candy as the smell of mint filled the space between us.

I glanced over at her barely perceptible chest. It would only be a matter of time before I surpassed her size; one more reason for her to hate me.

Finally, the sales clerk came back with a selection of bras to choose from.

I wanted to get a frilly number with a rose at the cleavage. Mother wanted to buy an ugly wire-rimmed number that resembled a medieval torture device. To my surprise, when the woman showed us a feminine yet sensible compromise, Mother allowed me to buy it.

Maybe she'd had her fill of humiliating me for the day. Or maybe she was just setting me up for the next heartbreak. I didn't know and didn't care. I just wanted to get out of there as fast as possible.

The sales clerk rang up our purchase, handing me the bag with a smile. I began to turn away, following Mother's lead, when the woman stopped me.

She reached under the counter and thrust a bunch of perfume samples into my hand.

"Here you go, miss. A pretty girl like you should have some pretty cologne."

"Thank you."

Mother scowled and held her palm out.

"I'm sorry. I don't have any more."

Mother took the packets from my hand and shoved them into her pocketbook. "Come, Geraldine, let's leave this lower-class establishment." Mother began to walk away at breakneck speed.

I ran to catch up to my tormentor, but turned to look back at the sales clerk. Our eyes met, and I saw the pity there. If she only knew.

Having no desire to antagonize Mother any further, I ran to catch up with her.

On the train ride home, Mother pulled a king-sized chocolate bar with almonds out of her purse. She broke it into sections, a third for me, two-thirds for her.

"I had a lot of fun today, didn't you?" she asked.

Unable to come up with a response, I just nodded and began to eat my chocolate.

"Yes, it's just you and me against the world. We're two of a kind, birds of a feather."

I shuddered at the thought.

"No one could ever break our bond. We have a special relationship. No matter how hard they may have tried, they could never have turned you against me. You know, I never belonged in that place. It was just their way of getting rid of me so they could try and turn my children against me. But they're not going to get away with it. They're going to pay for what they put me through."

All of a sudden, a tidbit of chocolate got lodged in my throat, and I began to choke.

Mother slammed me hard across the back a half dozen times. Finally, the candy flew out of my mouth.

Tears began to stream down my cheeks.

"Are you okay?" the doting parent asked.

She reached into her handbag and pulled out the 7-Up she had bought in Grand Central Station. Ripping the tab off, she handed it to me.

"Drink it slowly."

I sipped the sweet soda and felt myself start to relax.

"Better?"

"I could have died."

She pulled me to her bosom.

"I guess you owe me one," she said.

She leaned back, shut her eyes and went to sleep. I tried to do the same, but could not stop myself from keeping one eye open to watch over her.

After all, I was Mother's Little Helper.

Chapter 39

Several weeks into the school year, Grandma became ill. The doctor came to the house and examined her. He wanted to check her into the hospital to run some tests "just to be sure," but she refused to go.

"If my time has come, I want the Lord to find me at home," she insisted.

"Don't you think He knows the road to the hospital?" the doctor asked.

"Are you trying to tell me something?" she replied.

"Just that the devil can find you anywhere," he said.

She stayed in her bedroom, watching television from morning through night. She neglected her garden and stopped attending her club meetings.

Eventually, even going to Mass became too much for her.

"Just leave me be," she'd say.

We brought her meals to her on a tray. Sometimes she ate. More often, she left her food untouched.

One Saturday afternoon, I brought her in a bowl of chicken soup. I balanced the tray with one hand as I opened the door. The window shades were down and curtains drawn. When my eyes adjusted to the darkness, I realized Grandma wasn't in bed. I turned around and saw her spectral figure standing in front of the mirror that hung over the dresser.

"You can put the bowl on the night table," she said.

I did as she requested and started to leave.

"Wait, Gerri, come here," she said.

I walked over to her.

"You're getting to be quite a mature young lady."

"Thank you, Grandma."

She touched my shoulders and I felt a cold chill. Her internal fire was going out.

"Can I get you anything else, Grandma?"

"Won't you stay and talk with me for a wee bit? "

"Of course I will, Grandma."

Although I wanted to escape the disturbing stench of her decaying skeletal frame, I knew it would not be right to leave. It would be cowardly.

She took my right hand and wrapped hers around it, guiding me to the edge of the bed. I tried to stay still for fear she would fall off and shatter into a thousand pieces.

"How is everyone?"

"We're all fine. We're just worried about you. We all just want you to get better."

"Whatever the Lord sees fit to happen, so be it."

I nodded without thinking about what I was agreeing with.

"There's something I want you to have," she said.

She went to the jewelry box on her dresser and removed a gold necklace with an emerald pendant dangling from the center.

"Come here."

She undid the clasp and put the necklace around my neck. We both gazed at my reflection in the mirror.

"Stay right there."

She went to the window, opened the drapes, and pulled up the shade. A bright wave of sunshine hit the mirror. The gem gleamed in the golden light that danced off the glass. It was exquisite.

Grandma hugged me from behind, her image reflecting in the mirror, a shadow of her former self.

"I knew it would look beautiful on you."

"I can't accept it. I'm sure Mother or Aunt Colleen would like to have it."

"That's precisely why I'm giving it to you. I don't want those two fighting over it when I die. There's enough bad blood between the two of them as it is."

Well, that's true.

"Please, Gerri, take it. It would put my mind at ease. You're the one person in this family responsible enough to take care of it. There's a practical side to it as well. If there's ever a time when you need money, a time when you have nowhere else to turn, you can always pawn it. That beauty will fetch a pretty penny. I ought to know. I've had to do it myself on more than one occasion. But I always managed to scrape together the money to get it out of hock before it was sold."

"Well, if it means that much to you, I'll accept it."

"Thank you, Gerri Girl. I love you."

"I love you too, Grandma."

I stayed with her the rest of the afternoon.

As it was Saturday and her soap operas weren't on, we watched an old John Wayne movie instead. Each time the villain appeared, Grandma would shout to "the Duke" to watch out for the evildoer hiding up on a ledge or behind a tree. Before the credits finished rolling, she fell asleep in her rocker. I lay an afghan over her and kissed her wizened face one last time.

Grandma passed away on Wednesday of the following week. Mother found her propped up in bed with a Bible on her lap and an empty silver-plated flask beneath the covers.

When we went to clear out her personal effects we found a pirate's booty of empty liquor bottles and beer cans hidden in every nook and cranny of her bedroom.

Throughout the funeral process, Mother leaned on Daddy for support. He played the role of dutiful husband as skillfully as any actor I'd ever seen.

When the crowd at the funeral parlor began to disperse, Daddy pulled Grandma's flask from his pocket.

Raising it to his lips he said, "Here's to you, old girl."

He took a swig and was about to put it away when Mother grabbed his arm. She held her palm out to him, and he put the container in her hand.

At first, I thought she was going to take a nip. Instead, she walked over to the coffin and placed the flask next to Grandma's pillow, between her head and a framed photograph of my grandfather.

"What made you do that?" Daddy asked.

"I thought she ought to be buried with the two great loves of her life."

Daddy smiled and nodded his head in agreement. He pulled her to him and kissed the top of her head. "You'll always be my love, Lizzie."

She disengaged herself from his grasp with a violent jerking movement.

"Don't you mean one of your loves?"

He tried to get hold of her again, but she walked away too briskly, vainly trying to flee the bitter memory of love long since betrayed.

Chapter 40

"Gerri, it's time to leave for school. You don't want to be late, honey," Daddy called.

"We have tests today. I don't have to be in until this afternoon," I replied.

I did have a test, but had not studied and did not want to fail. Lying was becoming second nature to me. Maybe it was a genetic trait.

"Oh, okay. I'm going to the city. If you need anything, Sarge is right next door. Oh, and there's always your mother."

"Okay, have a safe trip."

"Don't open the door without looking out. And don't let anyone know you're alone. Promise me."

"I promise. Goodbye."

"See you later."

I heard him leave a few minutes later. The boys had gone to school, so I had the entire day to do whatever I wanted.

I decided to take a walk around Lake Owl's Head. Grandma had always said fresh air is the first step to a fresh mind. She had only been gone a short while, and I already missed talking to her.

When I reached the midway point, I was startled by a flock of geese taking flight. A moment later, a shot rang out, and I watched a bird plummet into the water. A hunting dog splashed into the lake and swam out to retrieve it.

As she returned to the shoreline, I noticed her master standing at the water's edge. A shotgun was dangling over his shoulder like a half-bent loaf of French bread. He grabbed the carcass from the dog's mouth and examined the trophy. Even from where I was standing across the lake, I could see the man break into a grin. He bent down and began to pet the dog furiously. The dog lapped up the attention. She was a faithful servant, with no will or mind of her own. Her only thought was to get approval, to receive praise for what a good dog she was. I wondered if her name was Gerri.

As I walked up the path to the back door, I heard Mother calling. She was standing in the backyard holding a string of Indian corn in her arms. "Why aren't you in school?"

"I wasn't feeling well this morning."

She gave me a skeptical look, but didn't question me further. "You look a little pale. Come inside and I'll fix you some lunch."

She started to move, but stopped as she remembered why she had come outside. "Oh, wait a minute. I was just going to nail this corn to the front door when I spotted you. Grab the hammer and nails from the shed, and I'll meet you out front."

I got the tools and met her at the door.

As I held the corn in place, she backed up to view it from a distance to see if it was centered correctly.

"How's this?" I asked.

"A little more to the left."

I shifted it.

"Better?"

"A little higher up."

I moved the stalk a few inches up the door.

"Good?"

She backed up to the edge of the lawn.

"Just a little bit higher."

I moved the corn once more.

Glancing at her out of the corner of my eye, I watched as she backed up into the road. She was holding her hands in front of her face, thumbs touching, index fingers projecting skyward, just like a movie director.

"Perfect."

I hammered the decoration into place, tapping gently so as not to crack the door.

Suddenly, the sound of screeching brakes pierced my eardrums. I turned to see a truck had smashed into a tree on the other side of the road. The driver climbed out of the wreck, teetering as he landed on his feet. He ran over to our side of the road, waving his arms frantically.

"It's not my fault. She was in the road. I couldn't stop. What was she doing in the road?"

I spotted Mother sitting at the curb, knees pulled up to her chest, arms wrapped around her legs. I ran to her and knelt down beside her. She had a small cut above her left eye.

"Are you all right?"

She didn't answer. She began rocking back and forth.

"Mother, are you okay?"

"I'm not going to the hospital."

She wrapped her arms around me, squeezing so tight my ribs ached.

"Don't let them take me, Gerri. Promise me you won't let them take me away."

The blood from the cut began to drip into her eye. I took a tissue from my pocket and dabbed at it. She winced.

"If you're hurt you'll need to see a doctor."

"I'm not hurt."

"But you have a cut. We have to get it fixed."

She tugged at the lapels of my coat violently. "Promise me you won't let them take me to the hospital."

The urgency of her plea frightened me.

"Please."

As the word hit me, I knew I had to protect her.

She looked up at me, eyes wide open.

"I promise I won't let them take you."

I helped her to her feet. The truck driver stood there, repeating over and over that it wasn't his fault. When the police car pulled up, Mother's hands began to shake. I took them in mine, and she began to calm down.

"What happened here?" the deputy asked.

The truck driver pointed his cap at Mother. "She walked right into the road. It wasn't my fault."

"Ma'am, are you all right?" the deputy asked.

I answered as Mother stared off into the distance, "She's all right. It's just a small cut."

He leaned over to examine the wound. "Looks like a pretty nasty one to me."

"My mother does not need to go to the hospital. It's just a minor cut."

"Ma'am, are you sure you don't want to have a doctor look at that?"

Mother squeezed my hand so hard it hurt.

"My mother does not need to go to the hospital."

"Why doesn't she speak for herself?"

Suddenly, she let go of my hand, and I watched in amazement as she began to move her fingers in a combination of patterns. I quickly realized she was doing her best impersonation of a deaf person signing.

The officer blushed as he backed off.

"Oh, I'm sorry. I didn't realize... I mean, it's not something you can tell."

An ambulance pulled up and two paramedics got out and started to help the truck driver.

"Hey, Joe, you need some help over there?" one called.

The deputy looked at us and shook his head.

"No, Matt, we're fine."

He tried to reach for her arm, but Mother pulled back so rapidly that she startled the poor man.

"Well, you just wash that out real good for her, okay?"

He gave Mother one last look and then went to assist the paramedics with the truck driver.

As soon as they left, I led her inside to the bathroom. She sat on the edge of the tub, and I started to apply some iodine to her head. She almost fell off, but I grabbed her just in time.

"Shit, Gerri, take it easy. That stuff stings."

"Sorry. I didn't know you could talk."

"Pretty good show, huh?"

She glanced at her watch.

"It's time for my soaps. I have an idea. You can make us some lunch, and we'll watch together."

She let me put the tape on the dressing before she flew to her bedroom.

The rest of the afternoon she described all the plot lines of each show as it came on, and I did my best to feign interest in her world of romantic intrigue and backstabbing family conspiracies. None of it really held my attention. After all, nothing those characters did could compare with the real-life drama of the Moran family.

As I watched her and listened to her that day, I began to feel sorry for Mother. She seemed so fragile, so vulnerable. Even when she'd been in the hospital, I never thought the delicate porcelain doll could break, never truly believed anything could hurt her. As I kept remembering the tremor in her voice, she seemed genuinely afraid. Almost as though she were human.

After the last credits for the last show rolled on, she clicked the remote and turned the set off. As she rubbed her head like a genie's lamp, a question popped into her head. "So, tell me again... why weren't you in school today?"

I answered without hesitation as I brought back the lie I had told to Daddy months ago.

"I'm having my woman's time. My muscles hurt."

She rolled up a magazine and whacked me repeatedly across the shoulders. I backed up to escape her blows, ready to hear her accuse me of skipping school. To my chagrin, she went into her night table and pulled out a bottle of pain medication. She tossed it to me as skillfully as a major league shortstop throws to a second baseman.

As she clutched her abdomen she said in a voice proud and strong, "Don't forget, Gerri Girl— I'm Queen of the Cramps."

Chapter 41

Paddy and I were coming back from taking baby John to Ferrytown Park the day the mysterious tragedy struck. As planned, we dropped John off to play with his cousin Michael at Sarge and Aunt Colleen's place before heading to our house.

"Daddy, we're home!" Paddy called.

No one answered.

I began to go upstairs when Paddy screamed.

"Gerri, come here!"

I ran to the living room to find him on the floor cradling Daddy's head in his arms. Daddy's eyes were shut. I grew weak when I saw the blood flowing from the back of his head.

"Call for an ambulance."

But I couldn't move. I just kept staring at the blood, paralyzed by the horror of what I saw. I don't know how long I had been standing there when Paddy began to slap me.

"Call for help."

Released from my trance, I ran to the telephone.

When I went back to the living room, I saw Paddy had propped Daddy's head up with a pillow. I had never seen my Samson-like father so helpless before, and it frightened me.

Paddy looked up and our eyes met. "It'll be all right, Gerri."

I don't remember them loading Daddy onto the stretcher or walking outside. The next thing I can recall is Paddy's anguished expression as he knelt at Daddy's side in the ambulance. The doors slammed shut, and they took off for town with siren wailing.

As they were leaving, Daddy's good friend Sheriff Hoffritz pulled up in his patrol car. As he approached, my eyes were drawn to a beer belly so large that the belt holding his revolver fell below his waist.

"What happened, Gerri?"

"Paddy and I came home and found Daddy lying unconscious on the living room floor."

"Wait here while I have a look around."

He returned after ten minutes.

"Let's sit in my patrol car."

He opened the door for me. We took a seat in the front, and he turned on the heater.

"Are you okay, Gerri?"

"Yes. I just..."

We both jumped at the sound of furious rapping on the window.

It was Mother.

"I saw an ambulance pull away."

Sheriff Hoffritz rolled down the window and tipped his cap.

"Elizabeth."

"Douglas."

Mother looked at me.

"What happened?"

"We found Daddy on the floor. He was bleeding from his head."

"Was it an accident?"

I looked from Mother to Sheriff Hoffritz. It hadn't occurred to me that it might have been anything other an accident.

"We'll be conducting an investigation, but there are signs it might have been a break-in gone wrong. Sometimes a burglar will panic when a homeowner walks in on him."

Mother nodded.

"Listen, Lizzie, we can't let the kids stay here tonight. Come with me."

We followed him to the back door where he pointed out how it been pried from the hinges.

"I'll take care of it after the detectives dust for prints."

"Detectives?" Mother asked.

"Yes. If the intruder has a record we might catch a break and find some fingerprints we can try to match. You never know with these situations."

Mother touched his forearm. "Thank you, Douglas. You're very kind."

"Just doing my job." He looked deep into her eyes. "Frankie didn't deserve this. All the volunteers at the firehouse will tell you he'd give you the shirt off his back."

Mother's reply was tinged with vinegar.

"Yes, he's a real humanitarian. I've often thought of nominating him for husband of the year."

The sheriff's jaw dropped, but he quickly resumed his professional demeanor. "Well, you ladies had better get going. I'll secure the premises."

We were in Mother's kitchen when the telephone rang, and she picked it up.

"Hello?"

She placed her hand over the receiver.

"It's Paddy Boy."

She began a series of nods with periodic interjections of "I see." She put her hand over the receiver once more.

"He wants to talk to you."

Her eyes narrowed as she handed me the phone.

"How's Daddy?"

"He's got a fractured skull. They have to operate. They think he may have some clots on his brain. Listen, Gerri, I'll be there soon."

"The sheriff said we couldn't stay in the house."

"The sheriff?"

"Yes, he pulled up when you were leaving. It looks as though someone broke in."

"Broke in?"

"Yes, the back door was hanging off."

"Listen, Gerri, I want you and Mother to go to Sarge's house until I get there. I don't want you alone."

"I'm not alone. I'm with Mother."

He paused for a moment.

"I don't want you alone with Mother."

I glanced at her.

"What do you mean?"

She was cutting an apple into sections with a paring knife. She speared a section and held it out on the knife blade to offer it to me. I shook my head.

"More for me."

Paddy continued.

"There's just something not right about this whole thing with Daddy. I just have a bad feeling in my gut."

I looked over at Mother again. There was something about her calmness, her detached coolness that made me nervous.

"Okay, we'll meet you there."

I hung up.

"Paddy wants us to go to Sarge's house. He doesn't think it's safe for us to stay here."

She burst into a toothy grin. "Ha. That's a good one. That's the last place we need to be. Colleen in a crisis is twice as nutty as normal Colleen."

"But Paddy says it isn't safe for us to be here by ourselves."

Mother smashed the apple core down on the table. She stood up and looked at me with the intense stare of a predatory beast. "Oh, Paddy says so, does he? Let me tell you something about Paddy." She waved her index finger as she spoke. "If Paddy were so smart, he wouldn't always be playing both sides against the middle all the time like some two-bit con man. Oh, I'm on to him and his ways."

She threw the remains of the apple into the garbage and began walking upstairs.

"No, we're not leaving."

She walked up a few more steps prior to pausing.

"We're not leaving now."

She walked to the landing before halting once again.

"We're not leaving ever."

She shut the bedroom door behind her.

I went to the living room and curled into a ball on the sofa, waiting for something, I did not know what. So I prayed for deliverance, hoping for divine inspiration to tell me what to do next.

It was dark when the ranting began, a low murmur barely perceptible at first. As it grew louder I could make out words.

"Paddy says we have to go. Oh, yes, let's listen to Paddy. He's the best judge of what to do. He's just like his father... just like him. Well, to hell with him! To hell with them both! I hate them! I hate them!"

I heard a heavy object being thrown. What was she doing up there? If only Grandma were still alive. She could handle her, but me... I only knew I had to get out of there.

I took the poker from the fireplace and ran to the back door, just as she started screaming the old phrase that would haunt me for years to come.

"Birds of a feather flock together! Birds of a feather flock together!"

I heard her fling the bedroom door open.

"Gerri, come here! Gerri, I need you!"

My hands were shaking as I fumbled to unlock the back door. I ran through the backyard, brandishing the poker in front of me like a deranged musketeer. When I arrived at Sarge's place, a pair of arms grabbed me and pulled me onto the darkened back porch. I struggled to break free from my captor.

"Let go! Let go!"

"Gerri, relax, it's me... Paddy."

He released me and the poker slipped from my hands. As my legs gave out, Paddy caught me in his arms.

"Come on. You're safe. You're with me now."

A light came on and Aunt Colleen stepped onto the porch. She took one of my arms while Paddy held fast to the other and they dragged me inside.

Chapter 42

I felt woozy as they lay me down on the couch.

"Get a damp rag," Paddy said.

Aunt Colleen came back with a sopping wet kitchen towel and proceeded to wrap it around my head like a turban.

"Colleen, get me the whiskey and a couple of glasses," Sarge said.

I sat up.

He took a crutch and pointed to the liquor cabinet.

"Colleen."

She brought him a bottle and two shot glasses.

"Come here, Gerri."

I took a seat on the hassock in front of him.

"I want you to watch me. Then, I want you to do the same."

He filled a glass, raised it to his lips, and swallowed with a jerk of his head. He poured me a drink and pushed it into my hand.

"I don't think I should."

"You've had a shock. You need something to calm your nerves."

"Mother wouldn't approve."

Paddy knocked on my head with his fist.

"Hello? Anybody home?"

Aunt Colleen giggled.

I raised the glass to my lips and swallowed the vile liquid. It hit me with a burning from my throat to my gut. I couldn't understand why Grandma would want to feel that hot. She should have put on a sweater.

"Let me have one," Paddy said.

Sarge put the bottle in the corner of the recliner. It looked like he had a glass tumor growing out of his backside.

"It's for medicinal purposes only."

Paddy held the back of his hand to his forehead. "But I think I'm going to faint." He fell to the floor, kicked his legs up in the air and closed his eyes.

"Me too!" Aunt Colleen screamed as she spun around and fell on top of Paddy's chest.

Sarge slid down from the recliner, clutching the bottle in his hands. He crawled over to them, unscrewed the cap, and poised the bottle over them.

"You want a drink? Here you go." He poured the whiskey over them.

Paddy sprang up, flinging Aunt Colleen to the floor, grabbed the bottle from Sarge and held it over his head.

"Who do you think you're playing with, old man?"

My aunt wrapped her arms around Paddy's leg.

"No, Paddy, don't!"

In a moment, Paddy regained his senses. He walked to the fireplace and smashed the bottle against the brick. Slowly, he sank to the floor, lowering his head into his chest as he hugged himself.

"I'm sorry. I don't know what I'm doing. I'd never hurt you, Sarge."

"Don't worry about it, lad. This day has been hard on all of us."

Paddy got up and gave Sarge his crutches.

"Go sit in my chair, boy."

For once in his life, Paddy did as he was told.

"Wait here," Sarge said as he disappeared into the kitchen.

Aunt Colleen began to pick up the shards of glass and managed to cut herself on a piece.

"Gerri, help me."

I examined the wound and saw it was just a scratch. She whimpered.

"It hurts."

I took the towel from my head and wrapped it around her hand.

"You have to apply pressure to a wound."

"Damn, Gerri, any child knows that."

Sarge came back and sat down on the hassock in front of a slumping Paddy. My brother lifted his head. Sarge reached into his pants pocket and pulled out a can of beer. Paddy took it and rubbed it like a genie's lamp.

"Thanks."

"What about me?" Aunt Colleen asked.

Sarge took another can from his other pocket and threw it at her. It landed behind the couch.

"You never could catch."

She crawled behind the couch to retrieve the can before stomping over to Sarge. She began to shake the beer can like she was mixing baby formula.

Wanting in on the fun, Paddy got up and began to shake his can.

"You wouldn't dare do that to a crippled old man," Sarge said.

Aunt Colleen and Paddy exchanged looks, and then simultaneously popped their cans, spraying Sarge with the suds. Paddy held his palm out and Aunt Colleen slapped him five. She took his hand in hers and led him toward the kitchen.

"Let's make some sandwiches. All this exercise has given me an appetite."

Sarge crawled back to the recliner. He did his best to wipe the beer suds away with his handkerchief.

"Are you all right?"

"Yes, just a little damp."

"That was a mean thing for Aunt Colleen to do. Why do you put up with her?"

He tapped his wedding band repeatedly as if tapping S.O.S. for his marriage. "It's for better or worse, Gerri Girl. Heaven help me, for better or worse."

Chapter 43

Daddy was still unconscious the following morning. Paddy said they didn't know when he would wake up. It could be a day, a week... or never. And if he did wake up, no one could say whether he would ever be the same again.

Sheriff Hoffritz had called to let us know he'd gone to see Mother and had persuaded her to see her doctor. Under his advice, she voluntarily checked herself into the hospital for the next week. But the doctor said she didn't want to see anyone. She told them she had no family.

The rest of us weren't so lucky. We had to go on, to find a way to survive, and stay together.

At first, it seemed as though we would be able to pull it off. Sarge and Aunt Colleen took John to their place to stay with them and Michael. Billy made a work schedule, and we all pitched in with the chores. Everyone recognized that Gerri could not do it all alone.

"If we all help out, the house will run like clockwork," Billy said.

Barely a week had passed when a crack appeared in his plan: Paddy started to stay out late. He became like a vampire, creeping home at dawn to escape the destructive powers of daylight. He neglected to do his share of the housework, even letting the laundry pile up into a monstrous blob of shirt arms and pant legs overflowing from the hamper to the floor.

One Friday evening, maybe when the blood supply was low, he came home just before midnight. We were sitting in the living room watching an old horror movie on television.

"Where have you been?" Billy asked in his best authoritative voice.

Paddy turned red as he flung his coat on the wing chair.

"Excuse me?"

"You heard me. It's past your curfew."

He grabbed Billy by the collar and pinned him to the couch. "Who do you think you are? You're not my father." Paddy pointed at him. "You're not even a man."

A look of pure beastly rage came over Billy's face. The intensity of his expression made me shudder. Suddenly, he pushed Paddy to the floor and began to pummel him with his fists, savagely, unrelenting in the viciousness of his attack.

"I am a man! I am a man!"

Blood gushed from Paddy's nose. Billy held his crimson-stained hands up before his face. Horrified, he released Paddy, and his victim fell to the floor. He offered his hand, but Paddy backed up on his rump to the doorway before he sprang to his feet and ran out the door.

Still in shock from what I had witnessed, I continued playing the bystander as Billy slumped to the floor. He pulled his legs to his chest, wrapped his arms around himself, and began to rock back and forth.

"I'm not bad. I'm not bad. I didn't mean to. I didn't. It's just he shouldn't have said that. I am so a man. I am so a man."

Slowly, I slid down beside him and put my head on his shoulder. Terrifying sobs emanated from deep inside him, from the place where you hide the secrets no one must ever know. When he grew exhausted and no more tears would come, we helped each other upstairs.

As he stood in the doorway of his bedroom, he reached over and hugged me.

"I love you, Gerri Girl."

"I love you, too, Billy."

He brushed a stray hair from my face.

"You know what?" I asked.

"No, what?" he replied.

"If I had to have a new father, you wouldn't be the worst."

"If I were a good father, I'd be able to control Paddy Boy."

We looked at each other and burst into laughter at the absurdity of his statement.

After all, everyone knew no one could control Paddy... not even Daddy.

Chapter 44

A week later, another crisis hit.

I was in that half-awake state before full consciousness when I felt someone grab me under my arms and pull me out of bed.

"Let go! Let go!" I screamed as I struggled to break free.

I had to fight for my breath as the fiend dragged me downstairs. His henchman slipped a mask over my face.

"Take some deep breaths," he said.

I began to choke as I spat up a sooty residue. Slowly, I grew aware of my surroundings as I recognized the fire engine lights flashing in the pre-dawn hour.

Paddy was standing near an ambulance, hands cupped over his mouth. Even in the early morning light I could see the fear etched on his face. Suddenly, a fireman appeared at the back of the ambulance and gave two thumbs up. A cheer went up from the other men, just as Paddy swooned.

I ran to him before anyone could stop me. Putting my hands under his head, I pleaded, "Paddy, Paddy, say something." He opened his eyes and replied, "There was a young girl from Nantucket."

I breathed a sigh of relief.

Suddenly, Billy popped up from the stretcher in the back of the ambulance, removing an oxygen mask from his face. "Gerri, Paddy, are you okay?" A paramedic pushed him back down. A fireman shut the ambulance door, the siren began to wail, and they sped away as dawn began to rise over the lake. The chief came over to us. Paddy rose to his feet, swaying unsteadily.

"Take it easy, son. We're taking you to the hospital to get checked out."

"That's not necessary. I feel fine."

"We'll just let a doctor be the judge of that, young man."

I outstretched my arms, and my brother hugged me.

Our house was badly damaged. Water dripped down the front, as if it were crying from the pain the fire had inflicted with the brutal flames. My own tears began to flow at the sight.

Paddy put his hand on top of my head before brushing several tears from my face with the fleshy parts of his thumbs.

"Don't worry, Gerri. It's not that bad. We're all fine."

The chief chimed in. "That's right. Things can be replaced. People can't. You're lucky to have such a brave young man for a brother. He saved you all. This boy's a hero."

Paddy shook his head. "No, I just did what had to be done."

"Well, not many people would have done what you did, even for family."

Paddy winked.

"Well, we are a very special family."

Out of the corner of my eye, I saw a figure trotting from the woods behind the house, heading straight toward us.

"Gerri, Gerri, I'm coming!" Aunt Colleen shouted as she barreled toward us.

"Aunt Colleen, slow down!" I shouted.

She collided into the side of the fire truck, landing face forward.

The three of us stood there for a moment, stunned by her sudden appearance.

The chief held his hands out to her in an offer of assistance.

"Are you all right?" he asked.

As she was about to take his hands, he jumped back and pointed frantically at the turkey on the leash in Aunt Colleen's arms.

"Dear God, what's that?"

"Oh, this is my pet turkey, Lizzie. Would you like to pet her? She's very friendly."

She thrust the fowl in his direction as if it were a dog or cat.

"Oh, no, thank you. I... have allergies."

He backed away to his car, opening it from behind as if afraid to turn his back on my aunt.

"Come on, kids. We need to go to the hospital."

Paddy was grinning from ear to ear as we followed the bewildered chief into his car.

He had just started the engine when Aunt Colleen started to rap on the car window. "She's really quite tame," she said while Lizzie gobbled, as if on cue. Aunt Colleen reached into her robe pocket and gave Lizzie a cracker. The bird snatched it and began to chomp on it, sending crumbs flying like confetti.

The chief held his hands out in a shooing motion. We weren't sure if the gesture was meant for Aunt Colleen or Lizzie.

Aunt Colleen knocked on the window again. "She can do other tricks, too." She put the bird on her arm and began to swing, with the dimwitted fowl dangling like a feathered trapeze artist.

"Go home! We have to leave now!" the chief yelled.

He beeped the horn, and Lizzie flew off in the direction of Lake Owl's Head, with Aunt Colleen racing after her.

"Hang on, kids," the chief said as he revved the engine and hit the pedal in a desperate attempt to escape.

We'd reached the first traffic light when he spoke again. "You mean to tell me she keeps that thing as a pet?" The chief shook his head.

"Well, she doesn't usually take it out of the house," Paddy Boy explained.

"She keeps it in the house? I knew there were some crazy things going on out here, but I never imagined..."

He looked at Paddy and me with a guilty expression.

"Sorry. I shouldn't have said that."

Paddy smiled.

"She's your aunt?"

We both nodded.

"Well, I guess we don't get to choose our relatives."

Paddy broke into a huge grin as he tapped him on the shoulder.

"No, sir, if only we could. We have many we would not have chosen to be related to." Paddy made a circling motion with his index finger at the side of his head. "And they're all cuckoo."

The chief smiled wryly, turned the siren on, and drove away at breakneck speed.

I sat there and fervently prayed for the rest of our trip that he wasn't taking us to Mother's hospital. They might commit the lot of us at a family group rate.

And once they had us in... they might never let us out.

Chapter 45

The luck of the Irish was with us; they released Paddy and me from the hospital the following afternoon. Billy had to stay another day as a precaution, since he'd breathed in more smoke.

Sheriff Hoffritz drove Paddy and me home.

As we pulled up to Sarge's place, Aunt Colleen and Mother were standing out front, Sarge behind them on the porch swing.

They ran down the steps together as we got out of the car.

"Gerri, I'm so happy you're back," Aunt Colleen said as she hugged me.

Mother grabbed Paddy around the waist.

"And how's our hero? How's my Paddy Boy?"

Paddy blushed. "Jeez, Ma, anyone would have done what I did."

Sheriff Hoffritz put his hand on Paddy's shoulder. "It takes real courage to pull someone from a burning building. Billy might not have made it if not for you, son."

Paddy shook the man's hand away. "Well, then I guess it's a good thing I out was out past my curfew, right? I wouldn't have seen the flames otherwise."

Sheriff Hoffritz stepped back to his patrol car. "The Lord works in mysterious ways."

He opened the car door.

"Elizabeth, if there's anything I can help you with, please call me."

"Thank you, Douglas."

As he drove away, we looked at each other, unsure of our next move, until Sarge called to us, "Why don't we have some lunch and let the kids know what we've decided?"

As we sat eating our sandwiches, I was taken aback by the level of civility my mother and aunt displayed. Their conversation was polite... an artificial politeness that frightened me.

"We've decided Billy and Paddy can stay here on the pullout sofa. You and John can live with me," Mother said.

"It's a matter of making the best of it until the big house is fit to live in," Aunt Colleen added.

"It's not as though we can't visit."

"Yes, we'll still have Sunday dinner together."

Mother slapped the table.

"Don't forget Thanksgiving is coming up. We can split the menu."

Aunt Colleen wagged her index finger at Mother. "Just don't get any ideas about eating Lizzie."

We all stared at her.

"I mean my pet turkey Lizzie. No one is cooking her."

"Of course not," Mother said.

Sarge looked at us with the bewilderment of an outsider. He hadn't known us during the infamous missing pet squirrel Thanksgiving.

Paddy put his hand on the dumbfounded man's shoulder. "It's a long story. One day we can share a bottle, and I'll tell it to you."

"I'm not sure I want to hear it."

Meeting over, we began to move the items we could salvage from the main house to our assigned living quarters.

Leaving the old place felt odd. At least I could take comfort knowing that Aunt Peggy and Grandma would be there in spirit to watch over the house until we returned. I could only pray that they were getting along in the afterlife. Sisters in our family did not have a very good record of friendship while still alive.

Chapter 46

W ithin a week of the fire, Sarge had a construction crew lined up.

Paddy promised to help with the remodeling. He talked his way into working for the contractors. "I'm going to make this place into a palace," he said.

As the days passed, we watched him transform into a junior version of his fellow laborers. He began to dress in flannel shirts and work boots. The construction foreman gave him a bright orange hard hat; one size too large, it wobbled on his head as he walked.

There was one item Paddy treasured above all the rest: his tool belt. Every afternoon he would come home from school and change into his work clothes. He would stand in front of Aunt Colleen's floor-length mirror and begin his ritual. Slowly, methodically, he would wrap the belt around his waist, fastening it with a quick wrist movement. One by one he would place his tools in their assigned compartments: screwdrivers, measuring tape, pliers, wrench. Finally, he would raise his hammer, spit on the head, and polish it with his handkerchief before twirling it into his holster.

One day, we were all gathered at the kitchen table when he came in and opened the refrigerator.

When he bent down and began to rummage through the shelves, Billy was the first to notice what happened. He tugged on my sleeve as he pointed to Paddy Boy. I felt the blood rush to my face cheeks when I saw the exposed flesh of his butt cheeks. The weight of the tool belt had made his pants slink down below his hips.

"Do we have any pickles?" Paddy asked.

"On the bottom shelf, in the back," Aunt Colleen replied.

She turned her head in his direction. As he bent lower, he exposed more of his fleshy backside. Her jaw dropped, and Sarge followed her eyes to Paddy.

Aunt Colleen was the first to make a joke.

"Is it getting drafty in here?"

Sarge joined in.

"I did open the window... but just a crack."

Even the normally serious Billy joined in.

"But... but... but I shut it."

Paddy found the pickle jar. He stood up, hiding his shame. He unscrewed the lid, and the jar opened with a whooshing sound.

"Don't hold dinner for me. I don't know when we'll be done working."

He was only gone a moment when Aunt Colleen began to giggle.

Soon, the rest of us couldn't contain ourselves, and the convulsive fits of laughter lasted a full fifteen minutes, until our sides ached and faces were wet with tears.

Now if Paddy hadn't been so full of himself, the subject would have been exhausted.

Unfortunately for the rest of us, he became an instant authority on construction. His conversation became peppered with expressions of construction expertise. If he pronounced a piece of woodworking as being "solidly crafted" he said it with the air of a challenge that none of us dared dispute. When he got started on the subject, you could not stop him.

Once he droned on for twenty torturous minutes about the virtues of one type of paint over another. I never would have believed that Paddy could be such a boring know-it-all.

I don't remember who started the nickname, but we began to call him "Droopy Drawers" behind his back.

Billy pulled me aside one day.

"I think Paddy needs a special project to keep him occupied."

"Like what?"

"I was talking to Father Quinn the other day, and he suggested the church lawn could use a new nativity scene."

"So naturally you mentioned what a construction genius Paddy Boy is."

"But of course, dear sister. After all, Paddy is the King of Construction."

Billy had no trouble convincing Paddy that he was the man for the job.

"I'll make sure it's the best display this town has ever seen," he boasted.

He drew up plans and bought supplies.

He cut back his hours remodeling the house. He explained how his coworkers felt, saying, "The guys understand. They know how important a job it is. Father Quinn wouldn't have picked me if he didn't know how good I am at construction. Word of mouth is how contractors get most of their jobs."

He kept his work in progress under wraps by means of tarps, but you knew he was there by the incessant noise. You could not help yourself admiring his work ethic.

The project took up his every free moment. Billy couldn't complain when Paddy did not help at home. After all, it had been his idea.

Before long the day of the unveiling ceremony arrived. It had been raining heavily all that week; however, that morning the rain had turned to a wet, slushy snow.

Sarge excused himself from the festivities because he couldn't walk very well through the muck with his crutches. The rest of the family would be there to support Paddy in his budding career.

Half the town had shown up, despite the lousy weather. It came as no surprise to any of us. Paddy had told anyone who would listen about his magnificent achievement. I wouldn't have doubted that he had invited most of them personally. The others were probably curious to see if the Moran clan would provide a good show. We did have a reputation.

I looked at the rectangular hill where the nativity was hidden behind a black velvet curtain. Paddy was standing at Father Quinn's side like a cherubic altar boy. He had put on his best suit and tie, the outfit reserved for funerals and weddings. Although it was still snowing, he left his overcoat open so everyone could admire how sharply-dressed he was.

My eyes were drawn to the gold cross pinned to the lapel of his coat. Billy must have loaned it to him... unless Paddy had helped himself.

The priest hushed the onlookers with his hands.

"Ladies and gentlemen, it is with great pleasure that I welcome you to the unveiling ceremony of our newly-designed nativity scene."

He put his arms on Paddy's shoulders.

"This young man has done a magnificent job, devoting his free time to create a holy shrine in honor of our Lord's birth. Let's have a round of applause for this obedient servant."

The crowd clapped enthusiastically. Paddy beamed as Father Quinn shook his hand.

"Now, let's say a prayer of benediction."

We bowed our heads.

"Lord, bless this nativity. We pray that it will inspire holiness in all who view it. Lord, bless this young man who has given so much of himself in this act of charity. This we pray in the name of the Father, Son, and Holy Spirit. Amen."

Father Quinn handed Paddy the rope that was attached to the end of the curtain.

"Here you go, son."

Paddy pulled the tarp off with a snap of his wrist to unveil his masterpiece.

The Holy Family sat raised on a platform. Their robes were painted in lustrous shades of blue and violet. White sheep with soulful blue eyes stood with the shepherds in front of the stage. Off to the back, the wise men stood patiently in the wings for their curtain call. In the middle of the figures sat the empty crèche awaiting the arrival of the star of the show, little baby Jesus.

The crowd broke into spontaneous applause.

I felt a glow just watching Paddy soak up the warmth of affection showered on him for his efforts. I walked up to Paddy to present him with the gift we had chipped in to buy him. "Here. We bought this for you."

Paddy took the wrapping paper off the shiny red toolbox and caressed it, rubbing his fingers over the surface where his name was engraved in gold lettering.

"Thank you. It's beautiful."

He kissed me.

A photographer from the *Ferrytown Gazette* came forward to take his picture. "If we get a good shot, we'll put your picture in the "Town Chatter" section this weekend."

Paddy posed with the professional air of a model fresh from the Paris runways. He kissed Aunt Colleen, then Mother. He pretended he was going to kiss Billy, but punched him in the arm instead. Everyone gathered around our brother to congratulate him. He was eating up the attention, basking in his triumph as though he had carved Michelangelo's David instead of a roughly-hewn collection of wooden statues for a small town church display.

No one noticed when Aunt Colleen climbed up on the platform.

I turned my head and gasped as I saw her lay Michael in the bed reserved for Jesus.

"Aunt Colleen, that's not made to stand on!" Paddy shouted.

But it was too late to stop the catastrophe.

He reached her just as the platform began to slide downhill as the moist ground beneath it gave way.

Mary fell off first, landing on her back.

Paddy snatched our baby cousin Michael, pulling him to safety just as Aunt Colleen tumbled on top of the Holy Mother.

Finally, Joseph landed on top of her to create a sandwich of holiness with a crazy Aunt Colleen filling.

Billy ran to help as the crowd buzzed.

The photographer took several shots of the chaotic scene, flashbulbs lighting up Paddy's distraught face as he struggled to remain composed.

Father Quinn and several of the men in the crowd helped Paddy untangle the mess. The display had not suffered any irreparable harm. After things settled down and the crowd had finally dispersed, we all pitched in to move the scene to more stable ground.

As soon it was firmly set, Paddy confronted Aunt Colleen.

"Why did you do that? Don't you have any common sense?"

"I'm sorry. I just wanted to see what Michael would look like as baby Jesus."

"Jesus? Jesus! What the hell are you talking about?"

"I'm sorry. I didn't know it would break."

Paddy shook his head as Aunt Colleen started to cry.

"Oh, come on now. Don't do that. You know us men have no power to fight the tears."

"I didn't mean to break it, Paddy. Please don't hate me."

Paddy put his arms around her. "It's all right. We can fix it. I could never hate you, Aunt Colleen. No one makes me laugh the way you do."

As suddenly as the tears had flowed, they stopped, and she tousled his hair in an impish manner.

"You're my favorite, Paddy. You always were."

She looked at me. "Oh, but Gerri is my favorite girl. Gerri, come here."

I went over to her and she hugged me.

Mother shook her head.

"Maybe we can go home now that Colleen's made a spectacle of our family in front of the whole town."

Paddy reached into his coat pocket and pulled out a wad of bills. "I want to treat everybody to hot chocolate down at the diner. Come on, Ma, it'll be fun to have all of us together."

Mother looked at the grinning Colleen and shook her head. "No, thank you. I've never been so embarrassed in my life, and I want to go home."

She touched Billy's arm. "Come home with me."

Billy looked at Paddy, then back to Mother.

"No, I think we should help Paddy celebrate."

Mother scowled at Billy. I had never her seen her look so angry with him before. It was so unlike him to disagree with her and take a stand.

"Fine, suit yourself."

One look at Billy's wretched expression told me the faithful lap dog regretted nipping his mistress.

She turned to leave and Billy took one step in her direction before Paddy took his arm to prevent him from moving, mouthing the word *no*.

Billy's pained expression was in sharp contrast to Aunt Colleen's glee. Being forgiven was not enough to satisfy her emotional craving. She needed another fix.

"Don't worry, Lizzie. I'll have your hot chocolate. And I'll have extra whipped cream on mine, since you're not coming. We don't need you. I'll have the kids all to myself."

Mother stopped walking and turned on her heels back to the receptive tentacles of her loving family.

"Paddy, I've changed my mind. I want your day to be special. I want to be a part of this family's joy. Let's go."

"Uh, okay, Ma, we're glad to have you with us."

He took her by the left hand, Aunt Colleen by the right, while Billy and I carried Michael and John in our arms.

"Oh, and Paddy, don't forget," Mother said.

"Don't forget what, Ma?"

"There's no place like home for the holidays."

Chapter 47

"**I**'m really worried about her. She seems... sicker than usual."
Sarge poured me a glass of milk and pushed the plate of cookies toward me.

"Try one. They're really good. Your aunt made them."

"Aunt Colleen?"

"Yes. She's an amazing chef."

I chose the smallest one, wary she may have inherited the Aunt Peggy baking gene.

To my surprise, it was a genuine Toll House success.

"What did I tell you? My Colleen can do anything if she just applies herself."

"Aunt Colleen?"

"Oh, you don't know her as well as you think you do. There are things I could tell you about her." He had a faraway look in his eyes for a moment. "But let's hurry up. She'll be up soon, and I know you two have a lot of shopping to do." He paused.

Aunt Colleen was taking a nap. One of her headaches had taken hold of her, and she had to lie down to relieve the pain. Her spells had always been a part of our lives, as long as I had known her. But recently, they had grown more frequent and intense, as if they would culminate in a final explosion.

"Don't you think you should take her to a doctor to be examined?"

"You know how she feels about doctors."

"Yes, but you could make her go."

He crunched into a cookie.

"Are you suggesting I could make her go against her will?"

"I guess not."

"She's not a child, Gerri."

I bit into my cookie.

"Isn't she?"

All of a sudden, Aunt Colleen appeared in the doorway. Sarge darted his eyes from side to side like he had an uncontrollable tic.

"Are you feeling better?"

It was difficult to tell if she had been listening to our conversation or not.

"Yes. I'll get the boys."

We were going to bring Michael and John to have their picture taken with Santa.

When she was out of earshot, Sarge leaned forward and took my hand, squeezing it hard. "Please watch out for her. I don't want her to be hurt. Promise me you'll look out for her."

"I promise."

I found her with the boys in her bedroom. Michael and John were dressed in matching plaid suits with red and green vests. Aunt Colleen clipped on their bow ties before she had them look at themselves in the full-length mirror. John touched his image.

"Me."

Michael copied his older cousin, except he kissed his face in the mirror instead of just touching it.

We put their coats on and headed to the door.

"We'll be back before dinner," Aunt Colleen said.

"Okay. Have fun, sweetheart," Sarge said with a thumbs-up.

Aunt Colleen went to him and tousled his hair.

"I'll let Santa know you've been a good boy. If anyone knows how good you've been, it's me."

When we arrived at the department store, there was a long line of crying and screaming children at Santa's Workshop.

Aunt Colleen, never known for her patience, left me with Michael and John saying, "I'll be back soon."

Keeping the boys under control wasn't easy. They kept taking their bow ties off of each other, throwing them to the floor with impish giggles.

We were almost at the front of the line when my aunt reappeared with a half-eaten doughnut in her hand. Her face was smeared with raspberry jelly.

"I have an idea," she said.

"Yes?"

"Why don't we take a picture with the four of us?"

"Aunt Colleen, it's supposed to be for the children."

"Don't be silly, Gerri. If I'm paying, I can get whatever I want. Who's going to argue with cold, hard cash?"

Soon it was our turn, and the helper elf escorted us through the golden ropes to Santa.

"Who have we here?"

Aunt Colleen plopped Michael on his lap.

"This is Michael. He's special because he's mine."

At that moment, my baby cousin took his bow tie off and flung it to the floor. Aunt Colleen retrieved it. When she'd clipped it back on Michael, she gave him a pinch on the cheek.

"You're a naughty boy."

He rubbed the red circle, but did not cry.

Santa pulled Michael closer. "Are you ready to have your picture taken?"

"We want a picture with all of us. Gerri, put John on the other side."

"We don't usually include adults in the picture."

Aunt Colleen pressed her face next to his and put her hand on his cheek.

Santa squirmed.

"I think you'll make an exception for me."

"Madam, the customer is always right," he answered as he removed Aunt Colleen's hand from his face.

He snapped his fingers while trying to balance the boys on his lap.

"Elaine, the young ladies want to be in the shot."

The shapely photographer in the Mrs. Claus costume peered out from behind her camera.

"They'll have to squeeze in really tight."

Aunt Colleen put her head next to Santa on the left while I knelt down on the right.

"Say Saint Nick."

The flash went off, and we blinked the blue circles away.

I lifted the boys down from Santa's lap and began to usher them out.

Mrs. Claus held open Santa's sack of toys while he reached in and gave the boys their presents with a jolly "Merry Christmas."

Aunt Colleen held her hand out.

"Where's mine?"

"They're for the children," Santa replied, no trace of jolliness in his voice.

Aunt Colleen stomped her foot. "Well, if I can't get a toy then I want another picture."

"This is highly unusual," Santa said.

"I want another picture or I'm not leaving," Aunt Colleen insisted as she crossed her arms over her chest.

Santa looked at Mrs. Claus for help, but she just shrugged her shoulders. Glancing at the line of waiting children, he relented with a snap of his fingers.

Santa grunted as Aunt Colleen climbed onto his lap and wrapped her arms around his neck. She pressed her breast against the white fur of his robe. Just as the camera clicked, she kissed Santa full on the lips. As she withdrew, she stained his beard with a trail of jelly.

"Have yourself a merry little Christmas."

Santa turned as red as his suit as he stammered, "You... you... too."

She jumped down, a huge grin on her face. The eyes of the shocked onlookers followed her as she scooped Michael up and spun him around. Whispers spread through the crowd like a gathering waterfall.

Turning my head in the direction of the murmur, I saw the shoppers staring in disbelief at the freak who would pervert a sacred Christmas ritual. It seemed an eternity before Mrs. Claus handed Aunt Colleen the Polaroid photos.

"Here you go," the woman said, passing them to my aunt as if she were delivering a load of soiled diapers.

Aunt Colleen examined them before giving a review for all to hear.

"Hey, look at Santa. He looks like I just gave him a case of the clap."

I had no idea what the phrase "case of the clap" meant, but judging by the reaction of the crowd, it had to be a very bad thing.

Aunt Colleen handed me the photos. "Take care of these until we get home," she said as she bent down to refasten the clamp on her snow boot.

I took John in my arms, lowered my head, and walked away in a desperate attempt to distance myself from her.

As I passed by, I overheard a young mother talking to her husband. "People like that shouldn't be allowed around respectable folks."

"Well, dear, it's obvious they have no breeding."

Our eyes met, and the contempt I saw there made my cheeks burn with humiliation. Judgment passed, we had been tried and convicted as unfit to socialize with decent human beings.

It was more than I could bear, and I began to run with my baby brother as Aunt Colleen took off after me with Michael in her arms.

"Hey, wait up!"

I kept running.

I soon realized I was only succeeding in attracting more attention and let her catch up.

"What's the big idea?"

"I have to go to the bathroom."

"Well, why didn't you say so? There's a restroom in the women's department." We walked at a brisk pace. She watched the boys while I went inside. Women laden with packages were jammed in the outer area waiting for a free stall. I went to the sink and splashed water on my face.

When a stall became free, I locked myself in, away from prying eyes. I pulled the photos out of my coat pocket and studied them with the curiosity of an explorer who happens upon a gory relic. I felt like the first adventurer who examined a shrunken head. I took my frilly lace handkerchief out and carefully wrapped both pictures in it, then tucked them away in my shoulder bag for safekeeping.

Family photos need to be treated with respect and treasured for the priceless historical records they are. You never know when the Smithsonian might contact you to request a valuable artifact to add to their collection.

Chapter 48

The following Monday, I went directly to Aunt Colleen's house after school. I had promised I would help her write out Christmas cards.

The first thing I noticed when I entered the living room was the picture of Aunt Colleen kissing Santa displayed prominently in the middle of the mantel. She had encased it in an ornate gold scallop-edged frame. You could not help but be drawn to it, like the eyes of the Mona Lisa as they follow you around the room.

I wondered what Sarge thought of it. Not every husband would brush a thing like that off... but Sarge?

"Isn't it great?" she asked.

She was beaming with pride at her artistic achievement.

"Well, I know you did it in fun, but don't you think you might hurt Sarge's feelings?"

She looked at me as though she couldn't comprehend that his feelings might have any bearing on the subject.

"Oh, that old stick-in-the mud. He did say it was vulgar. But who's he to talk? Your grandmother had it right. He is a dirty old lecher. You wouldn't believe the things he..."

She stopped talking and put her hands to her reddened cheeks as her thoughts turned elsewhere for a brief moment. She shook her head as if attempting to push her thoughts to the darkened corners of her mind. As suddenly as she had stopped talking, she resumed.

"Why are we wasting time talking about him? Let's get writing."

She had about fifty copies of the photograph with the four of us surrounding Santa ready to stuff into each envelope.

As I sat addressing the envelopes, I glanced at the sideboard and saw another framed picture of the four of us. The frame on this one was wooden, and there was a gift tag hanging down the side. I was too far away to see the name.

As I got up to examine it, Aunt Colleen suddenly jumped up and snatched the picture away. "It's a surprise gift to someone special." She took it to her bedroom.

When she came back, she tossed another pile of photos on the table. I picked one up and turned it over. They were copies of the smooching photo.

"Don't forget to send a copy of these."

"You can't be serious."

"Why not?"

"You can't do it. You're sending cards to half the town. My God, Aunt Colleen, you're sending a card to Father Quinn. It's not a good idea."

She gave me a scornful look as she began to insert the second set of photos into the cards.

"Either you can help me, like you promised you would, or you can leave."

"Aunt Colleen, I can't let you do it. You'll be the laughingstock of Ferrytown. Don't you know they call you crazy now?"

Her eyes narrowed to slits.

"Go."

I went out to the dock to think. Pangs of regret hit me in a tidal wave of guilt. I had called her the one word that she hated more than any other: Crazy, the word I had never said to her face before; I had thought it many times, but never said it aloud.

I tried to convince myself I had only been trying to protect her, to save her from the inevitable embarrassment her plan would cause her. Except I knew in my heart that it wasn't Aunt Colleen who was afraid of the resulting humiliation. She had never been ashamed of anything she had done in her entire life. She felt no guilt, no remorse. For Colleen, the world was Colleen, and no one else existed.

Still, I could not help fearing the consequences the rest of us would face if she sent out that picture. So I told Paddy as soon as I could find him.

"Don't worry. I'll make the problem go away."

"How will you do that?"

He just grinned at me. I did not press him for details.

Later he confided he had been a good boy and volunteered to bring the Christmas cards down to the post office to mail out. Or so he told Aunt Colleen.

He actually waited until the coast was clear and dumped them off the dock and into Lake Owl's Head. Unfortunately, the letters did not sink beneath the surface and began to float to shore.

"Damn it, Gerri. I should have put them in a sack with a cement block. That's how all the gangsters get rid of the evidence."

Over the course of the next several days, we scoured the lakeshore for letters that refused to stay down.

If I had been blessed with powers of extra-sensory perception, I might have recognized the incident with the letters as a warning sign of events to come. Poor visionless young girl that I was, I did not have the ability to see that it would not be the last time family secrets would refuse to stay buried in the lake.

Chapter 49

Aunt Colleen was determined to buy an artificial Christmas tree that year.

"I'm tired of pine needles everywhere. What we need is something that doesn't require vacuuming."

I had to bite my tongue to stop myself from laughing. She wouldn't have vacuumed. She never did. If any housework needed to be done, she had a knack for getting someone else to do it.

Even though I knew about her plan, the sight of the tree was still a shock when I opened the door. Sunshine hit the silver branches, creating metallic rays that temporarily blinded me.

Dropping my book bag to the floor, I took hold of a branch. I rubbed the slick foil between my fingers, and it made a crinkly sound that sent a shiver through my fillings.

"So, what do you think?"

Aunt Colleen was standing in the doorway, eyes searching for approval of her Liberace-inspired choice. Moving back, I took another look at the glaring monstrosity, trying to find some positive quality worth praising, in order to spare her feelings.

"It's..."

"Yes?"

"It's..."

She began to frown.

"Shiny as a quarter."

Embracing me from behind, she said in a self-satisfied voice, "I knew you'd love it. Sarge says it's tacky, but you know what an odd duck he can be."

Yes, he's the flaky one.

"Your brothers will be here soon. They're getting the decorations from the basement at the other house."

After my brothers arrived, I sorted through the ornaments with Billy, while Paddy tested the lights.

Aunt Colleen was rummaging through a box when she found her stocking. You knew it was hers because her name was in gold glitter four inches high. It was a foot wide and three feet long. She nailed it to the center of the mantel where everyone would be sure to see it. She hung up two significantly smaller stockings with "Michael" and "Sarge" written on them in tiny script.

"Getting any coal this year, Aunt Colleen?" Paddy asked.

"No, we'll leave that for Sarge McScrooge."

As if on cue, he appeared in the doorway.

"I'm not a Scrooge. I just think Christmas trees should be green."

She snorted.

Sarge sighed.

"Why don't I whip us up a batch of eggnog?" he asked.

Aunt Colleen's eyes grew wide. "Can we have the special dark rum?"

"You know you don't handle that very well."

She broke into a pout and stomped her foot.

"Oh, all right, I suppose we can make an exception for the holidays, if you promise me you'll behave."

Aunt Colleen made the cross-your-heart-and-hope-to-die symbol across her chest, and Sarge broke into a huge grin before he headed to the kitchen. When he was gone, she whispered to me. "See? That's how it's done. That's how you get a man to do what you want."

We continued with our task: lights strung, ornaments placed just right, tinsel tossed in strands of gold and red and blue. We added a few finishing touches before Paddy got on top of Billy's shoulders to put the angel on the top of the tree. Finally, Billy crawled on the floor and plugged the lights in, and we gasped at our gaudy creation.

"It's perfect," Aunt Colleen said.

As we stood admiring our handiwork, there was a knock at the door. We exchanged glances before Paddy went to answer it. He returned with a large package, wrapped in red and tied with a green ribbon.

"No one was there, but I found this."

Aunt Colleen looked at the tag, and disappointment spread across her face.

She handed it to me.

"Who's it from?" Billy asked.

I looked at the tag. "It doesn't say, but it's for me."

I put it in the corner under the tree.

Sarge called from the kitchen. "Can somebody help me?"

I went to lend a hand.

He had filled the punch bowl close to overflowing with creamy golden eggnog, a very generous dash of nutmeg floating on top. I waited for Sarge to return to his seat before carrying the magical elixir inside.

Aunt Colleen stuck her head over the bowl and sniffed. "I don't smell any rum."

Sarge reached into his sweater vest pocket and pulled out a key.

"Here, sweetheart, why don't you unlock the liquor cabinet and get it."

With a greedy look on her face, Aunt Colleen snatched the key and retrieved the bottle. As she was about to pour it into the bowl, Sarge blocked her with his cane.

"In your own mug, please. The kids want some eggnog, too."

"What mug?"

Billy, Paddy, and I jumped up simultaneously, bumping into each other in a race to the kitchen. The boys each took a glass mug, and I took the last two. We were about to go back inside when the phone rang. I picked it up while my brothers rejoined the others.

"Hello?"

"Did you get my gift?" It was Mother.

"Yes."

"Don't open it until Christmas."

"I won't. Are you all right?"

She hung up without replying. I went back to the living room and ladled myself and Aunt Colleen a serving each of eggnog.

"Who was on the phone?" Sarge asked.

"Just a wrong number."

No need to mention Mother's name and risk spoiling the party.

Aunt Colleen poured some rum into her mug.

"Let's have a toast."

We raised our cups.

"To the Ghost of Christmas Past."

Billy got up.

"To the Ghost of Christmas Present."

Finally, Paddy said, "To the Ghost of Christmas Future."

Aunt Colleen wrapped her arms around Sarge and gave him a peck on the cheek. "What do you say, my love?"

He put his forehead against hers and lay his hands on her shoulders as he said in a loud, bass voice, "Bah, humbug!"

Chapter 50

The workmen had finished repairs on the house, so I thought it would be the perfect place to hide the Christmas presents I had bought. Mother was too much of a snoop for me to hide them at her place. The cottage was out as well. Aunt Colleen had been known to look through closets and drawers for hours in her efforts to discover what she would be getting each year. I was grateful my brothers did not indulge in the find-the-present game. I guess they had no interest in looking for my presents. They knew all I could afford on my allowance were the cheapest quality five-and-dime handkerchiefs.

I got up early that Saturday morning, looking around to make sure no one was watching. Treading carefully, I dragged the laundry bag filled with gifts through the backyard, a pint-sized Santa Claus.

As I approached our house, I was startled by a noise near the garbage cans. My heart fluttered as a raccoon jumped down from a pail, knocking the cover off in the process.

"Silly coon. Shoo."

Entering the house, I was hit by the overpowering smell of paint and sawdust. We were planning on moving back on Christmas Eve, so I didn't want to hide the presents anywhere that someone helping move our stuff back might find them. I thought for a moment until I concluded the basement would be the safest place. It was seldom visited. Maybe my family believed Daddy when he said he had seen Aunt Peggy's ghost pacing the floor down there in search of a sense of humor.

The floorboards creaked as I crept down the steps, dragging my bundle behind me like dead cats in a sack. I pulled on the chain light, and the naked bulb swung back and forth, casting eerie shadows on the wall. Walking to the corner, I opened the armoire where Mother kept the old clothes she insisted on saving. She harbored a deep belief they'd come back into style one day, and she'd be sitting on a gold mine. Pushing aside her treasure trove, I stacked the gifts in size order on the floor of the wardrobe.

As I shut the door, my eye was attracted to a pile of outdated encyclopedias against the wall. Grabbing a couple of volumes, I cleared off the ripped leather recliner and sat down to read. I fast fell asleep. When I woke, shafts of light were peeking through the windows, illuminating particles of dust drifting carefree through space. My nose began to itch as they invaded my sinuses. As I waved them away with my hand, I heard voices echoing through the heating ducts. Positioning a chair next to the vent, I pressed my ear against the metal. They were female voices, but I couldn't make out any words so I decided to move closer to investigate.

I slithered up the stairs, one step at a time, trying to minimize the noise of the floorboards beneath my weight. When I arrived at the top, I was able to tell the voices were coming from the living room.

I got down on all fours, crawling to the doorway commando-style as I had seen Paddy Boy do many times.

As I inched nearer, I recognized Mother and Aunt Colleen's angry tones.

"Who do you think you are, taking Frankie's son?" Mother asked.

"The judge gave custody to Sarge and me. I have every right to keep him."

"I don't care about judges. He's my husband's son. You know the family rules. Promises were made. I want Michael."

"You can't have him. It's Gerri I should have. She always should have been with me."

"Fine, you can have her. You know I never wanted her. If you and Frankie hadn't been so careless we wouldn't have needed to pretend."

"You know what? Maybe I'll keep Michael and take Gerri, too."

"Don't even think about it. You're not breaking your promise to Mother."

"That old hag is dead. I declare all agreements null and void."

"I'm warning you. Don't even think about it."

"And just who's going to stop me? Maybe your knight in shining armor, Frankie, will come to your rescue. Oh, no, that's right. He had a little accident."

"What do you know about that?"

"All I know is that he should have listened to me and done the right thing."

"If I ever find out..."

Suddenly, I felt an urge to sneeze fill my nostrils. I moved sideways like a horseshoe crab skittering across the sand. Hold it in, I pleaded with my body as the overpowering itch tortured me.

At the kitchen, halfway to the back door, I lost control and let out a rapid succession of sneezes, one, two, three, loud and violent. I listened for a reaction and was met with silence. They had stopped talking.

I sprang up and ran out the back door, running faster and faster around the lake until I reached the opposite shore and collapsed on the ground.

I lay on my back, holding my hands over my ears in a desperate attempt to drown out their words replaying in my head, but they kept hitting against the inside of my skull like the keys of a typewriter.

"It's Gerri I should have. She always should have been with me."

All at once, a picture of Aunt Colleen kissing Daddy flashed across my mind.

"If you and Frankie hadn't been so careless, we wouldn't have needed to pretend."

I broke into a hysterical half-laugh, half-cry as the truth revealed itself to me in a shockwave of clarity: Aunt Colleen was my real mother. Daddy was still my father, but Mother, dear sweet Mother, who had never wanted me, was really my Aunt Lizzie.

"You're not breaking your promise," Mother had warned.

What was the promise? What kind of a twisted game had they been playing? Had they traded children the way my brothers swapped baseball cards? I broke into convulsive fits of laughter as a picture of what I had bought Mother for Christmas came into my mind: A mug with the phrase, "Number One Mom" on it. If Daddy was right and Aunt Peggy's ghost was searching in the basement for her sense of humor, she definitely would have found it once she happened upon that gift. As for me, I stopped laughing that morning.

As I lay shivering on the frozen shoreline of Lake Owl's Head, I was filled with a dark, anxious dread over my true identity. After all, if crazy Aunt Colleen was really my mother, what did that make me?

Chapter 51

I began to wander aimlessly by the side of the lake as I gathered my thoughts. I couldn't go home without a plan. If they had seen me, what would they do? If not, what should I do about what I'd heard?

As I walked, their words kept echoing in my head, crashing against my skull like silver spheres in a pinball machine.

I kept moving, feet gliding me forward like jellyfish floating over ocean waves, until I found myself in front of the church nativity scene. Gathering up a bunch of evergreen branches, I made a nest to sit before the Holy Family. I closed my eyes, interlacing my fingers in my lap, and I began to shiver.

I had read many stories about gods and goddesses who would intervene in the affairs of mere mortals. Perhaps if I prayed hard enough, concentrated all my will, I could make Mary and Joseph come to my rescue.

Please, Father Joseph, please, Mother Mary, save me. Help me, Holy Family. Make me forget what I heard. Make it all like it was before I knew.

Please.

Opening my eyes, I raised them to the statues, fingers crossed.

Oh, no! Not them!

I fell backward as I saw Mother's face on Joseph, Aunt Colleen's on Mary. Turning over, I buried my head in the snow, pounding my fists on the ground. *Not fair! Not fair! I've been good. I've done nothing wrong. Why can't just one wish come true?*

My fists continued to rage against the injustice of it, beating against the cold, damp earth until I realized I was hitting them against the sharp edge of a jagged rock.

Pulling myself up, I stared at my cut hands, wounds seeping blood, stigmata of my pain.

Slowly, I turned to confront my tormentors, only to find the faces of the statues had changed back to Joseph and Mary.

I got up and moved closer, peering into the empty crèche. It was almost time for the baby to arrive. Jesus had been very fortunate. He had always known who his folks were, and how he got there. And unlike me, his mother had wanted him.

I moved on, walking over to Ferrytown Park. A group of boys on the field tossed a football back and forth.

Was I like that football, passed from one relative to another, propelled by the selfish desires of adults who treated children like mere possessions?

My heart skipped a beat as one of the boys kicked the ball over the goalpost.

Yes, that was me.

I fled, sprinting up Union Hill, crossing the town square, until I reached the firehouse. The garage door was open, and the shiny red metal truck glistened before me. There was a light under the closed door to the inner sanctuary where the volunteers socialized while awaiting impending disaster.

As I stood staring at the engine, an irresistible urge took hold of me. Jumping on the running board, I grabbed hold of the rope to the bell and struck the alarm.

Clang!

I felt an electrical spark shoot down my arm at the noise, and I immediately did it again.

Clang! Clang!

It was thrilling.

I could not stop.

Clang! Clang! Clang!

Over and over, I had to make the bell sing: *I am here! I am Gerri!*

Suddenly, the door to the other room flew open, and two burly men came rushing toward me.

"What is it? What's wrong?" the taller one asked.

I started hitting the bell again until he took me by the waist and removed me from the running board.

"Is there a fire? Are you hurt?"

I tried to answer, but no words would come.

There were footsteps behind us.

"What's going on, boys?" a familiar voice asked.

I turned and locked eyes with the fire chief.

"Well, look who we have here."

The other two men exchanged glances.

"Friend of yours, chief?" the shorter man asked.

"You might say we're old acquaintances."

"She was clanging that bell like a madwoman."

The chief got down to eye level with me.

"Is there an emergency, sweetheart?"

All I could manage by way of an answer was to shake my head.

He nodded. "I'll take it over from here, lads. Go keep an eye on the chili before we burn the firehouse down."

They did as they were told, but not without giving me sideways glances before shutting the door behind them.

"So, do you want to talk about it?"

"I... don't think so."

"Well, why don't I give you a lift home? It'll be dark soon, and it's a long walk back to Lake Owl's Head."

He noticed the cuts on my hands and took them into his.

"How did this happen?"

"I fell."

He gave me a skeptical look.

"Fell, huh? That your story?"

I nodded.

"We'll go to the bathroom to clean them up before I take you home. I want you to promise me one thing first."

"What's that?"

"Promise me that if anyone ever hurts you that you'll let me know. Can you promise me that?"

How was he to know that it was too late? I had already been hurt so much that nothing could take away the pain.

"I promise."

"You're a good girl. Now, let's get some iodine and bandages on those cuts and get you home. I'm sure your mother will be looking for you before long."

If only he knew I had no idea which mother that would be. Would it be crazy mother number one or crazy mother number two? Either way, the thought of her searching for me left me fighting a dose of bitter bile as it welled up in my throat.

After he finished administering first aid, we got into his car, and he buckled me into my seat.

"So, Gerri, how would you like it if I put the siren on while we drive you home?"

"That would be great."

I was filled with genuine excitement when the flashing light started to wail. It was a rush to hear the screaming in my ears.

"Get ready for the royal treatment. When you have the siren on, everyone has to pay attention to you."

Wow, maybe I can get one and carry it with me wherever I go.

The chief gripped the steering wheel, put his foot to the pedal, and peeled out of the driveway as he announced, "Ready or not, here we come."

Yes, ready or not, here I come.

Chapter 52

We had promised Billy we would attend Christmas Eve Mass together; however, Mother informed us she would meet us there. As he was still underage, Billy wasn't supposed to drive at night without an adult licensed driver in the car. He announced he was willing to forego the rule this time for two reasons: to promote the spirit of family unity, and to celebrate the birth of the baby Jesus. Billy was good that way. He was always willing to make sacrifices for the sake of promoting his own saintliness. If I had to choose between Billy's holiness and Paddy's sinfulness, I would go with Paddy every time. At least it was honest.

When we arrived, the church was packed to overflowing with congregants. Because of the large number of parishioners, we weren't able to sit together. My brothers and I were seated midway from the back. Aunt Colleen, Sarge, and Michael were ushered to the first row.

Father Quinn marched down the aisle, surrounded by his flock of adoring altar boys. He beamed as he genuflected, his robes swishing with a dramatic flourish as he glowed in the spotlight. It was the night he waited for all year long, the time his star shone the brightest.

He began the magical chants and we responded.

I had trouble concentrating on the words, as an uneasy feeling made me turn around and search the faces of those behind me. Seeing nothing unusual, I tried to shake off the vague and unsettling sense that something was out of kilter.

The priest continued with his poetical readings.

Eventually his mantra drew me in, casting a spell over me. The rhythm of the words and music swathed me in a blanket of false security.

We lined up for communion and drank the body and blood of Christ, vampires thirsting for eternal life. I suppose Mother must have been disappointed when my dress did not tear. Secret dieting has advantages.

As I marched back down the aisle, my eye was drawn to the stained glass window where Mary cradled her dead son in her arms. She looked as though she were overcome with grief. If that were my mother, she'd only be worried that my tattered loin cloth would reflect poorly on her. If I were too thin, she'd pick on me the same way she did at my being overweight.

Returning to my seat, I knelt to pray. As I bent down, another wave of cold dread came over me, and I turned my head to review the crowd.

Just then, a grossly overweight man behind us crouched down to pray. The bench groaned under his weight. I saw Paddy break into a grin as he looked at the rotund man. My brother elbowed me in the side and tried to get me to laugh as he filled his cheeks with air to puff them out like a walrus. It made me angry to think how thoughtless and cruel my brother could be, especially when he knew I had been on the receiving end of many a similar taunt. He turned his attention back to the front when he saw I would not take his bait.

Still feeling ill at ease, I turned around and spotted Mother. She was kneeling, rosary beads clutched tightly in her fingers, eyes shut. She crossed herself and opened her eyes. When she lifted her head, our eyes met. She nodded and gave me a small queen-like wave. I gave her a weak wave back, just as the portly man struggled to an upright position, blocking my view of petite Mother.

I felt a tug at my sleeve.

"What are you doing?" Paddy asked.

"Waving to Mother."

He cocked his head and tried to catch a glimpse of her.

"I don't see her."

Try as hard as I could, I was unable to find her again among the many faces.

Mass continued on in an endless, repetitive drone, broken up by hymns that were dusted off once a year to see if anyone could remember the lesser-known latter verses without resorting to humming.

Finally, when the last amen was said, we put our coats on and shuffled through the throng out to the car.

When we got there, Mother was leaning against the fender, arms crossed.

Billy hugged her. "Hi, Ma."

She kissed him on the cheek with a loud smack.

Paddy Boy pushed him to the side and kissed her on the forehead. "Merry Christmas, Ma."

She held her arms out and tried to take John from me.

He clung fiercely to me.

"Come to Mother."

He would not let go.

Mother backed up.

"Oh, he's playing hard to get. He'll come around. Men always do."

Sarge and Aunt Colleen arrived.

"Merry Christmas, Col," Mother said.

"What are you doing here?"

"What do you think I'm doing? I'm attending Midnight Mass like the rest of my family."

"I thought witches only attended the Black Sabbath."

Before Mother could respond to the dig, Sarge stepped forward.

"Merry Christmas, Lizzie. How is my favorite sister-in-law?"

"Just fine. Merry Christmas to you, too, my dear old brother-in-law."

"Don't you think we'd better get heading home? There's a definite nip in the air tonight. We don't want the little ones catching cold on Christmas day, do we?"

Billy opened the door and helped Sarge in. Aunt Colleen slid in next to him, plopping baby Michael in as though he were just another Christmas package. She slammed the door shut.

Billy and I stood facing Mother, not knowing what to do next. Should we seat her next to Aunt Colleen and risk more viciousness on the day of our Lord's birth? Surprisingly, Mother broke the tension when she spoke with a strangely detached calmness.

"Gerri, can you walk me home?"

I looked to Billy for guidance.

"We can fit you in, Ma. You don't need to walk."

Mother looked at Aunt Colleen, then back at me.

"No, I think I'll walk. But I would like some company. Gerri, can you come with me?"

"I..."

"Come on. We have a lot of catching up to do."

Billy nodded.

"Okay, Ma, we can take the shortcut through Ferrytown Park."

I was about to hand John to my brother when Mother put herself between us.

"No, bring him with you. He is my baby, you know."

Billy took John from me.

"No, it's too long a walk. He'll freeze his little toes off."

Mother stared at him with the eyes of one who has felt the sting of betrayal. For only the second time I could remember, Billy had taken a stand against her.

But a moment later, she reversed course.

"No, you're right. He's just a baby, after all. You always were the sensible one in the family, Billy my love."

Perhaps she had become filled with the spirit of the holiday. Or maybe she had sipped too much communal wine.

Billy managed a weak smile.

"Take care, Gerri. We'll see you back home."

He got in, handed John to Paddy, and started the engine.

As they drove off, Mother intertwined our arms, and we began to walk down the dark path toward home.

Round yon Virgin, Mother and child.

Chapter 53

When Mother unlocked the door, I was greeted by the sight of our old Christmas decorations arranged in a mocking display of holiday memories.

"Let me have your coat."

It was so unlike her that I was dumbfounded. She helped me take it off and hung it on the same hanger that she put her own on, smothering my coat with hers.

We went to the living room, and she turned on the Christmas tree lights. The bulbs flashed like fireflies on a lazy summer evening.

"What do you think?" she asked.

"It's beautiful," I replied.

She went to the mantel, taking a snow globe and shaking it as she walked.

Holding it under my nose for inspection, she asked, "Remember this?"

I examined the scene of an Eskimo boy and girl rubbing noses, but could not place the object.

"You might have been too young. We bought it when we took you to see Santa one year."

She shook it again as if she would loosen the memory from the inner recesses of my brain.

"I'm sorry. I don't remember."

"That's all right. I didn't know I still had it until yesterday. It's funny, you know, the things you hold onto."

"I'm sorry you went to the trouble of showing it to me."

She put it down on the coffee table as she motioned for me to sit next to her on the sofa.

"I didn't bring you here to look at that silly old thing."

She placed her hands on my shoulders and made a solemn face.

"I do have something important to show you. I want to talk to you first."

What was she up to now? Was she going to tell me the story of my birth? Would the shepherds gather 'round to hear the news?

"I know my sickness has been hard on everyone, especially you. I can't imagine what I put all of you through, never knowing how I would react from one minute to the next. "

She pulled on the sleeves of her sweater.

"It must have been hell for you. But I'm done blaming myself. Gerri, I have a disease."

"A disease?"

"Yes, Gerri Girl. I'm a victim of manic depression. My mood swings, my fits of anger, they're all symptoms. The doctors don't know why some people get it. But it does seem to run in families. Do you know most alcoholics are depressives?"

A picture of my smiling Grandma passed across my mind.

"Anyway, I wanted to let you know I have it under control. Things are going to be different from now on. I want to show you why."

She went to the kitchen and returned clutching a prescription bottle in her hand.

"These are my lifesavers. They keep me on an even keel. Of course, I'm still seeing my therapist."

"I thought you already took medicine."

"It wasn't the right one for me. But these... these are wonder pills."

She shook the bottle like she was playing the maracas.

"Gerri, it's like I'm starting my life over. For the first time, I can put a finger on why nothing has ever seemed to go right in my life. It wasn't my fault."

She put her hand on my shoulder. "Can you promise me you'll try to forgive me? Do you promise me we can start over?"

I did not know what to think or say. Suppose this was just another one of her cruel tricks... what then? Still... I could not resist her. The spell of her words drew me in.

"I promise."

She smiled as she stroked my hair.

"Thank you."

Her face took on a serious expression.

"Do you think we can go to the main house now and tell your brothers?"

I went to the closet and got our coats. Taking it from me, she wrapped my coat around my shoulders. She opened the door, but hesitated on the front step for a moment.

"Gerri, I'm afraid. What if they don't understand? Do you promise to stay by my side?"

"Don't worry. I promise to stay by your side."

Satisfied I would forever be Mother's Little Helper, she shut the door behind us, and we went forth to spread the good news of Lizzie's rebirth.

Chapter 54

When we arrived next door at the big house, the boys weren't there.

I watched Mother as she pretended to be interested in the late, late movie. Every time Bing Crosby would appear on screen with Ingrid Bergman, she would sigh and say, "Now if they had priests like that when I was a girl, I never would have stopped going to church." Despite her joke, I could tell she was more than annoyed that my brothers were out so late.

So we sat in the living room and waited... and waited... .

Another movie had just begun when the back door opened. Mother leaned forward, her knees knocking against the coffee table.

Paddy stuck his head in the doorway saying, "Well, look who we have here. It's the sisters of charity."

Mother thrust her watch in his direction. "Where have you been?"

"Been?"

"Yes, I remember you boys got in the car and were headed home. Why are you so late?"

He hung his head.

"Aunt Colleen invited us in for eggnog and cookies. We couldn't say no."

"You couldn't say no to Aunt Colleen?"

Billy came in and knelt in front of her, wobbling as he tried to stay upright.

"Well, it is Christmas," he said.

As he spoke, the smell of rum wafted across the room.

"Are you drunk?"

He kissed her ring finger as if she were the pope. "Just filled with holiday spirit."

She grabbed his lapels and pulled him across the table.

"You smell like a brewery."

He belched.

"Oops. Sorry."

Paddy laughed.

She let go of Billy and our fallen saint fell on his backside.

"You find this amusing?"

Mother leapt up, lunging at Paddy Boy like a wild woman. He jumped to the side. There was a loud thud as she hit her head against the doorjamb. Stunned for a moment, she sat there.

Paddy offered his hand.

"Ma, are you all right?"

She wrapped her arms around him, pushing them both forward. They crashed into the Christmas tree, knocking it to the ground. Paddy wriggled free and plopped on the couch beside me.

Billy began to tremble.

"Stop... stop... no."

Mother pulled broken ornaments from her hair. A sliver was embedded in her cheek, just below her left eye. A drop of blood dripped down her face like a tear.

Paddy pulled out his handkerchief as he started in her direction.

Suddenly, she reached behind her and threw a silver angel at him. But he ducked and it hit Billy on the chin, right on his scar. We held our breath.

Billy crawled over to Mother and put his face next to hers.

"What's the matter? Couldn't find a teacup this time?"

Paddy Boy burst into a belly laugh.

Mother whispered to Billy.

The two of them grabbed Paddy by the legs, pinned him to the floor and began to tickle him mercilessly.

Finally, he couldn't take any more of their torture.

"I give, I give."

They let him go, and the three of them got into a huddle. The trio nodded in agreement, and I shuddered as they eyed me. Before I realized what was happening the three of them pounced on me, lifting me over their heads and into the backyard. They dropped me into the snow and began to chant, "Snow angel! Snow angel!"

What could I do except flap my arms and legs until their request was satisfied.

They let out a cheer.

I got up, made a snowball and hit Paddy in the face. Mother laughed. Paddy scooped up a pile of snow and dumped it down her back. Billy threw a missile at him.

Soon the four of us were running back and forth, engaging the enemy, then withdrawing, only to attack again. We eventually wound up at the dock, exhausted, cold, soaked through to the skin.

We sat down, Billy next to Mother, Paddy against me. No one said a word as we leaned against each other like puppies in a litter.

Finally, when sunrise broke over the lake, we got up without saying a word and went home, arms intertwined, warm despite the chill. We were almost like a family.

In only a matter of hours, that feeling would be shattered forever.

Chapter 55

The next morning, I woke about ten. No one else was awake. I could hear Paddy and Billy snoring with that wheezing sound all the men in our family made. Being careful not to wake them, I crept downstairs to the kitchen. This would be my first attempt at making Christmas dinner on my own, and I was anxious for everything to turn out just right.

As I was mixing the glaze for the ham, I heard the front door open and shut.

"Hello?" I called.

I went to look and found the latch chain hanging loose.

Sprinting upstairs, I found Mother had gone.

It struck me as odd that she hadn't said goodbye, but I brushed it off as no more unusual than anything else she had ever done.

So I continued with my preparations, sampling everything, despite the voice in my head that told me I would be as big as a house by New Year's, and a young lady needs to watch her figure.

I switched the radio on and tried to let the carols drown out the ghost of Christmas Mother Past.

An hour passed when there was a frantic knocking at the back door.

"Who is it?"

"I can't find them! They're gone!"

It was Aunt Colleen.

I unlocked the door and she fell into my arms, shaking violently.

"Who? Who's gone?"

"The babies. They're gone. I went to wake them up this morning, and they weren't in their cribs."

"When did you see them last?"

"I checked on them just before I went to sleep. They were clinging to each other in Michael's bed, you know how they do."

"Where's Sarge? Maybe he took them for a walk."

She looked at me in disbelief at the absurdity of my statement. He could barely get around in good weather, much less in snow-covered lawns with two toddlers.

"No, Gerri, he's still sleeping. But Gerri..."

"Yes?"

"I did a terrible thing."

She took a prescription bottle from her pocket.

"I put the powder from my sleeping pills in his eggnog."

"You did what? How could you do such a crazy thing?"

She lowered her eyes.

When she raised her eyes, I saw a look of regret I had never seen before.

"Sometimes he wants me to do things... dirty things... and I don't want to do them... especially not on Christmas."

I put my index finger and thumb on her lips and pinched them shut, removing them slowly.

"We need to call the sheriff."

She dropped to her knees and began to tug on my legs.

"No, please don't. They'll lock me away in the loony bin. You don't know what it's like in those places. I've been there. Don't. Please don't."

She began to tremble.

I pulled her up, hugging her tightly to try and calm her down.

"No, Gerri, promise me you won't call."

Her face was etched with so much pain that I could not resist her plea.

"I promise."

She kissed me repeatedly as she took my hands in hers.

"Let's search the house again. Maybe they're playing hide-and-go-seek."

We ran hand in hand to the cottage.

As soon as we entered the bedroom, I noticed the window was open. I went over and glanced outside at tracks in the snow.

"Follow me."

Instinctively, I knew where they would lead.

Aunt Colleen spotted the note taped to the back door.

As soon as she read it, she dropped it and ran off at breakneck speed.

"Wait!"

I bent down and read the words: *Dear Col, meet me at the lake. Love, Lizzie.*

Racing through the snow, I stumbled and hit my head on a tree stump in the backyard.

It took a moment for me to regain my senses and catch sight of Aunt Colleen, just as she reached the center of Lake Owl's Head.

Mother was standing there, the boys on a sled in front of her. They were still in their bedclothes. Even at that distance, I could see them shivering from the cold.

This couldn't be real.

It couldn't be happening.

Time slowed down to a blur of images and sounds: cracking ice, splashing water, intertwined bodies fighting to untangle themselves.

I was there but not there, watching the scene unfold as if I were watching a movie.

Desperately, I tried to will myself back to the moment.

Putting one foot in front of the other, like Frankenstein's monster, I forced myself to walk as I looked on in horror.

Mother had her arms around Aunt Colleen's neck while John clung onto her.

I did not see Michael.

I was within twenty feet of them when I heard Aunt Colleen's urgent cry. "Gerri, save us!"

Mother tightened her grip around her sister's neck, but Aunt Colleen managed to break free for just an instant, and she began to let loose the secret in a voice so loud it echoed across the lake: "Gerri, I'm your..."

With a rage-contorted face, Mother clamped her hands over Aunt Colleen's mouth and dragged her under. They disappeared into the lake along with John.

I took a step forward when the ice started to crack in a zigzag line straight toward the dark hole.

Oh, God, what do I do?

I had to get to them, to do something. But the more I struggled to move, the more paralysis set in, as my fear overwhelmed me with the thought of joining them in the water. My limbs grew numb, and I fell limp to the ice, my face sticking to it. Digging my nails into the frozen mass, clawing until blood flowed in rivulets into the crack, down to the watery grave.

I looked one last time at the hole in the ice where they had gone under, and knew I could not save them. I had to save myself.

I lay down on the ice and curled up into a cold, hard, unfeeling ball before closing my eyes and letting myself pass into a black void of nothingness.

That's where they found me: unable to speak, unable to describe the horror I had witnessed, unwilling to confess my guilt.

Mother's Little Helper, promise-maker, promise-breaker. Babies had drowned, and I had done nothing to save them. Sometimes I think I'm the most cowardly, selfish pig on the face of the earth.

But sometimes I think you just have to let go of your burdens, let them sink like bodies into the water, never to be seen again.

And sometimes, yes, sometimes, I think I may be just like Mother. After all, the apple doesn't fall far from the tree. And that's the most frightening thought of all.

Chapter 56

"Upstate Family Drowns In Christmas Tragedy" – read the headline in the city paper. It was speculated that one sister died trying to save the other in a heroic attempt that failed. Maybe I had imagined Mother's choke hold on Aunt Colleen's neck. Perhaps she deserved a posthumous medal for valor.

"Lake Owl's Head Claims Local Family" – announced the Ferrytown Gazette. Mother, Aunt Colleen, and the boys were the latest names added to an already lengthy attendance list of death recounted by the paper. Tardy slips issued, permanent detention in a watery grave their ultimate punishment.

When the newswires picked up our story, we, the surviving children, were labeled as the "Moran Orphans," a title that would haunt us for many years to come. Almost immediately, charitable organizations designated us their cause of the moment. A circus-like atmosphere began to surround our newfound celebrity. We became media freaks in a sideshow of misfortune: *Step right up and see the pitiful victims. Careful, folks, don't get too close. They might bite.*

The circus began at the funeral.

As my brothers and I emerged from the limousine, we had to shield our eyes from the cascade of blue-and-white camera flashbulbs. An unruly flock of reporters were lined up behind barricades, each vying for dominant position. As we walked past, I was repulsed by the ugliness of the vultures feasting on the carrion of our pain-ravaged faces.

I could feel the anger rising in Paddy Boy as he tightened his grip on our intertwined arms. Billy covered us with his overcoat in a vain attempt to shield us from the greedy scavengers, as we ran into the church for sanctuary.

An usher escorted us down the aisle to the first row, next to an already seated Sarge. I had never sat so close to the front. The first pew was usually reserved for very important persons, like visiting dignitaries. Perhaps they thought we were the ambassadors of death.

Glancing around, I was astonished by the sight of hundreds of floral arrangements. There were lilies on the altar, chrysanthemums perched on memorial tripods, leafy green plants on wooden stands.

The grandest displays were the pieces draped over the caskets. White roses lay in an overflowing profusion on the exquisitely-carved wooden boxes holding Mother and Aunt Colleen, smaller ones for the boys. The flowers made me think an attempt was being made to trick naïve onlookers into believing they were viewing a delightful garden. But I wasn't fooled. No, I knew that if I opened the lids I would find only the decaying remains of my worst nightmare.

As the mourners filed in, I began to feel increasingly uneasy as they tried to catch glimpses of my brothers and me without being seen. Each time I would spot a spectator in the act, he would pretend to be looking elsewhere. The hideous game made my stomach ache as the acid started to churn.

After several annoying rounds, I decided to satisfy their morbid curiosity by positioning myself on my knees facing the crowd. Faced with my confrontational challenges, the gawkers soon forfeited the match.

Suddenly, I felt a tugging on my forearm.

"Gerri, turn around. That's not how a young lady sits," Billy scolded.

I shuddered as I recognized the tone of voice. Turning around, I studied his face to check if he had miraculously morphed into Mother. Much to my relief, the only resemblance was the Audrey Hepburn cheekbones they had in common.

The service began, and I focused my attention on the speakers. From the outset, I had to control myself from breaking into derisive laughter as they uttered phrases like "strong family bonds" and "sisterly devotion," speaking about my family. The knot in my stomach grew tighter.

As they continued with their lies about a family that never existed, I began to fantasize about dragging them down from the lectern, slapping them across their faces, and shouting, "You didn't know us! You didn't know us!"

Instead, I sat quietly till the end of the service. As infuriated as I was at the charade, I was not ready to experience the pain honesty would inflict on me. Deep wounds need time to heal, especially open and festering ones.

The following day, the media glare continued as we drove up to the cemetery gates. I suppose we should have been grateful that the uninvited guests were kept at bay by a contingent of state troopers guarding the entrance. But they could not stop the hungry photographers, perched atop their automobiles, from snapping pictures as we passed through the gates.

We gathered around the coffins that were mounted on metal frames above perfectly-formed holes in the ground. My brothers and I stood, while Sarge sat on a wooden chair, metal crutches at his side, like machine guns at the ready.

The biting wind forced me to wrap my scarf across my face to protect it from the painful cold. The brief thaw that had allowed the ice on Lake Owl's Head to open and swallow the dead had been replaced by an arctic blast.

They say that in life, timing is everything; maybe my family had been born with faulty biological clocks.

Or maybe we were just one more shining example of the luck of the Irish. Poor bastards, we never could escape our fate.

Looking at my brothers, I sighed as I remembered when Daddy passed the flask to Mother the day of Grandma's funeral. I wished he were with us. My heart ached as I pictured him alone in his nursing home bed, a man dead but not dead, whose fragile existence was marked by the whooshing sounds of a respirator.

I began to shiver. Paddy Boy noticed and wrapped his arms around me. A moment later, Billy took off his muffler and wrapped it over my scarf to create a double layer of warmth. We exchanged small smiles, and I began to feel better.

I scanned the crowd for familiar faces and saw the fire chief and his volunteers directly across from us. Their caps were polished to gleaming spit-shine perfection.

To their left, the mayor was standing next to Mother's former nemesis, the ever-dowdy Mrs. Whitcomb. I wondered if she felt good to see what had become of the woman who had humiliated her. Was she mourning or gloating?

There were others—school teachers, shop owners, soccer team members—almost everyone we had come into contact with on a regular basis in Ferrytown.

As I was looking them over, I was struck by how few of them had ever been inside our house, as though the walls had been impenetrable to outsiders. Visitors had been rare, and had required special permission to enter our inner sanctum. There had been a few exceptions, but I guess no one cared. Our house was the one you avoided, our family social outcasts, gossiped about by those seeking to feel superior.

I turned my attention to the priest mouthing words that came out as frozen puffs of breath. I did not hear what he said as I watched his lips move. My eye was drawn to the magic wand he was using to sprinkle water over the coffins. I hoped he had not been fooled into believing he would be able to raise my family like a magician, *Abracadabra, one two three, up and out, say I to thee*! It would not have been proper to trick a priest.

A mere five minutes later, the show was over, and we said our final farewells to the departed. As I approached the caskets, a wave of grief hit me, and I began to sob convulsively. Paddy tried to comfort me with a hug, but the sadness must have been contagious, and he, too, began to cry.

Billy wiped my tears with his handkerchief, oddly calm, as the mourners began to file away.

"The Holy Spirit is with you," he said.

Paddy dried his tears on his coat sleeve and sneered in contempt at our perpetually holier-than-thou brother.

"I'm with you, too," he said as he took one of my arms.

Billy grabbed the other and they engaged in a brotherly tug-of-war over me as we walked to the limousine in an uneasy union.

The driver opened the door and directed us in with a wave of his cap. My brothers fought to force me to sit beside them. I disentangled myself and instead sat down next to Sarge.

"How are you, sweetheart?" he asked, as he took my hands in his.

I shrugged and quickly took back my hands and thrust them into my pockets. Ever since Aunt Colleen had said Sarge made her do "dirty things" I had tried to avoid contact with him, especially taking care not to be alone with him. I never told my brothers what she had said. How could I tell them that their war hero idol, someone they considered an uncle, was a pervert?

Paddy reached into his coat pocket and pulled out a flask. He unscrewed the cap and took a swig before Billy snatched it from him and took a healthy swallow.

"Pass it here," Sarge said.

He chugged several doses of the Gaelic medicine and was about to hand it back to Paddy when I grabbed his wrist.

"Me, too," I said.

Sarge looked at Paddy, who in turn looked to Billy. My elder brother stared into my eyes as if assessing my needs before agreeing to my request.

"Let her have a drink. Just don't get used to it. It's a one-time deal," Billy said.

I took the flask, raised it to my lips, flung my head back, and let the liquor slide down my throat. A burning sensation hit my gut, and I knew I had made a mistake.

"How is it?" Paddy asked

"Warm," I answered in a frog-like voice, as I struggled to keep the vile liquid from rising up and spewing out from between my lips.

The others laughed, and I felt hurt by their callous disregard for my feelings. But I did not tell them how their laughter stung me. After all, I had asked to be one of the boys. Be careful what you wish for... .

Paddy grabbed the flask from me and shoved it back in his pocket. "I'll save some for you when you're older," he said with a wink and a grin.

We settled back in our seats, each alone with our thoughts, as we sped through the frozen wasteland to uncertain futures in a world that soon loses sympathy for lost and forgotten souls.

Chapter 57

T hree days later, Billy left for the seminary. Although he was a year shy of the required age to enter, an exception was made, and he was admitted to start training for the priesthood. I suppose his connections and history swayed the decision in his favor. It helps to have friends in high places.

"I'll keep you in my prayers," he said as he boarded the yellow school bus.

Stopping on the first step, he reached down and hugged me as he whispered in my ear, "I love you, Gerri Girl. And God does, too."

Straightening up, he made the sign of the cross over me before rushing to his seat to take his place among the righteous army of pimply-faced teenage boys.

I went back to the cottage.

Cardboard boxes sat lined up for the movers to load onto their truck. Sarge was going to move in with a cousin in Schenectady.

"The memories are too painful here. I can't stop seeing the dead," he had explained.

"But didn't you see a lot of dead people when you were in the war?" Paddy asked.

"Yes, but they were just casualties. They meant nothing to me, not really. Not like my Colleen. Not like my Michael... my poor little boy."

His eyes welled up with tears, and he turned his head away.

Paddy got up, put his coat on.

"A man needs his privacy," he said before leading me to Lake Owl's Head.

We walked the entire perimeter of the shoreline that day, neither of us acknowledging that we might not see each other again for a long time.

Social workers had arranged for both of us to be taken in by separate sets of foster parents. Normally, it would have been much more difficult to place older children right away. But our status as the "Moran orphans" had made us treasured possessions for do-gooders seeking to cash in on our fame.

Paddy was having none of it. He had made a plan to run away before they came for us. His friend Willie Six Toes had an uncle who could use a street-smart lad to assist him with his nefarious schemes. Paddy saw this job opportunity as a means to prosperity.

"I'm not going to work all my life. That's for suckers. I'm going to become filthy rich," he said.

"And what will you do with all your money?" I asked.

His face took on a solemn expression and he took my hands in his. "I'm going to come back for you and build a palace for us to live in, princess."

"Oh, Paddy, that's so sweet of you."

He blushed. Dropping my hand, he kicked a stone with his boot. "Either that or blow it all on loose women and the ponies."

I punched him in the arm.

Instead of punching me back, he pulled me to him and hugged me.

"I love you, Gerri Girl. Promise me you'll never forget it." He laid his hands on my shoulders. "Promise me."

"I promise."

"Good. Now let's go down to the diner and have an Irish breakfast. All this mushy talk is making me hungry."

The next morning, I could not stop laughing inwardly as the man and woman from the social services agency conducted a frantic search for my brother. After they gave up, they escorted me to the car, keeping a strong grip on my wrists in case I should decide to make a break for it.

As we walked down the driveway, I felt something hit me on the shoulder. Looking around, I could not determine what had hit me or where it had come from. The male social worker noticed my searching and tried to alleviate my fears.

"Don't worry, the sheriff will find him," he said as he helped me into the back seat of the car.

Halfway down the driveway, I spotted Paddy Boy perched on the roof.

I could barely contain my laugher when I saw him turn around, bend down, and drop his pants to moon us by way of a goodbye. I did not know how much I would miss his indomitable spirit until he was out of my life.

Less than an hour later, I arrived at my new home.

My foster parents showed me around before allowing me to settle in the bedroom I was lucky enough to have to myself.

"I hope you'll be happy here," the mother said.

I nodded, but could not suppress a yawn.

"You must be exhausted after all the…excitement of the past few weeks. Why don't you take a nap? I'll call you when lunch is ready," she said as she gently shut the door behind her.

I sat on the bed, but did not lie down. I was too much on edge to relax.

Putting my suitcase on the bed, I unzipped it and dug into the innermost recesses to find my hidden treasure. As I sat munching on my chocolate bar, I was seized by a hunger no candy could ever sate. The hollow feeling in my stomach was too large to fill; the void was cold and dark and too painful to bear. The hurt grew progressively worse until finally I could stand it no more and had to make it stop.

In a frantic act of desperation, I ran to the bathroom, found a bottle of aspirin, and swallowed pill after pill before curling up in the bathtub, praying for the end to come.

But even as the blackness overtook me, I knew I could not wipe out the awful truth that hurt so badly I wanted to die. I was alone.

When I woke, I found myself in a hospital bed. Trying to sit up, I realized I was strapped in by the arms and legs. The pungent smell of disinfectant made my nose itch, and I sneezed.

"God bless you," he said.

Turning my head in the direction of the voice, I saw a doctor standing to my right.

"Welcome back, Geraldine. I'm Doctor Stone."

Instinctively, I tried to raise my hand, but could not because of the restraints.

"Let me get those off."

Gently, he released me from my bondage before grabbing me under the arms to prop me up on a couple of pillows.

"Thanks," I managed to utter, despite my sore throat.

"I'll bet your throat must smart."

I nodded.

He poured me a glass of water, helping me take a sip. I felt relief as the coolness washed over my raw flesh.

"Better?"

I nodded again.

"Good. Now that I've done you a favor, I want you to do one for me."

What could I do for him?

"I want you to promise me you'll try your very best to get well. Can you do that for me? Can we shake on it?"

I began to lift my hand, but was too weak to move it more than a few inches.

Doctor Stone leaned over, interlaced our fingers, and shook our hands as I smiled in agreement.

It was one promise I hoped never to break.

A Letter Home

Dear Lizzie,

I suppose you're wondering why I'm writing you now. I could tell you that I'm trying to tie up loose ends, to make sense of the mess our lives became. But that would be a lie.

I could tell you I'm writing to say how much I miss you and want you back and don't care what you do or how you treat me. But that, too, would be a lie.

Should I let you know that in spite of everything we went through, in spite of the hurt, in spite of the madness, I'm still here?

But the question I always ask myself is why? What right do I have to be here when the others aren't?

I guess being in the right place at the right time isn't always enough. I could have run onto the ice when it began to crack. I could have risked my own life to save you.

But sometimes you have to summon the courage to save the one person no one else can save. Sometimes you have to save yourself.

Don't get me wrong. It's not that I didn't love you. I always did and still do and always will, despite the pain. It's just that when you love someone, you expect to be loved in return.

I'm not blaming you. You couldn't help it. You were who you were, and I am who I am.

I'm tired of listening to all those whiny patients in group therapy who keep bitching about what a terrible childhood they had and how they can't get over it. One day I'm going to smack them across their pathetic faces and tell them to get on with their lives.

If I can do it, so can they.

I've accepted the fact that you weren't my mother; you were just the woman married to a man who had a baby with your sister.

How you didn't go mad sooner, I'll never figure out.

But I'm not going to try.

I'm putting it all to rest.

Finally, I know who I am.

I'm not Gerri Girl or Mother's Little Helper, Paddy's sister or Frankie's daughter.

I'm a survivor.

I promised myself that I would never give up, and if there's one thing you taught me above all else, it's that a promise is a promise.

Well, I can't think of anything else I want to say, except to say hello to Grandma and John and Michael. Wait, I forgot one more person. Say hello to my real mother.

Tell Colleen I love her.

Sincerely,

Geraldine Francine Moran

I dug up the dirt around her gravestone and buried the letter deep in the earth, where the words could reach her rotting corpse.

Then I wiped my hands on my jeans, stood up, and shook my fists toward the heavens as I shouted across the cemetery in a voice loud and strong: "I'M QUEEN NOW!"